THE BRIGHT SIDE OF CHRISTMAS

HOLLY RIDGE
BOOK 1

MORGAN ELIZABETH

To the eldest daughters who make the magic happen for everyone else.

A NOTE FROM MORGAN

Dear Reader,

   I *loved* writing this book. Truly.

   Stepping into Holly Ridge felt like the perfect breath of fresh air I needed. I started my career writing a small town romance series (shout out to the Springbrook Hills series, my babies!), so writing another one that embodied everything I love about small town romances (a tight-knit family, meddling friends, nosy neighbors, traditions upon traditions that somehow, everyone knows about) was everything to me.

   The idea of battling neighbors came to me this time last year while having my annual watch of Christmas Vacation, and I couldn't stop thinking about someone who hated Christmas moving next to Clark Griswold, but make it the whole street. The chaos! The hilarity! The grumpy sunshine/dislike to lovers of it all! Perfection, if you ask me.

   This book was cathartic in more ways than one: as the mom who is obsessed with Christmas but more often than not, burns herself out by the 24th, trying to make all of the magical moments happen, and also a recovering people pleaser who hates letting people down. Like

Wren, over the years I've had to come to terms with the fact that people will always take advantage of your kindness, and that realization is never fun. Thankfully, I have my own Adam, who does everything in his power to make sure I set and, most importantly, *maintain* my boundaries. (I'm working on it, at least.)

If you find yourself in the same boat, I hope you also get to experience the magic you create this year and find time to slow down and enjoy the season.

This book, while a cozy Christmas romance, does have a few moments that you should be aware of: Wren is dealing with grief from the loss of her grandmother, and Adam grew up with emotionally neglectful parents. Please make sure to protect your own mental health at all times and set the story aside if need be! Reading is supposed to be our safe space. Also!!!! For the first time in a LONG time, this book isn't a *true* no third-act breakup. There is no true breakup in this story, but there is a third-act relationship bump. As a vehement third-act breakup hater, I promise it's not much of a third-act breakup if we're going by my personal definition, but yours might differ from mine.

Anyway, I hope you love our trip to Holly Ridge as much as I did!

Love you to the moon and Saturn,

Morgan

PLAYLIST

Deck the Halls - Nat King Cole
   is it new years yet? - Sabrina Carpenter
   Marjorie -Taylor Swift
   A Troubled Mind - Noah Kahan
   I've Got My Love to Keep Me Warm - Frank Sinatra
   Like Christmas - Jonas Brothers
   Eldest Daughter -Taylor Swift
   Gingerbread Lover - Ivoris, Chevy
   Couldn't Make it Any Harder - Sabrina Carpenter
   Daylight - Taylor Swift
   Underneath the Tree - Kelly Clarkson

ONE

Wren

"I think he's a serial killer," my best friend says as I sit on my couch, cutting endless amounts of shapes from colored construction paper. My fingers are going to go numb soon, but it has to get done before next week, so a break really isn't an option.

As I often do when I'm in the middle of a project, I deeply regret signing up to do all the decorations and snacks for the school-wide Thanksgiving party at the elementary school where I work. Unfortunately, considering no one else was signing up for it, I knew that if I didn't offer, it simply wouldn't get done.

It's what my grandmother would have done, too.

I push that thought aside, instead looking up at Hallie. She's standing at the window that faces my neighbor's home, watching him like she's on an investigative lookout. I'm surprised she doesn't have some kind of long-range camera in hand, taking black-and-white surveillance shots.

"Jeez, Hal, he's not a serial killer," I say with a laugh and a shake of my head.

"Do you have proof of that?" She pauses her intense investigation, looking over her shoulder at me with a raised eyebrow.

I tip my head at her curiously. "How does one obtain evidence that their new neighbor is not a serial killer?"

"You talk to him, for one, something *no one* has been able to do."

That much, at least, seems to be true. My new neighbor moved in almost two weeks ago, having bought the house sight unseen in *cash*, according to Jeanie Holmes, one of the two real estate agents in our small town of Holly Ridge. No one knows anything about the mysterious man, except that his name is incredibly average. (Searching for *Adam Porter* brought up at least three dozen results, the most being a real estate mogul who must spend a considerable amount on ads, as he took up almost every result on the first page. That Adam Porter, though, lived in Michigan, a far cry from northwest New Jersey.)

"Nat is going for a Mafia don in hiding." Natalie Deluca, my other best friend, *would* vote for a Mafia don in hiding.

I'm sure Adam Porter is here for some incredibly boring and run-of-the-mill reason, but given the strange purchase details and the lack of insight on our newest resident, I'm not surprised the rumors have started to fly off the handle.

Holly Ridge isn't just a small town. It's a close-knit community where everyone knows everyone and everything *about* everyone, whether you want them to or not. An outsider randomly moving in with no one being able to discern any information about them is not just strange—it's unheard of. It also breeds wild stories, such as him being a serial killer or in witness protection, just two of the many ideas Hallie has thrown out in the last hour since she noticed his car pull into his driveway. She came here to help me assemble decorations, but even when I invited her, I knew she was mostly going to chat and keep me company while I worked.

"I highly doubt a Mafia don would choose Holly Ridge to hide out in."

"Exactly. That's why serial killer makes so much more sense," she says matter-of-factly.

As I set the hundredth orange triangle aside, my fingers cramp. "None of it makes sense, Hallie."

"I just don't know how you sleep at night knowing a potential serial killer lives right next door to you." I've known Hallie since preschool, when we both showed up on the first day in the same dress, so her dramatic responses are nothing new to me.

"Like a baby," I say, although these days, I'm actually not sleeping much, not with a million and seven projects on my plate. But that's neither here nor there. "Honestly, Hallie, think about it. Why would a serial killer move to a small town? Wouldn't a big city be the better choice?"

She scoffs in disbelief, waving a hand at me. "Exactly what a serial killer would *want* you to think."

I let out a laugh as I cut the last orange triangle, deciding I need a break before I move on to turning them into pie slices. Might as well knock out two birds with one stone. I stand up, brushing scraps of paper off my black yoga pants. "Fine. I'll go over there and ask him." Hallie's head snaps toward me, her face panic-stricken, and I have to fight back a giggle.

"You're just going to go over there and ask him if he's a serial killer?" She stares at me, aghast, as I move toward my front door and slip on my shoes. "You can't do that, Wren. That's how you become number one on his list. You already have the whole cutesy, innocent heroine in a horror movie who lives alone and *almost* makes it to the end thing going on."

I shake my head with a laugh. "No, I'm not going to ask him if he's a murderer. But he's home right now, and I need to ask him when he's going to start decorating."

"Ah, decorating committee duties," she says with a nod. "That's a good cover, actually. Ask him about his decoration plans, keep an ear out for the pleas of women trapped in his basement, check to see if his house is furnished, that kind of thing."

I pause and stare at her, shaking my head. Sometimes, I can't tell if she's joking or being serious.

"Hallie, if he were keeping women locked in his basement, I would know."

"Would you?" she asks, skeptically.

"I mean, I would like to assume I would notice if my new neighbor were dragging women into his house."

"Not if you're constantly making pumpkin pie garlands and cutting everything out for hand turkey popcorn balls or whatever other bullshit you signed yourself up for."

I don't respond to the jab, knowing it won't get me anywhere.

Hallie doesn't get my need to help where I can and constantly tells me I need to relax more. But she doesn't understand how it's just in my blood: it's what I do. I'm Wren King, daughter of Peter and Susan King, granddaughter of Dottie King. My grandmother told me from the moment I was able to understand that Kings help people, always, and from a young age, I took that to heart. I'm proud to be someone everyone can count on to lend a helping hand.

"Hush," I say with a wave of my hand, not wanting to hear her speech on how I need to prioritize myself again. "Get to gluing those cotton balls on while I go over there, will you?"

"Hell, no. I'm standing here on watch with 911 on speed dial just in case he drags you inside against your will." Her lips tip mischievously before she adds, "Though, that might not be too bad. I hear he's ridiculously hot." I roll my eyes at her dramatics but leave without saying anything else, knowing that if I do, I'll never get this done.

I'd been meaning to go next door and introduce myself to my new neighbor anyway. When he moved in, I tried to say hello, but he didn't answer when I knocked, so I left my welcome basket with fresh muffins, a few new-home essentials, and a welcome packet I put together for everything one might need to know about our little town: community events, takeout menus, a list of important numbers, and the like. The next morning, the empty basket was on my front porch along with a note that simply said, *Thanks. -A.* Since then, I've tried to catch him numerous times, but I haven't managed to do so.

When I walk up his pathway, I catch sight of him moving in the window and give him a little wave and a friendly smile. I might be imagining it, but I think he might groan when he sees me. Ignoring that, I move up the three steps of his porch, a familiar routine because this house used to be owned by Mrs. and Mr. Demauro, whose daughter was in my grade. When I'd go to my grandmother's house, which I now own after she left it to me, I would often go next door to see if she could play.

After I knock, I wait for a long moment. Long enough that I wonder if he actually *did* see me. Maybe he didn't, and he didn't hear my knock. I'm contemplating whether I should knock again or ring the bell when the door opens, and the choice is made for me. When it does, a towering man stands in the doorway, staring down at me, unspeaking.

"Hi!" I tip my head up to my new neighbor, who is about a foot taller than I anticipated and *far* more handsome than Jeanie let on, or that I could catch in the small moments I saw him going in or out of his home. His hair is dark, longer on top than it is on the sides, with warm brown eyes and a thick layer of scruff along his cheeks. His flannel shirt is unbuttoned, revealing a tight white T-shirt that stretches across a broad chest, paired with a casual pair of jeans that fit far too well. If Hallie were here, she'd probably ask him to turn around so she could see his ass.

Eventually, my gaze makes it back up to his eyes. That's when I realize he has not returned my smile. Discomfort settles in my gut for a second before I know I can't really blame him. There's a stranger on his front steps, practically ogling him, and there's a good chance he saw my best friend weirdly watching him from the window.

"I'm Wren. I live next door." Silence hangs between us, and I give in to the urge to fill it. "The white one." I tip my head to the side toward my home and stare at him, feeling increasingly uncomfortable as he remains quiet. Still, I'm determined to make a good impression. "I keep meaning to come over and introduce myself, but life has been so wildly busy. So... Hi! I'm Wren!" I let out a nervous giggle that makes me sound like an idiot, I'm sure, but it must do something, because finally his stone facade cracks the tiniest bit. His face stays stoic, but his eyes light as if, despite himself, he's entertained by me.

"Adam," he says. The word is finite, but I nod and shrug at him.

"I know. Small town, word spreads." His jaw goes a bit tight like he isn't fond of that, so I quickly add, "Not that there's been much to spread about you, of course. Your name and where you moved are all I've been able to get around town." A blush burns over my cheeks as my unfortunate habit of verbal vomit comes out.

Finally, I get a genuine reaction: the lift of a thick, dark eyebrow and the tiniest tip of the corner of his lips.

He's amused. That's a good sign, right?

I don't think serial killers get amused by rambling women, do they?

Unfortunately, the rambling only gets worse.

"My best friend thinks you're a serial killer," I admit, then instantly wish I hadn't because *who says that to a virtual stranger?* My panic fades almost as quickly, though, melting into something much more pleasant because with my words, his lips spread into a smirk.

It's not even a full smile, just a slight tilt of his lips like my antics amuse him, but my *god,* it's a good smirk that settles warm in my belly.

"And you?" he asks.

I stare for a moment before realizing what he's asking.

"I was leaning more toward you won the lottery and are hiding from your greedy family." He tips his head ever so slightly, like he's assessing me and taking me in, so slightly it must be unintentional, and I wonder if maybe I'm right, after all. When he doesn't give me the truth, or really, anything, I fill in the silence that has grown between us once more. "Anyway, I just wanted to stop by, say hi, and introduce myself formally. If you ever need anything at all, I'm your girl. It's kind of my thing around town. You need some help, call up Wren King!" His brow furrows, but he nods, then steps back just a bit as if he's done with the conversation and going to close the door.

Quickly, I add, "Oh, also, as head of the decorating committee in town, I must ask, when do you plan to start decorating for Christmas? If you'd like, I can come over to help out. Many hands make light work, and all."

"I don't," he says in that low, gravelly voice. I shrug and give him a slight, conciliatory nod.

"No worries, just figured I'd offer since you might not be comfortable asking for help since you just moved here and all." I stare at him some more, the chill of mid-November starting to creep beneath my sweater. I probably should have thrown on a jacket, but honestly, I didn't think I'd be standing outside this long.

He shakes his head, confusing me.

"No. What I meant was, I don't plan on decorating. Not my thing."

"I'm sorry?"

He shrugs as if he didn't just say the most unbelievable thing. "It's not my thing. Christmas, decorating. Not for me."

"But...but you live on Bluebird Lane." He raises an eyebrow at me. "It's...it's..." I force myself to take a deep breath to calm and center myself when I hear my voice going high-pitched. You always win people over much more easily with a friendly face and a calm demeanor. "It's tradition. This is the most decorated street in all of Holly Ridge, and that's saying something because we *love* decorating here. The town has been fully lit for almost thirty years; this street is going on sixty." It's a tradition started by my grandmother, and I have the honor of continuing it this year.

"Well then, it sounds like you won't need me to take part; plenty of festivity to go around," he says, then goes to close the door.

I don't know what comes over me, but I put a hand out, stopping it.

"The entire street will be lit up. We have a Land of Sweets theme going this year, you know, like in *The Nutcracker*? It's going to be spectacular, but we need everyone involved to make it extra magical. The lights bring people from all over to come check it out." His jaw goes tight with my words, but I'm too panicked to really understand it, much less heed the warning.

"Well, I guess you're just going to have to deal with this one staying dark this year." Any trace of amusement disappears from his face, and my gut drops.

I don't mean it, really, I don't. Arguing isn't really my thing, but the way he's so casually brushing off my request lights some kind of irritation in my chest I can't seem to tamp down. "Why? It wouldn't have to be anything crazy, just a couple of strands of lights, something easy. I'll even do it for you! I have tons of extra decorations; you won't even have to buy any."

He shakes his head. "You don't have to do anything for me. I'm fully capable."

Hope sparks in my chest as the panic about failing in my very first year as decorating committee head, of letting everyone down, dissipates.

"So you'll put up some lights?"

"No," he says simply. That hope shatters to the ground like a delicate ornament.

My jaw tightens, and I kind of want to stomp my foot, throw a full-blown temper tantrum right here on his front porch. "Why not?"

He sighs, and I can tell he's losing whatever patience he had for me, but I can't find it in me to care.

"Because I don't like Christmas, and I didn't move here to get into some kind of community decorating contest. I'm just trying to live my life."

"You don't like Christmas?" I ask, aghast. "Why not?"

"I just don't. It's my least favorite time of year."

He says it so plainly, as if he just told me he doesn't like pizza or chocolate instead of admitting he doesn't like the most magical time of the year. My jaw drops. Not liking the holiday season is...unthinkable. Absolutely ridiculous. Who doesn't like *Christmas*?

Before I can come up with anything to say through my shock, some argument to pull him to my side, his phone starts ringing. He looks toward his kitchen where the sound is coming from before turning back to me.

"I'm going to have to answer that. Have a nice day, Wren." And then he closes the door in my face.

I stand there for far too long, probably looking like an idiot staring in shock at a closed door, before I slowly turn and trudge down his walkway. With each step, the shock melts away, irritation filling its place.

"I think you're right," I say with a sigh, slamming the door behind me and kicking my shoes to the side. Hallie is standing beside the window facing my neighbor's house, so I know she probably watched the entire, thoroughly embarrassing interaction. I lean my back against the door and sigh.

"I always am," she says. "What am I right about this time, though?"

"He's a serial killer."

Her eyes grow wide. "Oh my god, what did you see? Blood on his hands? Rope hidden in a corner? Or did you hear shouts or something?"

"Worse," I say. "He said he hates Christmas."

TWO

ADAM

"Got anything new for me?" my agent asks when I hit *accept* on my phone.

"Hey, Greg, how are you? I'm great, settling into my new home well, thanks so much for asking," I grumble. I already regret answering his call, even if it did get me out of talking to my neighbor, who looked like I just told her I actually *was* a serial killer when I told her I don't like Christmas.

"You moved?" Greg asks with genuine confusion in his words. I take in a deep breath and let it out slowly, moving across my living room to the side window facing my neighbor—Wren's—house. "Oh, yes, that's right, to some middle-of-nowhere town, right? Wanted to clear your mind or some shit." The downside of not having any real friends in this fake-as-fuck industry is that the only person I've told my problem to is, in fact, Greg. "Well, did it do the job? Are you feeling inspired?"

I sigh as Wren finally makes her way down my front walkway, frustration in each step. Despite my shitty mood, I find myself smiling at the look of it.

"You know how the muses work," I say, trying to play down my issue.

"Look," he starts. "Writer's block is totally normal. Really, it is. But we promised multiple artists some options by the new year—"

I cut him off, that all too familiar flare of frustration that's been toeing into anger blooming in my chest.

Greg has been my agent since he signed Midnight Ash when I was barely eighteen years old. When Trent decided to pursue a solo career and the band came to an end, I approached him about collaborating on songwriting and production. Despite my frustration with the man and the way he kind of makes my skin crawl, he's really fucking good at his job, and he's the reason my office is lined with awards and the reason I have worked with so many amazing artists over the years.

But if I'm being honest with myself, he's also a big part of the reason I'm facing the worst burnout of my career.

"No, *you* promised, Greg. You promised people things on some timeline you created without consulting me, knowing damn well I don't work on *your* timeline. I work on *my* timeline. I'll have the material when I have the material, but you calling me up every few days to ask if I have anything new isn't helping." I think about the empty sheet music and the blank pages, which only make me more frustrated. "I'm doing what I can, but I've been creating nonstop for years. I need to recharge. I need time. If that's not something you're willing to work with, then maybe it's time we go our separate ways."

As I knew he would, Greg loudly objects. "No, no, no, Adam, don't be like that. You know, I just get excited about new material. I love working with you, you know that."

He loves the paychecks he gets, is more like it. He loves that he gets the money without the headache of a performer who comes with an ego or the stress of bad press and tabloid rumors, since I'd rather stay under the radar.

Greg continues to talk in my ear, spinning stories of apology, saying I'm his favorite client and that he was just joking. As I often find myself doing when talking to Greg, I zone out. The thing is, I don't need the money. As the bassist for Midnight Ash for ten years before we split up, and having written some decent hits that bring in consistent royalties, I don't need the money. Especially when it's just me, and I don't need much of anything to keep myself happy.

But despite telling myself that over and over, I can't deny that I *want* it. I *want* to overcome this.

Playing music and writing songs bring me happiness and have always been a much-needed escape.

Except for the recent glaring fact that I *haven't* been happy. I keep having the nagging thought that *something* is missing—not that I'll be sharing that with Greg, or anyone, for that matter.

While he talks, I continue to watch my preppy little neighbor stomp away, her shoulders set tightly. Her loose chocolate curls bob as she walks down my walkway before making a tight turn toward her house, the red ribbon tying back the top half of her hair dancing happily in contrast to her agitated movements.

"I'd love another holiday hit like 'All Lit Up'; that would be fucking sick. I could get someone in the booth right away, use it for this year even."

"I'm not doing another fucking Christmas record," I say quickly. My biggest hit to date was some random junk I wrote in ten minutes, and it has gotten more streams than any of the songs I've put my entire heart and soul into. Number two and three in my most-streamed songs I've produced and written are also holiday songs. It's become a sore spot for me, and I decided last year that I wouldn't write holiday songs anymore.

How good of a songwriter could I really be if my biggest hit is some holiday-themed bullshit? It's become such a thorn for me that hearing "All Lit Up" or any of the other Christmas songs I've written, which happens from November to December and, recently, creeping into October, makes my skin crawl. I've begun to dread the holiday season, knowing that my personal failure will once again haunt and taunt me.

It's probably also why the writer's block is hitting so hard right now, although I won't be telling Greg that.

I should probably have been a bit less of an ass. Still, I made a rule long, long ago for myself: I would never pretend to be someone I'm not, be it for my parents or fans or my manager, and Greg toeing the line as he always seems to do reminds me I don't actually want to be on this call at all.

"And listen, Greg. I told you, I'm not working on your timeline. Never was, never will be. If you want a piggy bank that performs when you tell it to, check out social media for one. I'm sure they'll jump when you say jump. That won't be me. I'll let you know when I have something for you." I pull the phone from my ear and end the call.

Getting into this business at such a young age, with Midnight Ash getting picked up when I was barely eighteen, and even long before then, when I was battling my parents' expectations of me, I learned quickly that you either stand your ground and protect your boundaries, or you'll get steamrolled.

Greg doesn't actually care about me; he wants to see if I have something new that will make him even more money than he already has.

I put my phone on Do Not Disturb in case he calls back, then set it on a table, crossing my arms on my chest as Wren walks up the steps to her porch and opens her door with more force than is needed before slamming it loud enough that I can hear it from here. And despite the dark cloud that always seems to hang over my head when I'm reminded of my writer's block, I smile.

That night, I stayed up late, scribbling in a notebook into the dead of night and trying to come up with something to get Greg off my ass, and once again coming up with nothing.

Six months ago, I hit a wall with my songwriting. Every time I sit in front of the piano or hold an instrument, nothing comes. I put a pen in my hand, and where I used to spill out words onto paper, there's silence. I bought a pretentious typewriter, hoping it might help, but instead, I spent nearly two weeks trying to find one I liked and another week procrastinating on playing with paper and ink types instead of writing a damn word. When all of my procrastination attempts ran out, I realized I was the problem.

I convinced myself I needed to get away, go somewhere quiet, and remind myself who I am or something like that. The city was too loud. I figured that must be the source of my creative block, and a change of scenery would fix my problems for good. How could my muse whisper to me when people were yelling all hours of the day?

Four weeks ago, I remembered someone mentioning this tiny town in Northwest New Jersey, Holly Ridge, and found a place for sale, buying it sight unseen.

Peace and quiet and anonymity. That's what I needed.

And I found it here, but I'm still...stuck.

I initially thought it was just a matter of settling in, so I spent days unpacking and assembling furniture in rooms I'd likely never use. I painted a room, then decided I hated painting, changed out light fixtures, and cleaned every inch of the home as if it were a profession. But eventually, I had nothing left to do but stare at a piece of paper once again.

Nothing.

Across the way, a light upstairs in Wren's house switches on, and my head raises to look. Despite my indifference to my neighbor, I've been intrigued by her since I moved in. She's always doing something, always up late in her office, which happens to be right across from mine. Sometimes, she seems to be writing on paper, which makes me wonder what she does for work, especially since she's up early every morning.

Even though it makes me a bit creepy, I watch her from where I sit for the next hour.

I don't write.

I don't do anything productive. Instead, I watch her, hunched over at her desk. I watch her rub her eyes tiredly. I watch her yawn plenty. Eventually, I watch her stand up and look at her desk as if she's frustrated she isn't done yet, but has to succumb to her exhaustion. Then she walks away before the light flicks out.

I sit there, staring at the dark window for a few moments longer, and then it comes to me.

It's small: five chords that could be nothing at all, but it's the first little hint of a melody that's come to me in months. I quickly scribble them down, though nothing comes after, even as I sit there for twenty more minutes, willing more to come. Eventually, I sit back and rub a hand over my face before checking the clock and deciding it's probably time to head to bed, though I do it with a little less hopelessness than the night before.

Maybe tomorrow, inspiration will hit.

THREE

ADAM

The next morning, I open my front door to head out for my run, and Wren is standing on my front porch, hand raised as if to knock, her face a mask of shock. "What are you doing?"

"Oh, uh, hi! I was just about to knock," she says with a friendly but nervous giggle. She's in a jacket this morning, the bottom of a burgundy dress poking out beneath the hem of it, with thick dark tights covering her legs and a pair of low-heeled shoes on her feet. With the flouncy bow she always seems to wear in her hair, she looks sweet and innocent.

"What are you doing?" I ask. That's when my eyes drift to what's in her hand: a green wreath with a cheery, bright red bow that matches the one in her hair.

"Oh, I was going to bring this to you! It's from my parents' place —they own Three Kings Christmas Tree Farm."

I stare at her and don't say anything. She bites her lip, the white of her teeth denting her pretty pink lips. My mind trails off, thinking of reaching up to pull that bottom lip free with my thumb before I knock myself back into reality. A reality where I don't note how plush and pink my neighbor's lips look.

"Why?"

She blinks at me. "I'm sorry?"

"Why are you bringing that to me?" There's another moment of hesitation before she tips her head to the side.

"Well...you don't have any decorations. I thought I'd make it easier and bring you one." She tips her chin to my door like I'm an idiot. "You already have a nail in the door, so I just gotta..." She reaches to hang it up, and I step in front of where she's looking. Her jaw goes tight, the sweetness leaving her face.

Unfortunately for me, the cute *doesn't* leave her face. In fact, the pout actually makes the cute more prominent.

"I'm not hanging that up," I insist. She puts one hand on her hip and glares up at me. Up because she's a short thing, I'm six-two, and she can't be taller than five-two.

"Why not?"

"Because I don't want to. I don't want any decorations."

She rolls her eyes and sighs as if I'm being dramatic.

"It's just a wreath, Adam." I like the way my name sounds on her lips, but I ignore that, too.

"I told you—I don't like Christmas. I don't like decorations."

"And that's why I'm here. I'll do it for you. We can't have you being the only house on the street with no lights. It's tradition. This street has been fully lit every year for sixty years." With the way she's speaking, I have to wonder if she's ever been told no, if anyone can ever ignore her cuteness and turn her down. I suppose I'll be the first.

If she were asking me about anything else, I might fall for it. But unfortunately for her, my undying hatred for Christmas and the feeling of failure it brings is stronger than her sweetness.

"I'm not decorating, Wren. Might as well get used to that now."

Her jaw goes tight, and she assesses me before she surprises me by smiling wide as she takes a step back. "Oh, you'll be decorating. You can mark my word."

I choke back a laugh at her determination. "Good luck with that."

She shakes her head, eyes sparkling. "I don't need luck. Not when I have Christmas spirit." She can't be real. It's like she's the star of some shitty made-for-TV Christmas movie with all that outlandish sass and cheer. I lost the battle to my laugh and let out a scoff, but it doesn't seem to bother her. Instead, she just shrugs. "You'll see."

Then she turns on her heel and makes her way down my front walkway, turning right down the sidewalk, then back up hers. Once she's inside, I close the door to my own home, groaning as I rub a hand over my face despite the fact that I was about to go on a run.

I am so fucked.

Not because she's clearly determined to be a pain in my ass, and I came here to find peace and quiet. *No.* No, I am completely fucked because I can't deny that when she walked away with a bit of extra sway to her steps, I watched her ass move with each and every swish of her hips.

The following morning, I open my door to take my morning run. While I don't see Wren on my front step, a knocking sound has my steps faltering. I turn in confusion, trying to find the source, but I don't have to look far. It's a wreath on my door, hanging from a nail that I should have removed but didn't. With dark green pine branches and a giant red bow, it isn't anything extravagant, but it's still a Christmas decoration.

It confuses me.

Mostly because I did not put it there.

I stare at it for a moment longer before the chill starts to seep into my bones. Staring at the godforsaken decoration won't do a thing. I'll take my run and handle it afterward, I guess.

But the entire time, I can't stop thinking about the green monstrosity on my door.

Thirty minutes later, I'm rounding the corner and catch Wren out on her front porch, locking her door behind her. I do my best to ignore the woman, reaching for my door before I hear it.

"Nice wreath," she calls across the gap between our houses.

I glare at her over my shoulder and see she's juggling two bags, a coffee thermos, and her giant water bottle while balancing a cardboard box on her hip. Her body is angled to face me, feigned innocence written over her face.

"I'm sorry?" I'm slightly out of breath after my run, and my fingers are frozen, but despite that, I turn to her, crossing my arms over my chest.

"Nice wreath. Looks good on your door, don't you think?" There's a hint of a smile playing on her lips, and she's doing a bad job at trying to hide it.

"Did you put it there?" I ask, even though I know the answer. If she wants to play this game, I can play right back.

"Why would I do that?"

"Oh, I don't know, because you're pissed I'm not taking part in your stupid decorating scheme?" That one hits a little too close, her jaw going tight, and I feel the warmth of a win rush through me, though it's not as sweet as I would have thought.

"Have a very merry day, Adam," she says, instead of continuing to argue, and then turns to move toward her car.

I turn back to my door, turn the doorknob, and walk into my warm house. But despite desperately needing a shower and to get my day moving, I stand at the window and watch her get into her old, shitty car that should probably have been replaced years ago and drive off.

When she's done, I sigh and head to the kitchen to grab a drink. I'm downing that and deciding on what I want to eat before I head upstairs and stare at a blank paper for hours on end once again, when my phone dings with a new incoming text. When I lift it, Trent's name is on the screen.

Trent, the former lead singer of Midnight Ash, for whom I still write songs.

I should have left it on Do Not Disturb.

TRENT:

Hey, man, anything new for me? The label's bugging me about getting into the recording booth with something new, but you know I'm loyal to you.

I groan and fight the urge to throw my phone against a wall or worse, respond with what I'm actually thinking.

No, you're not; you're loyal to no one but yourself. You know my songs are likely to perform well for you, and I'm the only one who can handle your diva antics.

I type out and delete a dozen replies, half of which would probably get me blacklisted in this industry, before I finally reply.

I'll let you know when I do.

Irritation fills my veins, both at Trent for only ever contacting me when he needs something and at myself for this never-ending writer's block. Then I head outside, grab the wreath, and walk along the sidewalk to her front porch, where I toss the godforsaken thing down before trudging back home and trying to write the next big hit.

When she gets home from work, even though I tell myself I'm not, I'm paying attention. From my office, I watch her approach her front door and, despite the three bags and two cups in her hands, bend down to grab the wreath from where I left it. She looks across the way to my house, and I can't confirm since it's getting dark and the angle isn't great, but I imagine her jaw going tight with determination.

I wait to see if she'll bring it back across the way, but she doesn't. That's why when I open my door the next morning and see it hanging merrily on my door again, I'm surprised. I leave it again, and this time, I don't see her when I return from my run. Instead, I watch her house from inside until she leaves for work. Then, I head out, ripping the wreath off my door and tossing it onto her porch once more.

On the third day, I walk out, and there's no wreath. Even though I'm happy to see my blank door, I can't help but feel the slightest pang of disappointment that this game is over.

The disappointment is short-lived.

When I return from my run, the wreath is back on my door. Across the way, a stern-faced Wren stares me down, her arms crossed on her chest. Her cheeks are pink with cold, making me think she's been waiting for me to see how I'll react. I shake my head at her and reach up to remove it, but stop. This time, instead of just being hung on the nail in my front door, the wreath is tied with a combination of tape and wire. I can't just easily take it off. With the amount of electrical tape on there, I think it would take me ten minutes and a knife to remove it.

Unfortunately, it isn't that thought that has me confirming I won't be taking down this wreath a third time.

It's the happy look that takes over Wren's entire face when she sees my hand drop with resignation, as if she knows that means I'm going to let it stay.

I wonder if that's how she always gets her way: a pretty smile and a bit of determination. She could steamroll the entire town that way and get everything she wanted.

I know it would work on me.

But for now, I'll give her the wreath. After all, what could one Christmas decoration hurt?

FOUR

ADAM

The next morning, when I head outside for my run, I realize what it could hurt. On either side of my walkway is a single two-foot-tall candy cane sunk a few inches into the frozen ground.

"Wren," I say in warning when I see her stepping out of her house. She gives me wide, innocent eyes, and I want to be annoyed—really, I do—but instead, I find myself fighting back a laugh instead.

Don't encourage her, Porter. She clearly doesn't need it, I tell myself.

"Yes?"

"Why are there candy canes on my lawn?"

She looks to where the plastic sticks, finding them instantly. "Huh. No idea. I thought you were just getting into the Christmas spirit. Did you not put them there?"

"You and I both know I didn't."

She shrugs like it's no big deal, then heads down her walkway. "Must be someone in the neighborhood trying to spread some holiday cheer. Have a good day, Adam!" She gives me a cocky grin before ducking into her car and driving off. I let out a huff, grabbing the candy canes and tossing them onto her lawn before heading out.

The next morning, the number of candy canes had doubled, though I have no idea when she put them into my lawn since her car was already gone when I stepped outside at seven a.m. When I return from my run, I pull them out of the lawn again, only for them to reappear the next morning.

By Saturday, I have a small trove of decorations on my lawn, and I've come to terms with the fact that the candy canes, at the very least, are probably staying. We're up to six, and when I tried to pull them out yesterday, I realized she did something to make them much more difficult to remove. Even though she wasn't outside watching me, when I turned to glare at her house, I caught her in the window for a split second before the curtains shifted closed as if she was hiding away.

After that, the candy canes stayed. The next day, a snowman joined their ranks.

It has not escaped my notice that this is the most fun I've had with anything even slightly resembling Christmas in a long, long time, but that's neither here nor there.

After another long day staring at a blank paper, I decide getting out might be what I need. I head downtown to The Mill, seemingly the only bar in town, around six o'clock, and instantly regret it when I walk in to see all eyes on me. The space is dim but clean, featuring dark hardwood floors and beams, with a dozen tables of various sizes and heights lining the room's sides. On one side is a bar with bottles lining the walls, a half-dozen stools, and a jukebox in the corner.

The tables are each full, which is when I regrettably remember it's Saturday. Of course, the only bar in town is busy on a Saturday night. I catch a few women at a table staring before they turn away quickly, whispering to each other, but I keep my head down, making my way to the bar on the left side of the room. Finding a stool, I slide onto it and take in a deep breath once my back is to the crowd. Sure, people are probably still staring, but it's at my back, so I can ignore that. I look around for a bar menu, but don't find one by the time the bartender hands over the drink he was making to a customer and moves my way.

"Hey, how's it going?" the bartender asks.

I tip my head in what I think is a polite nod, then give him my order. "Whatever you recommend on draft, please."

The bartender's face goes confused for a moment before he turns to grab a glass and begins pouring from one of the taps. When it's full, he slides the frosted glass across to me. I reach for my wallet to pay, but he shakes his head.

"No need, we'll set you up a tab. So, how's it going? How's your day?" It's the second time he's asked this, and that's when I realize he isn't asking as some kind of habitual greeting. He actually wants to know.

I recall my call with Greg the other day, where I made a sarcastic quip mocking him for not even bothering with the nicety. Yet, this utter stranger seems genuinely interested in my answer. Something about that settles strangely in my chest, but I push it aside and answer out of obligation.

"I, uh...not bad. You?"

"Oh, just living the dream back here, can't complain." Once more, I think he's being sarcastic, but then I really take him in and realize he's not. He means that with his whole chest. He has nothing to complain about because he's happy as can be working at this bar. "Colt, by the way. I own this place."

"Adam," I say, reaching across and shaking his hand. Panic surges for a split second when he hesitates, thinking he might have put pieces together of who I am, but then the look clears, and he gives me a broad, genuine smile.

"New here?"

"Is it that obvious?"

"Small town. You learn to take note of new faces when you know everyone who lives here." I still haven't wrapped my mind around that concept; it's something I didn't really think about when I decided a small town would be the best to disappear into, not that I ever planned on hitting up a local bar.

Thankfully, Colt gets called away to the other side of the bar before I can respond, but a moment later, the bell over the door jingles. With it, a squeal from one of the tables draws my attention. The woman who had been eyeing me when I walked in is standing and rushing to the door, her arms outstretched as she pulls another woman into a hug.

I recognize the newcomer instantly as my neighbor.

Wren.

Wren, who wears the little bows, left me muffins on my front step, even though I was home and just didn't want to engage with a stranger when I first moved in. Wren, who seems determined to spread cheer everywhere she goes. Wren, who looked like I shot down all of her dreams when I told her I wouldn't be decorating for the holidays, and who has taken it upon herself to *force* me to decorate.

Wren, whose ass I couldn't stop staring at when she walked off.

Wren, whose ass I can't stop staring at *now*.

"You got something going with little Wren King?" Colt asks, jolting me out of my daze, and I realize then I must have been staring. Embarrassment burns over my face, but I pretend it's anything but.

"Who?" I ask far too quickly to be smooth.

"The girl whose ass your eyes are glued to."

"My eyes are not glued to anyone's ass," I lie with a stiff shake of my head.

"Sure they aren't, my dude."

Silence fills the space, and I realize he isn't going to fill it until I respond. Usually, I'm fine with that. Typically, I strive for silence.

But here, where everyone is close and chatting, and I'm the loser sitting at a bar alone, I don't like it.

So I explain.

"She's my neighbor."

"Oh, fuck, I forgot the Demauro house was up for sale. You bought it?"

"Seems like it."

"How are you settling in? I'm sure Wren has gone full-blown welcoming committee."

For some reason I can't quite explain, I decide to expand. "We're in a war right now."

"A war?" he asks, quirking an eyebrow at me, intrigued.

"She wants me to decorate my house, but I don't like Christmas."

There's a beat before he lets out a deep belly laugh, head tipping back. "You sure picked the wrong place, then, my man," he says when his humor dies down.

"Yeah, I'm learning that." Once more, silence hangs uncomfortably between us, and even though I'm usually at ease with quiet, I feel the need to fill it. "She keeps bringing decorations to my place. Used industrial tape to hang a wreath on my door after I kept taking it down, and I think she may have quick-cemented candy canes along my pathway. This morning, there were a couple of lollipops in my yard." Those were not nailed into the ground, so they slid out easily and found their way onto her front step.

He nods stoically, as if he doesn't find this behavior alarming or surprising. "Wren is a lot of things, but one of them is a King. I grew up with her brothers and did some work for her dad when I was a kid. They're some of the most stubborn people I've ever met."

"So it's a family trait." I shake my head and let out a little sigh of knowing defeat. "Got any tips for me?"

"Give in now," he says. "No one is more determined to spread cheer than Wren King. She's the head of the decorating committee, just like her grandmother before her. Her parents own a Christmas tree farm, and she volunteered to run the Christmas Festival this year even though she's got her hands full with her job. Still, she pitches in if anyone needs absolutely anything around town, so she does a little bit of everything around her, paid or not. Making things, house-sitting, volunteer work—you name it, she does it."

It reminds me of her office light, how she's up late, always seeming to be doing something different late into the night. I thought it might have been some kind of side hustle, but volunteering to help other people does seem more on brand somehow, even though I barely know her. Before I can ask any of my dozen other questions, though, a familiar scent of cherries and vanilla trails over to me, and a small brunette slides into the stool beside me, sliding an empty pitcher across the bartop.

"Heya, Colton, Adam," Wren says, tipping her head toward the bartender. I fight every instinct to turn toward her, instead keeping my head straight. Maybe that should be my new tactic: perhaps if I just ignore the woman, she'll give up and leave me alone.

Even though I don't know her all that well, I somehow already know that is absolutely not the case.

"Hey, Wren, table needs a refill?"

She nods, and even though her gaze burns on my profile, I don't turn to look at her. She lets out a little laugh, entertained by my ignoring her, before turning back to Colt. "Yeah. Beer this time, if you don't mind."

Colt tips his head the slightest bit, and I take note.

"Beer?" I can't help it, I shift the tiniest bit to get a glimpse at her. Her focus is on Colt still, and she shrugs, giving him a small, self-deprecating smile.

"It's what the table voted on."

Colt gives her a look as he reaches for a pitcher and turns toward the tap as if he knows it's no use arguing with her.

"You don't drink beer, Wren."

"All good, I'm not going to be here much longer, anyway." She bites her lip and looks back at the table. "Can you also put it on my tab?"

I should shut up.

I should pretend she doesn't exist.

But I don't. "So you're not going to drink it, but you're paying?" I ask, raising an eyebrow. She turns her focus back to me, a playful gleam in her eyes, hiding the utter exhaustion that lingers on her face, before she shrugs like it's no big deal.

"It's my turn."

"But you're not going to drink it."

"The table voted on it, and Maxine paid for the last round. I'm not going to be selfish and not pay just because I won't be drinking it."

I tip my head. "You didn't get here all that long ago—I can't imagine you even took part in the last round."

A blush blooms on her cheeks, and it's sweet. I like that I've caught her off guard, a small win in our battle of wills, but it only lasts a moment before she lifts an eyebrow and the corner of her lips tips up, clearly moving to the defensive.

"Nice to know you were watching me, I suppose."

I sit there stunned, realizing I walked right into that one. My jaw flexes as I try and figure out how to counter, but my new...friend? cuts in.

"Hear you're on a mission to get your new neighbor to decorate his house?"

I turn my head toward him, and he gives me a shit-eating grin in return.

No, definitely not my friend.

"*And* you're talking to people about me?" Wren asks with a smile just as wide as Colt's. "One might think you're obsessed with me, Adam."

"No," I say, trying not to seem as flustered as I feel. "I was simply complaining about my annoying neighbor who keeps leaving her junk on my lawn." It's bait, my own effort to get her riled up, but unfortunately, she doesn't give in to it easily. Instead, she pulls her shoulders back, triumph taking over her face before she explains to Colton.

"Well, as you know, as head of the decorating committee, it's my mission to maintain the thirty-year tradition of every house in Holly Ridge being lit up for the holidays. Our new neighbor is adamant that he won't be decorating, but I'm working to make sure he doesn't disrupt our streak." It sounds like a speech, like she's running for office instead of trying to get me to put up some lights.

"I don't like Christmas. I don't like decorations."

Colton lets out an entertained laugh, watching our back-and-forth.

"Well, maybe you shouldn't have moved here. This town is lit up from Halloween to New Year's, so you're in for some misery," Wren says with a tight jaw.

"I have no problem with other people decorating. I just don't want my house lit up like you can see it from outer space."

Colton slides the pitcher in front of her, and she gives him a sweet smile that slides off her lips when she turns back to me.

"A few strands of lights won't make your house visible from two streets over, much less space."

"The same way that one house going dark won't make yours shine any less brighter."

"But it's a *tradition*," Wren says, throwing her hands and nearly whining now. I bite back the way it makes me want to laugh and shrug instead.

"Your tradition, maybe. Not mine."

"It's the town's tradition. You're in the town, so it's now your tradition, I would think," Colton adds. When I look at him, there's an entertained look on his face, and he's clearly enjoying my irritation.

This entire town is wack.

"That's not how that works," I say.

Someone calls Wren's name from the table she came from, and she stands, giving them a *one-second* gesture, before turning back to me.

"Well, I'm taking it upon myself to ensure that you have holiday spirit this year."

"You can't make me decorate my house, Wren."

She stares at me, taking me in for a moment before a grin spreads across her face. "I can't?"

It's less of a question and more of a challenge, something that settles somewhere deep in me. Not in a bad way, either. That's when I come to the complete realization I'm in for it with Wren King. She is going to push my every button in her mission to get her way.

If that hadn't already been obvious, I might be surprised. But I'm not.

What surprises me is that I might just let her.

"No, you can't."

"Hmm. Well, I guess we'll see, won't we?" And then she walks off, pitcher in hand, and I tell myself not to stare at her ass as she does, at the way the edges of her sweet dress sway with each step across the backs of her thighs.

I realize I completely lost the battle when Colt starts laughing loudly, snapping my attention back to him. He's shaking his head at me with a wide grin.

"Good luck with that, man."

I flip him off but don't argue.

How can I, really?

Instead, I watch her as she pours drinks for her friends, then sits in front of an empty glass, smiling and nodding to whatever they're saying.

"Does she do that a lot?" I ask without really thinking.

"What?"

"Ignore what she wants for the greater good?"

"Oh, yeah. She's best friends with my little sister, and the two of them couldn't be more different. Hallie? That girl will knock over any and everyone to get what she wants. But Wren wants everyone around her to be happy, even if it means she never gets what she wants. Youngest of three, but you'd think she was the responsible, self-sacrificing oldest sister instead."

I turn back around, staring at my half-empty glass and letting his words sink in. A part of me doesn't like that—Wren never getting what she wants.

A sweet, gorgeous woman like that should always get her way.

She has to know that if she just smiles and flips her hair, she could get anything she wanted. It's the playbook she's been using on me, after all.

Seemingly unable to control myself, I glance over my shoulder, catching one of the women she's with handing her a glass of beer. Wren lifts her hands and shakes her head, but her friend must insist, so she accepts it with a small nod. Although she sets the glass before her, she doesn't take a sip.

"What does she drink?" I ask, continuing to watch the table like a fucking creep.

"What?"

I turn back to him. "What does she normally drink? You said she's not gonna drink the beer, right?" He takes me in for a long moment before he looks at me, assessing in a way I don't necessarily like.

"Anything sweet." *Of course*, the woman who is all sugar plums and fairy lights likes sweet drinks. "Though it's late and she's volunteering bright and early tomorrow, so she probably won't even have a real drink tonight. If she weren't humoring her friends like she is now, she'd probably have ordered a Shirley Temple. But she won't want anyone to feel bad for getting beer, so she'll just nurse that for the next hour before she leaves."

A fucking Shirley Temple.

I take her in, then, in a way I haven't let myself yet. She's in a white turtleneck with a burgundy dress over top, a pair of translucent, dark tights covering her legs, and little boots on her feet that are hooked into the railing of the stool she's sitting on. As she always seems to do, she finished the outfit with a matching burgundy bow in her hair, tying back her loose chocolate brown curls that float down to the center of her back.

She looks like a woman who would unabashedly order a Shirley Temple at a dive bar.

She also looks like the kind of woman who, if asked, could tie the stem of the cherry and not even know what it implied.

I am so completely fucked.

That fate is even more evident with my next words.

"Put one on my tab."

Another pause before he lets out a loud laugh, shaking his head. But he doesn't ask any other questions, not as he puts the grenadine and ice into a tall cup, not as he tops it with a handful of cherries and then some ginger ale. Not even when he leaves the bar and carries it over to her. I watch her until he taps her on the shoulder and she turns to him, not wanting to see the interaction.

I should have told him to tell her it wasn't from me. I'm not sure why I even did it at all, especially since when she puts two and two together, she's probably going to be even more of a pain, thinking I'm nicer than I actually am.

"She's staring at you, man," Colt says when he's back behind the bar, forearms leaning on the polished bartop, a shit-eating grin on his lips.

"Good for her," I say, resisting the urge to look over my shoulder. Is she happy? Annoyed that I stepped in? Confused?

It doesn't matter, I tell myself.

Even my subconscious doesn't buy it.

I stay, chatting with Colt, much longer than I intended, switching to a soda after my beer is gone. Despite myself, I enjoy sitting at the bar, the casual atmosphere. It's low pressure, with Colt coming over to have small talk with me between customers, introducing me to various people as if I were actually part of this town now, instead of the interloper I feel like.

FIVE

ADAM

Wren leaves about twenty minutes before I do, not that I was watching. Eventually, I decide I should go try to write, so I settle my tab and say goodbye to Colt. As I drive in the dark, I note that Wren wasn't lying. Every house in town is decorated, nearly every one already glowing bright. I have to begrudgingly admit that it does look friendly, welcoming, and festive.

When I turn onto Bluebird Lane, it's even brighter. My house looks strangely depressing as the only one not lit up.

Not that I care, of course.

As I pull into my driveway, I note that Wren is kneeling out front, wrapping a string of lights around the post of her mailbox. She waves at me with her usual, cheery demeanor, and I give her a slight wave in return. I might not want to take part in her chaos, but that doesn't mean I have to be a total asshole. That's what I'm thinking as I step out of my car and spot something out of place on my front lawn.

A blow-mold snowman is smiling up at me. A snowman that wasn't there when I left. A snowman I surely didn't buy. There are also two more candy canes, making almost half of my walkway a candy cane lane, of sorts.

When I look back at her, there's a small smirk playing on her lips that I fight not to return. She probably came back from the bar, put them up, and then decided she needed to decorate her mailbox at ten at night just to see my reaction.

You have to appreciate her tenacity, at the very least. Not many women would stare at me like that, challenging me as if I hadn't turned them down a dozen times already. After a moment, I sigh, realizing this battle is already lost.

"This you?" I call out across the lawn.

"Just a little Christmas spirit!" she says, that smirk widening into a grin.

"Wasn't the wreath enough?"

She shakes her head. "That one was basically charity. Don't you want the local kids to see your house and know you're not some grumpy old man?" I stare deadpan at her in answer, and she lets out a small, frustrated sound that shouldn't be cute. "Your house looks haunted," she whines.

I could argue, but I'm learning that gets me nowhere with Wren, so I sigh in defeat instead.

"If I leave them, will you leave me be?"

"I don't know. Are you going to add lights to your house?"

I return her smile then, unable to hold back, and for some reason, I'm enjoying this back-and-forth of ours. "Probably not."

"Then probably not."

I let out a chuckle, then shake my head, heading up my walkway. "You're not going to win this battle, Birdie." I don't know where the nickname comes from, just that she always looks like a delicate little bird. But when her face lights up at my words, I can't find it in me to regret it.

"That's fine. I'm happy to fight the good fight," she says as I step into my house, shaking my head with a light chuckle.

I spend an hour at my kitchen table with a notebook, trying to get some writing in. A dozen pages are balled up on the table, but I leave them to clean up in the morning when I decide it's getting late and I should head to bed. When I pass the door to my office on my way to my room, a light catches my eye, making me pause and turn toward the room. As I enter, I notice the light in the room across from my office in Wren's house is on once more. Tonight, she's working on a new project, a sewing machine in front of her as she feeds red fabric through it. Her long hair is in a haphazard bun on the top of her head, and she's washed her face of the makeup she was wearing at the bar, revealing the tired look of her eyes. I sigh when I check the time, realizing it's after midnight.

Even though I'm tired myself, I sit at my desk, intrigued to see just how late she stays up. She continues to work as I listen to music and jot down words, trying to make something work. My mind is so stuck on all things Christmas decorations that I find myself jotting down words, lines, and a few notes before I realize they're all holiday themed. I push the paper aside and am about to give in for the night when finally, she stands, turning off her light and leaving. I check the time. 1:02 a.m.

I usually go for my run at seven, no matter how late I stay up, and even though I'm usually the kind of person who doesn't need much sleep, I can feel in my bones that I'll be tired tomorrow. If she's doing this night after night and then waking up at the crack of dawn to head out for the day, I don't know how she's not dead on her feet every day.

Not your problem, Porter, I remind myself. *She's a nuisance. Not your problem.*

The next morning, I wake to find the rest of my candy cane walkway had been completed, and can't even muster the annoyance to be annoyed. I do look across the way to see a smiling and waving Wren, though.

"Morning, Adam."

"No more decorations," I say, but the sternness I'm trying to keep in my tone seems to have left the building.

"Or what?" she asks, playfulness in the words.

My breath stops in my chest at the taunt.

A million responses move through my mind, each more inappropriate than the last, and I push each one back, but one makes it through my filter. "Or else I might have to retaliate." The threat does the opposite of what I intended, making her face light up, her eyes twinkling with mischief.

"That's a risk I'm willing to take." And then she's prancing down her driveway, her sweet skirt swaying behind her as she goes.

Let the games begin, I suppose.

SIX

Wren

The next morning, I place a two-foot-tall gingerbread man on Adam's front lawn and stand back, admiring my handiwork. He still has no lights, but we're making slow progress. With less than a month until Christmas, I think I will manage to bring him around to the bright side and convince him to light up his house.

Just then, Adam steps out onto his front porch wearing a pair of gray sweats that should be illegal (I'm sure Hallie would have something to say about the noticeable bulge in his front) and a matching gray hoodie. For a split second, he almost looks like someone from one of those trashy tabloids Nat reads, but I lose my grip on who his doppelganger might be before quickly shaking my head to clear my thoughts.

His eyes scan his yard, already trained to look for some new addition, and when he spots it, his head turns to where I am as if he already knew I was there.

"More decorations?" he asks with a raised eyebrow.

"I don't know what you're talking about," I say, fighting to keep my face neutral and innocent.

"You're playing with fire, Birdie."

A wave of warmth washes over me at the nickname, the same way it did when he said it last night, but I push it aside, putting my hands on my hips and tipping my head in challenge.

"Is that supposed to scare me off?" He shrugs as if the answer is *yes*. "I have two older brothers. Threats of retaliation were a Sunday morning tradition in my house." He gives me a small smile then, one he's clearly trying to hide but does so ineffectively. It sends that increasingly familiar hit of warmth through me, like a glass of warm, spiked cider on an empty stomach. It even gives me the same light-headed feeling.

"I don't think anything could scare you off if you set your mind to it."

"I can be very persistent when there's something I want," I say. "And I *am* going to make you decorate your house by the end of the season, Adam Porter."

"Is that so?" he asks, raising a thick eyebrow in my direction.

"I'm not going down without a fight, at the very least."

"Then I guess this is war, isn't it?"

He's been kind of an ass, but I'm finding I very much like this version of Adam. The fun, playful one. It's much better than the grumpy one who sits in his boring, undecorated house by himself.

"I guess it is," I say. Unfortunately, as much as I'd like to continue this back and forth, I do have to get to work, so I step toward my car and give him a little wave. "See you later, Adam."

When I park in my driveway after work, I note with glee that Adam still hasn't taken any of my decorations down. I'm enjoying this game between my neighbor and me, and I spent a good chunk of my day plotting up schemes for how to take it to the next level. I step out of my car, grab my things from the trunk, and trudge up the walkway toward my front door. As I approach my house, I notice something is off. But since the multiple bags and boxes in my hands are threatening to fall, I don't stop to pinpoint what it is.

When I step outside to get my mail ten minutes later, though, I realize what it is: my nutcracker is missing. I look left and right, trying to see if I moved it and forgot, then look around my porch to see if maybe he fell over, but there's nothing.

The centerpiece for my Land of Sweets display this year was a stunning online find. He was a bit battered and bruised when I got him, but with some sandpaper and a fresh coat of pastel-colored paint to better fit my vision, he was even better than expected. He's huge, nearly five feet tall, and heavy since he's mostly made of wood, and he was standing guard on my porch this morning when I left for work.

And now he's gone.

I'm coming to terms with either having to make do without or buying a new one when I feel eyes on me. I look to my right and see it for a flash: a pair of broad shoulders, a brooding gaze with an entertained smirk, and eyes that meet my shocked ones right before a curtain is pulled closed.

Somehow, I know.

I know Adam Porter has something to do with my nutcracker going missing.

I guess this is war, isn't it? he said this morning.

With a slight growl, I turn on my heel and make my way down my front pathway.

My day was absolute garbage. I had one student bite another, and the parent of the biter tried to blame it on the other kid's parents. Somehow, I agreed to bake all of the items for a bake sale fundraiser that will take place on Sunday at the holiday shop the school runs for the kids, and on top of that, when my mom called during my lunch, she asked if I could manage to make a quilt for her friend's granddaughter before Christmas. As seems to be my way, I stupidly agreed, even though it throws any plans of going to bed at a reasonable hour in the next week *completely* out the window.

And then, to top things off, as I was leaving work, Jan Klein made a snide remark about how the decorations on Main Street looked a bit lackluster compared to last year and said she hoped I had plans to *finish them up*. I bit my tongue and thanked her for her input instead of telling her we put up the same decorations as last year, and if she wanted to add more, she was more than welcome to do so on her own time, like I secretly wanted to do.

It's not that I don't want to help everyone. I love being the person in town everyone can count on, really. But with my new role as head of the decorating committee, I'm finding it challenging to balance my own goal of making my grandmother proud, my desire to make it the most festive year to date, and my need to help everyone who needs it.

The truth is, despite just how much I have to do right now, I would really like to nap for about a week, and the weight of all of these responsibilities is getting to me.

However, the exhaustion I felt in my bones just minutes ago seems to have evaporated as I move down my pathway, across the sidewalk, then up Adam's walkway. In fact, there's almost a *pep* in my step as I stomp over there. And even though I'm annoyed as can be, I'm also a bit eager for whatever confrontation we're about to have.

I only have to knock twice before the front door opens, Adam shifting to lean into the door frame with his arms crossed on his chest. He's in a long-sleeve shirt that clings to broad shoulders and thick muscles, but I force myself to keep my eyes on his face.

Don't fall for the hot arms, Wren. You're here because he stole your nutcracker. You're supposed to be stern, not swooning.

He smirks down at me before he speaks, not helping my urge to swoon in the least. "Can I help you?"

"Where is my nutcracker?" I ask, setting my hands on my hips and giving him the best glare I can muster. It's the kind I give my students when they're doing something they shouldn't, and I have to stop being the cool young teacher and instead be the disciplinarian. His smile goes wider, and my *god*, the man should do it more. I can't say he isn't good-looking when he's all brooding eyes, irritated glares, and annoyed jaw clenches, but this teasing look is absolutely panty-melting material.

His eyes shift to the side, looking expectantly at the window beside his door, and I follow his gaze, then gasp when I see my nutcracker in his window.

"What have you done to him?" I exclaim, noting a T-shirt for the band Atlas Oaks pulled over his head and a black sock on the top of his staff, hanging limply like a sad flag.

"Oh, calm down, it's a sock and a shirt. I didn't take a chainsaw to him."

"This is sacrilege. He's a symbol of Christmas spirit! Not...whatever that is." I wave a frantic hand toward the window.

"I think sacrilege is a bit dramatic. But he's my hostage now; I can do what I want with him."

I glare at him, my irritation brewing as we bicker on his front step. I have so many things to do, and none of them involve arguing with my neighbor.

The irritation directed at him is new for me. I always have a firm hold on my emotions, especially the negative ones, and can usually tamp them down and greet people with friendliness, no matter how I'm really feeling. Unfortunately, it seems my neighbor knows precisely which buttons to push.

"Come on, Adam. Give me my nutcracker back. He's the entire centerpiece for my decor!" It sounds like a whine even to my ears.

"Oh no, how will your eighteen million lights and decorations survive without your five-foot nutcracker?" he says, deadpan.

I roll my eyes. I find myself doing that a lot with him.

"Eighteen million is an exaggeration."

"Is it, though?" he asks as if he doesn't believe me.

"I can't give you a total because I've never felt the need to count them, but it's definitely not eighteen million." I shake my head, realizing I'm focusing on the wrong thing. "But we're getting off track: are you going to give him back to me?"

"You have to give in to my demands before you get him back."

Clearly, I'm losing my mind, something that must be caused by a mix of Hallie telling me nonstop about how hot my new neighbor is— *"Serial killer or not, Wren, the man is hot. I might be able to look past the potential murderer aspect if I got his head between my thighs,"* was what she said when we spotted him at the bar the other night—and the fact that I haven't gotten laid in well over a year because suddenly, I'm picturing an entirely inappropriate set of *demands* from Adam Porter.

Or maybe I just really need sleep, because I almost convince myself that his eyes flare with my question, almost as if his mind is going in the same direction as mine.

But there's no way.

The man can't stand me.

"Take back your decorations. And don't put any new ones up," he says, pulling me back from that dangerous track.

"No," I state, crossing my arms on my chest.

"Then you're not getting back your nutcracker. You're going to have to find some new symbol of Christmas spirit or whatever."

I fight the suddenly consuming urge to stomp my foot and whine. "This is ridiculous. I have a lot to do tonight besides argue with you."

He crosses his arms on his chest once more and tips his chin down to look at me questioningly.

"Yeah, what's up with that? Does Santa have you working doubles? You're up until the ass crack of dawn doing God knows what every night—"

"Are you watching me?" I ask, and for the first time, I contemplate Hallie's serial killer theory.

"Your lights are always on. As you know, your house is right next to mine, and my office faces yours." That explains that, I suppose. "So I can see that you're up until three a.m.—"

"One," I correct. "I don't let myself stay up later than one, not three a.m. or *the butt crack of dawn.* And it's not every night." He raises an eyebrow and tips his head, and I let out a frustrated breath before adjusting my response. "It's every night right now, but not normally. The holidays are just a bit extra crazy."

"Do you not require sleep during the month of December? I don't think one can actually survive on Christmas cheer alone, not even you."

I glare.

"I have things to do. Unlike you, I care deeply about this community and ensuring that everything for the holidays is perfect so everyone can enjoy the season."

"Except for you?" It throws me off, and my head moves back with confusion, but he clarifies. "You work your ass off to let everyone else enjoy their holiday season, but there's no shot you have any free time to enjoy it yourself."

"I enjoy it just fine. I love helping people out with their decorations and making their gifts, and—" I pause as he watches me with skepticism before shaking my head and stopping myself. "This is off topic and, honestly, none of your business. My sleep schedule has nothing to do with whether or not you're going to decorate your house or give me back my stolen property."

"I don't know. You think my focus is in the wrong place, but I think I'm the only one of us pushing for the right thing. You seem to take care of everything for everyone—when was the last time someone took care of you?"

My jaw tightens. "I don't need someone to take care of me. I've got it handled."

"Sure you do."

"You think you know everything and you're better off than me because...what? No one relies on you? No one can count on you to help them out? It just makes you a jerk."

"How am I the jerk in this situation? You're working nonstop for everyone in your life, and no one seems to care if that means you barely even sleep, but sure, I'm the asshole."

"You won't even put up a couple of stupid Christmas lights! You're willing to ruin a thirty-year tradition just to prove a point!" I take a step closer, and heat rolls over him in waves. The exhausted, stupid part of me wants to curl into it, but that part is an idiot.

"And yet I have left up every one of the decorations you've put on my lawn, Wren."

My pulse pounds, and I ask the question I've been wondering since he stopped trying to remove them.

"And why is that, Adam? What's the grand plan there? Are you giving me hope so you can rip it away? If you hate Christmas decorations so much, take them out yourself! Break them! Throw them away! Call the cops!" My voice is raised now, and I poke him in the chest with each option, and each one feels good, like I'm letting all of this pent-up emotion that's been unwittingly building for weeks out on *someone*, even if somewhere in my mind, I know it's not the right person.

But that feeling transforms quickly. All of the breath leaves my lungs when his hand moves, lifting quickly and wrapping around my wrist before pulling me in until my chest is against him. His hand settles on my hip, and the contact burns even through the layers of clothes.

I'm surprised when he speaks next, his words a low rumble.

"I fucking hate Christmas, Wren, but every time I walk out my door, there's something new on my lawn from you, and I can't seem to make myself be mad about it. Part of that is because if I time it right, I can look across the way and see you standing there with that little proud smile on your lips, and it makes my fucking day. So they're still up, but don't get me wrong, it's a selfish move."

I have to tip my head back to look at him from this distance, and he tips his down to look at me.

In that moment, I realize it wouldn't take much for him to kiss me like this.

My mind runs through the scenario: I could move to my tiptoes, and he could bend a bit more. His arm would curve around my back and tug me in close, and then maybe he would drag me inside and—

Okay, this is going too far. Maybe he's right. Maybe I *do* need to go to sleep earlier.

Not that I'll be listening to his advice any time soon.

I'm still trying to organize my thoughts and think of a way to respond to his confession, but I'm saved when a familiar voice speaks.

"Is that you, Wren?" I recognize it as Mr. O'Donnell from three houses down. It snaps me out of my daze, and I blink, turning to look at him standing on the sidewalk, his dog on a leash at his side.

"Yeah, it's me."

"You got a second? I wanted to ask a favor of you."

I clench my teeth and fight back a groan.

"Later, Wren," I hear behind me, and when I turn back to Adam, he's stepping back, that guard back on his face, but with a cocky tilt of his lips.

It's hot.

And I freaking hate it.

Instead of giving him the validation of a response, I turn away without another word and move toward Mr. O'Donnell, even if it means I'll probably be adding another item to my to-do list when I'm done.

At least I'm not stuck talking to Adam anymore.

SEVEN

Wren

As soon as I get back into my house and close the door behind me, I groan loudly with defeat. My mind reels trying to fit in picking up Mr. O'Donnell's grandson from the airport on Saturday morning, which I stupidly just offered to do, in with the million other things I have to do. I mentally rearrange my calendar before texting Hallie to see if she can scoot the baking we were supposed to do on Saturday morning to Friday. She's in, but that means I need to finish the top piece of the quilt tonight, most likely. I stupidly thought I could go to bed at a reasonable hour tonight, given that the exhaustion is starting to seep into my bones, but this changes my plans. I eat dinner at my coffee table, finishing up the first trimester report cards, then get into my cozy clothes before heading up to my office to sew.

It might be the fact that I'm stressed and tired, but as I cut the squares for the quilt, my mind moves to my grandmother teaching me how to make fabric blocks for quilted stockings we made for the whole family when I was nine. My heart gets that familiar heaviness at the memory, something that's been happening more and more since the holiday decorations started to go up. This was her favorite time of year, and everything reminds me of her. She took the town decorating and the holiday festival seriously, which is why I have taken on so many of those responsibilities myself, knowing no one else would prioritize them the way I would. I'm determined to make this the best year yet, determined to honor and memorialize her in this special way.

As I've done since she passed in February, I push that grief back, filling in the void with more tireless work. Keeping myself busy is the best way to fight back against the gloom of losing her.

It's not too late when the first yawn happens, and the cup of coffee I made myself is barely taking the edge off. At around ten, the light across the way flicks on. My head lifts, remembering Adam telling me he could see me working at night. Adam enters the room, and I can't see much of it, but I watch as he moves through it before sitting at a desk that faces the window. When his head turns in my direction, I quickly tip mine down, returning to my task at hand with a fervor. An embarrassed flush burns my cheeks, and I hope he can't see it. In the meantime, I simply pretend I've been hard at work nonstop. After a while, though, I get the nerve to look up again.

When I do, I see he's staring at me. Not just staring—he waves at me when he sees me looking back at him. I give him a half-hearted lift of my hand before moving back to my work. Ten minutes or so later, I lose the battle of will and look up again. He must see the shift in my movement, because he looks up, too. I try not to think about what that means, that he was that aware of my movement. But when he lifts a finger and presses something against the window, I lose that train of thought.

Instead, I focus on the white piece of paper with dark, messy writing scrawled across it.

Go to bed.

I roll my eyes at him, then reach for a dark marker of my own and a piece of scrap paper.

You first.

I lift an eyebrow at him, and even though my eyes are tired, I catch him smiling just a bit. Then he shrugs and stands, turning off the light and walking away. I sigh and go back to my project, but guilt wraps around my insides. When I look at my phone, I see it's 12:40 a.m. My personal limit is one o'clock, but...how much could I really get done in twenty more minutes? And I *am* tired, which makes everything take longer. I'd be much more efficient with more sleep.

And Adam went to bed as soon as I said I would if he did first.

Not that that matters.

Still, I wrap up what I'm doing, neatening up the area quickly before turning off the light in my office and heading to bed a bit earlier than usual.

The next morning, I dig through the box of extra decorations and gasp excitedly when I spot the box of unbreakable ornaments. On my way out the door, I hang them on the small bush outside Adam's house before heading to my car. As I reach for the driver's side door, he steps out onto his porch, taking in my handiwork with a small smirk on his lips. I remember what he told me about his keeping the decorations up being a selfish action, and warmth fills my belly against my will. When his gaze moves to me, he lifts an eyebrow.

I give him a sassy little wave, then get in my car and drive off, grinning the whole drive to school.

Work is a bit easier than the day before, with no one biting anyone else and no parents emailing or calling me with complaints, thankfully. When I get home, I open the front door, push it open with my shoulder, and toss my bags onto the couch, but pause when I see something on the floor. Closing the door behind me, I bend to grab it before standing and unfolding the paper.

It's a plain piece of computer paper with magazine clippings of letters writing out a message and a Polaroid picture glued to the bottom half of the paper.

A photo with a figure I instantly recognize.

My nutcracker.

Fulfill our demands or the nutcracker gets it, the paper reads. The photo is a Polaroid of my pastel-colored nutcracker with the town newspaper with today's headlines in front of it.

I can't help it: I giggle.

I *giggle.* This man has stolen my property and is threatening to damage it, and I'm giggling. And planning what kind of decorations I can put on his lawn next.

Maybe the sleep deprivation is truly getting to me. My mind drifts to his insistence that I take care of myself, and the humor seeps out of my body.

He said I work to make everyone's holiday magical but have no time to enjoy it myself, and for a split second, the tiniest hint of frustration I hadn't realized had been locked away flares to life. For a moment, I question if he's not right, if I'm doing this for everyone else at the expense of my own happiness.

But I quickly lock that thought away and throw away the key. What does he know? I take care of myself just fine and *am* enjoying myself. I enjoy helping out those around me, especially during a busy, stressful season like Christmas. Who cares if I'm a bit tired and have slightly less free time in December if it means everyone around me has the most magical holiday season possible?

My mind once again drifts to my grandmother and the dozens upon dozens of memories I have of her pitching in to help out around town.

"It's important we all do what we can, especially this time of year," I remember her telling me when we were wrapping up gifts for the toy drive late one night. I was probably twelve at the time, and I was staying at her house to help prepare the finishing touches for the holiday festival that she had been planning for as long as I could remember.

"But you're doing all the work, Grandma," I had said.

She shook her head and gave me a soft, patient smile. "No, sweet girl. I'm doing what I can. I'm happy to give a little extra time to those I care about. It makes me happy. It makes those around me happy. Can't see any reason not to do it, if that's the outcome."

I've always taken that to heart, helping everyone and anyone, often before they even ask for help.

Adam wouldn't know community and cheer if it slapped him in the face. Of course, he wouldn't see the value in sacrificing a little sleep for that.

At eleven thirty p.m., I'm pinning together quilt blocks when I feel eyes on me and look up, catching Adam staring at me across the way. A blush burns over me, and I become self-conscious, thinking of him looking at me, so I keep my head down for a full ten minutes, refusing to let myself look up. When I finally let myself glance up, his head is down, but it lifts as if he was watching for me. He points at a piece of paper taped to the window.

Go to bed.

I can't tell if it's the same one from last night, but I shake my head at him and wave a hand at him before starting to sew more squares together.

The next time I look up, he's gone, the light is off, but that note is still there. It puts a rock in my gut, though I ignore it. Soon after, my bobbin tangles, and I sigh, then decide to leave it for tomorrow and head to bed a bit early at quarter after twelve.

But it has nothing to do with Adam's note.

Not in the least.

When I get home from work the next day, there's another note slipped under my door, and excitement fills me as I pick it up.

No, not excited.

Being excited to read a hostage note for a nutcracker would probably denote that my mental state is crumbling.

Take down the decorations or else.

Today, the photo is of the nutcracker next to a hammer. I let out a laugh, then fold up the note and place it on my kitchen table with the other one. In retaliation, I add a couple more glittery lollipops to his yard. I spend the evening prepping cookie dough for the bake sale, cleaning the kitchen, and wrapping up schoolwork before taking a shower and slipping into some comfy clothes. I baked and set aside four cookies for myself—a little treat for making it to the end of the day—and then grabbed the plate before heading upstairs to my office to work on some decorations for the upcoming school-wide holiday party. A co-worker was supposed to do it, but she asked if I would mind taking it over for her, and she would cover Valentine's Day. I agreed, knowing I already have all the stuff to make some simple decorations and garlands.

When I settle in, Adam's office light goes off across the way, the note taken down sometime between last night and now. I push away the strange jolt of disappointment before throwing myself into working on some of the decorations for the holiday party in two weeks. I'm about halfway through one of the big banners when the light flicks on.

Without my mind's permission, my eyes pop up, looking at the window across the way. He's entering the room, wearing a well-fitting short-sleeved shirt that, even from this angle, I can tell hugs his biceps perfectly.

Nope, no Wren. We don't care about his arms, remember? He's bossy and rude and hates Christmas.

Unfortunately, I've always been a sucker for good arms.

His eyes are locked on me across the way.

Instantly, I put my head down and continue with my sewing, pushing fabric through the machine and trying to concentrate. Eventually, I crack and then glance up. He's sitting at the desk, head down, but he must notice I'm looking once more, because his head pops up as well. Then he reaches over, grabbing for a paper and pressing it to the window.

Go to bed.

I shrug, then shake my head before looking down at my project again. Ten minutes later, my curiosity wins once more, and I look up. This time, his head is no longer tipped down; instead, he's sitting, gaze locked across the way with his arms crossed on his chest. When he sees me looking at him, he reaches over once more, pressing the note to the window again.

Go to bed.

Underneath, he's added another word in his thick, no-nonsense handwriting.

Now.

I check the time, seeing twelve thirty on the clock.

I can't let him win, even if my eyes are starting to lose focus and my work isn't as neat as it used to be.

I shake my head, and he glares at me, then pulls the paper down, scribbling on it.

Add lights to the wreath.

I read it once, then rub my eyes before reading it again. Lights to the wreath? I tip my head to the side, exhausted and not fully understanding, and he looks like he's about to sigh before letting the sign drop and writing another.

If you go to bed, this one reads.

He's *bribing* me.

And unfortunately, I'm totally about to fall for it. I don't want to give too much away, I shrug, then grab a piece of paper of my own.

Lights on your porch?

A long moment passes as he reads it, his face clearly displeased, before he writes something and presses the paper to the window.

Don't push it.

I fight a smile, knowing it was probably a lost cause but not wanting to seem *too* eager about his offer. Lights on the wreath would mean that, at the very least, the entire street has lights.

A huge win, I think, as I write down my response.

I was going to bed anyway.

Even from across the way, I can see his eyes roll, which is why, when I clean up and turn the lights off, I'm grinning. It stays on my face as I clean up and get ready for bed, and when I finally do, it's still playing on my lips.

EIGHT

Wren

"You need a break," Hallie says on Friday afternoon as she helps me bake cookies for the bake sale. At the staff meeting on Tuesday, Stephanie asked if anyone was willing to bring in some treats to sell while the PTO puts on their annual holiday shop for the kids, and the room was absolutely silent. I know those funds help the graduating fifth graders have a party at the end of the year. If no one signed up, it wouldn't happen, so I volunteered.

When I did, a relieved sigh went through the room, which I usually assume was because everyone was glad the fundraiser would still happen. Now, I have a little voice in my head that sounds far too much like my neighbor.

What if everyone was just relieved I pitched in so they wouldn't have to step up themselves?

Like I've done every time since that voice started speaking, I shake my head, knocking it free, and move on, continuing to scoop dough onto a cookie sheet and appeasing my friend. Hallie isn't wrong: I *do* need a break, but I also know one is coming soon. I just need to get through the next few weeks.

"It's almost winter break, and then I'll have ten whole days to relax." My best friend, for as long as I can remember, stares at me, clearly not buying what I'm selling her. I sigh in defeat and amend. "Eight, if you remove Christmas." She continues to stare, but I stand strong.

"And you aren't signed up to help with anything else during your break? You're going to take it easy and catch up on sleep?"

I bite my lip, carefully avoiding her eyes and concentrating on portioning dough.

"Wren," she says in a chiding tone.

"What am I supposed to do? Not to help people? It's just house-sitting and checking in on Mr. and Mrs. Peters's cat while they're away."

I don't mention that I will probably end up babysitting my niece a couple of times, and I already told my parents I'd help them do post-holiday cleanup at their Christmas tree farm while I'm off.

Not that I'll be telling her that.

"Yes! At least not at the expense of your sanity! No one expects you to do everything, Wren." I give her a look because lately, I've been thinking that's not true. She raises an eyebrow and counters. "If they do, it's because you have set those expectations with your utter lack of boundaries."

"I have boundaries!"

Hallie scoffs out a laugh.

"Where? Tell me a single boundary you have set and maintained, Wren. It used to be working on weekends, and we both know that shit's long out the window." I flip through my mind, trying to think of something I can give her as proof, but come up empty. "And then it was not volunteering for anything extra, which turned into not volunteering until you were explicitly asked." She tips her head to the dozens of cookies and brownies individually packaged for the bake sale. "But I already know you offered to bake all of that without even asking if anyone could split the duties."

I set my scoop aside and move to the tray I took out of the oven earlier.

"It's just extra chaotic right now because this is my first year in charge of the decorating committee and the town festival." I slide the spatula under a cookie, averting my eyes from my best friend's knowing gaze. "I just want everything to be perfect this year. It's the first year..." I let my words trail off, afraid that the emotions I've kept in a brightly wrapped box and tied with the most perfect bow will escape. I don't have to say it, though, because Hallie is my best friend and always knows.

"I know, babe. I do, really, and I get it. I'm sure your grandmother is watching and so proud, but just like me, she's nervous. She was the biggest proponent for your boundaries, always telling people to do shit themselves and stop asking you for help."

I look at her knowingly. "Yes, and every December, all of *her* boundaries also went out the window. It's just what happens."

My grandmother was head of the decorating committee in Holly Ridge from the time she was twenty-eight until she passed away earlier this year. She was my favorite person in this world and loved nothing more than this town. She cherished helping it and making it into a real community —values she instilled in me. When she was sick, I told her I would continue her legacy and make this holiday the best one yet. I still remember the soft look she gave me, the way her hand moved to cup my cheek.

I know you'll keep the lights shining bright, Wren.

I might be tired, and I might be stretched thin, but I'm doing it for her. I'm doing what she would have done if she were in my shoes, and every day I go to bed hoping I'm doing her proud.

"You and I both know this was a problem well before the season hit, Wren. You're going to burn yourself out."

Before I can answer, my phone beeps with a new text notification, a welcome interruption from having to respond to her. I set the last cookie onto the cookie rack, then reach for my phone to check the screen. I fight not to react visually to the text Carrie Staub, one of the moms on the PTO, just sent me, but I fail and let out a loud groan.

"What?" Hallie asks, stepping closer, then reading the text over my shoulder.

CARRIE

> Hey, Wren! So sorry to ask you last minute, but I can't make it to set up tomorrow. Any chance you can fill in for me?

"Tell her no," Hallie says, words firm. I sigh, then turn to her, resting my back on the counter as I stare at my phone forlornly.

"If I don't, it won't get done."

"Or she'll find someone else to do it. Or do it herself, God forbid."

I lift my phone up to remind her of the message. "She said she can't do it."

Hallie gives me a soft look, the kind you give kids when they ask about something that is obvious to adults.

"Or maybe she just doesn't want to and knows you will," Hallie says, grabbing a cookie and moving to my kitchen table to sit, facing me.

I pause for a second and blink at her before shaking my head. "She wouldn't do that. People don't do that."

"I love how you see the best in everyone, Wren, really, I do, but people do that shit all the time. And unfortunately, you're just too sweet and kind to notice or question it."

I stare at the text, confused.

Do people actually do that? Do people do that to *me*? I know I've become the person in town that can be counted on, but people only ask me when they don't have another option, right?

I'm lost in those thoughts when Hallie's concerned voice pulls me back into the present. "Uh, Wren, what is this?"

"What's what?" I ask, shaking my head and setting my phone down, deciding I can answer later, especially when I see the genuine panic on Hallie's face.

"Are you being threatened?"

"What are you talking about?" She waves a piece of paper, then I laugh, realizing she's holding one of the ransom notes from Adam.

"What the hell is this, Wren? It's creepy. Should we call someone?"

I shake my head, reaching for the three other notes I've received and handing them to her. "No, my nutcracker has been stolen and is currently being held hostage. It's not a real threat or anything." *I don't think*, I don't add.

"Stolen by who?" She sifts through the papers.

"My neighbor."

Her concern has morphed into intrigue with this new piece of information. "The hot one?"

"The grumpy one," I correct.

"Same difference. Why would he steal your nutcracker?"

"Because I've been sneaking decorations onto his lawn, and he doesn't want me to." I reach for a cookie on the cooling tray, trying to distract myself from thoughts of Adam with its sweet, melty goodness.

"Oh...kay?"

I explain further, telling her about our back-and-forth of my putting decorations on his lawn and how, at first, he removed them, but for some reason, he's stopped.

I leave out our nightly exchanges, since even though I've come to anticipate them, they might fuel her serial killer theories.

I also leave out how he told me he stopped taking them out because he likes watching the joy it brings me. *That* would definitely fuel her hot-neighbor fantasies, which might be even worse.

"So it's like a kinky elf on the shelf?"

I choke on the bite of a cookie I just took.

"It's not kinky, Hal. My god, not everything has to be sexual," I say once I can breathe again.

"A man is sending you Polaroids, and that man looks like Adam Porter. That makes it sexual by default."

I let out a laugh and shake my head at my best friend. "I don't think that's how that works."

"It is, trust me. I would know." I pause, mid-bite, and stare at my best friend, trying to decide if she's being serious. She gives me a mischievous look that makes me a little nervous. I open my mouth to ask a question, though I don't know what it is, but she stops me before I can. "You know what we should do?" Her tone makes those nerves ratchet up further.

"I have no idea," I say slowly. Hesitantly.

"We should break into his house. Try to steal it back."

I stare at her, then shake my head. "Hallie..." There's a warning in my tone, the kind a mother uses when she's trying to be supportive, but also knows her kids are giving her the absolute worst ideas ever. In this friendship, I am always the mother.

"Oh, come on. It will be fun!"

I try to appeal to her common sense. "I don't know if breaking and entering is the right choice for a man who, not long ago, you said was probably a serial killer."

She waves a hand at me and walks to my front door to retrieve her jacket.

"I don't think he's a serial killer *now*. My current theory is that his dad is Santa Claus, and he doesn't want to take over the family business, so he's hiding away. It would explain why he hates Christmas, after all."

I blink at her, fighting the laugh that would just encourage her. "You've really put some thought into this, haven't you?"

She gives me a *duh* kind of face.

"Of course I have. I've been asking around, trying to see if anyone knows anything about him. It seems the only people he's talked to are Jeanie, and I'm convinced she signed an ironclad NDA when she sold the house, and Colton, who is as tight-lipped as can be." Hallie rolls her eyes at the idea of her older brother not giving her gossip, though he has spent all of the years he's owned his bar doing just that. He says that being a bartender comes with an honor code he refuses to break. Of course, that means Hallie does everything in her power to try and get him to break said honor code constantly.

Even though she acts like Jeanie is a gossip, the real source of all the town's knowledge is Hallie.

"Maybe no one knowing anything means he wants some privacy." I reach for the pan with the unbaked dough, grab it, and move toward the oven.

"Come on," she says, grabbing the pan from my hands and putting it to the side. "The ovens are empty—we'll put this batch in when we get back after our successful recovery mission."

I stare at her, knowing from a lifetime of being friends that once Hallie gets an idea, there's no talking her out of it.

"What if he's home?" I ask, and she shakes her head.

"He was getting into his car when I got here two hours ago, and his car still isn't out front. The coast is totally clear."

I twist my lips, trying to think of a way to dissuade her, but also, a small part of me likes the idea. I can't seem to fight back a smile at the thought of Adam coming home and finding the nutcracker missing. Will he come to my door and ask about it? Steal something else?

"Do you still have the key to the back door that the Demauros gave you?" Hallie asks, and I nod.

"I don't know if it will work, though."

"No better time to try, right? You try the back door, and I'll go up front and pretend I'm ringing his doorbell, keep an eye out, and you sneak in the back."

"Why do I have to sneak in?"

"Because it's your nutcracker, and I'm a much better lookout."

She's not wrong. Between messing with my brothers and Hallie's, we're well-versed in sneaking around to get what we want. Over the years, we've learned that I often get distracted by something or someone and forget that I'm supposed to be creating a diversion if needed.

I stare at her, knowing there's no way I'll be able to talk her out of this, then sigh. "Fine. You call me, and I'll keep my phone on me. Start yelling if he pulls up, and I'll slip out."

She gives me a triumphant look, and I move toward the front of the house to slip on my shoes while Hallie follows, then leaves out the door. Once she's outside, she calls me, and I answer but don't speak. Instead, I reach for my keys and head out the back door.

I get into Adam's house easily, the spare key Mr. and Mrs. Demauro gave me when I house-sat for her still working. My heart is pounding as I look around the once-familiar space, noting how empty it is. Everything seems to be painted white and clean. While Mrs. Demauro has lots of colorful art and photos, Adam has left his walls bare.

I fight the urge to look around more, wanting to find out what I can about my mysterious neighbor, but I know we might not have much time, and I need to move quickly. Stepping through the kitchen and into the living room, I spot my nutcracker in the front window, then begin making my way there.

Before I can reach it, though, I'm up against the wall, a body pressed against my front and brown eyes looking down at me.

NINE

Wren

When my back hits the wall, I yelp, my phone falling to the ground with a clatter. Panic surges through me before it melts into something different altogether as my brain processes that Adam Porter is hovering over me, one hand on the wall beside my head, the other resting on my hip after gripping me there to corner me.

"What are you doing here?" he asks after a moment. My eyes are locked on his, and stupidly, I note that they're not brown, like I initially thought, but the prettiest greenish-hazel color, and the lashes are long and dark. Why do men always seem to have the longest, darkest eyelashes, while women are left to resort to gluing little things onto their eyelids or caking on layers of mascara to get anything close?

"Wren." My name rumbles through me, making my mind return to the task at hand.

"Hey, Adam. Funny seeing you here."

That was the best I could do?

But when a smirk forms on his lips, any regrets of not having a better response melt away. "In my own house?"

I shrug as best as I can. "I thought you weren't home. Your car isn't out front."

"It's in the garage. What are you doing here?"

I roll my lips between my teeth, and his eyes follow the movement. My heart pounding has nothing to do with him watching my lips and everything to do with getting caught, but it surely isn't helping.

"I'm on a mission," I finally reply in a faint whisper.

"A mission?"

"I'm infiltrating enemy territory to get my fallen comrade back." His lips tip for the tiniest of seconds before it's gone, the entertainment fleeting, but there.

"How did you get in? I think this would be considered breaking and entering."

"Just entering, actually. I had a key."

His brow furrows. "Why do you have a key for my house?"

"I used to house-sit for the Demauros. Not my fault that you didn't change the locks."

"Of course you did." He pauses, and silence hangs between us. His chest is pressed to mine, his face just inches from mine, and I wonder if he can feel my pounding heart. If so, I sure hope he's just assuming it's because I've been caught in his house.

"Are you going to give me back my nutcracker?" I ask, staring up at him, heart pounding. "I feel like I earned it at this point. I made it this far."

He hesitates for a moment before speaking.

"What do I get out of it?" he asks.

"I'm not taking down the decorations."

"Then counter," he insists.

Again, my heart is pounding in my chest. His eyes drop from mine, then focus on my lips, then back to my eyes, and my lips part, his breath coasting over them in a terrible replacement of what I really want at this moment.

Suddenly, I don't care if I ever get that nutcracker back.

For some reason, I find myself wanting Scrooge himself to kiss me.

"Ask for what you want, Wren." The words are a quiet rumble that settles in my bones. I wonder if he can read my mind, if he knows I'm thinking about some other counteroffer that is so far from decorations, it's not even funny.

"Ask for it, and I'll give it to you," he whispers, confirming my fears. His eyes dip to my lips and back up. "You never ask for what you want, but I'm telling you right now, you will when it comes to me, Birdie."

The only thing I can think of right now is a kiss.

My mind can only focus on ways to try and get him to dip his head a bit. Would that be a good counter? Would he accept a kiss as payment? Maybe I could get the kiss *and* my decoration back. That would definitely be a successful mission, right?

Before an answer can leave my lips, though, a familiar voice is calling out, "Well, this looks cozy."

There's a pause, then my eyes go wide with panic as the realization of what almost just happened fills my mind. When he sees it, Adam steps back, putting three feet between us. I linger against the wall for a second too long, I'm sure, to seem natural, but I'm unable to stand straight after being so close to him. I also can't move my eyes from Adam, and I watch as his lips tip in an almost imperceptible way, like he's well aware of his impact on me and happy about it, before his face goes blank and he turns to Hallie.

"Did I interrupt something?" she asks, stepping into the living room. "I thought I would come in here to rescue you, but I don't know if you actually need any rescuing."

"What are you doing here?" Adam asks, looking between my best friend and me. Before I have to explain once again, Hallie speaks.

"You're holding her nutcracker hostage. We're attempting a reconnaissance mission."

Adam fights back a smirk, face remaining stoic, but I see it for what it is: a mask.

"So you two really broke into my house to get a nutcracker back?"

"You're the one sending my best friend ransom notes like the Zodiac Killer."

"Okay, Hallie—" I start, seeing that this is going to start spiraling soon, my headstrong best friend battling against my incredibly stubborn neighbor.

"She's the one leaving her shit all over my lawn."

"So you're holding her beloved nutcracker as repayment? Isn't that a bit childish? She's just trying to bring a little bit of cheer to the town. It's tradition, after all, for the whole town to be lit up."

"I just don't see why that has to be *my* problem. I don't like Christmas; I don't know why my house being undecorated is such a big deal," he counters.

"Because you're a part of the town! We decorate in this town," Hallie says, voice rising as she throws her hands up in frustration. It's interesting watching the argument for this side of things, when usually I'm in Hallie's position.

Unfortunately, despite how entertaining this all is, today has been a long day, and I have at least a dozen more cookies to finish baking before I can even think about heading to bed. I try to mask a yawn, but Adam's attention is instantly on me.

"You look exhausted," he says, taking a half step closer to me. There's an irritated look on his face, as if the idea of my being tired genuinely annoys him.

"Oh, just what every woman wants to hear," Hallie says, and he turns his head to glare at her, though his body stays pointed toward me.

"I didn't say she doesn't look gorgeous. I said she looks tired, probably because she's up until one a.m. every damn night, working her own fucking Santa's workshop."

"Are you stalking her?" Hallie asks with wide eyes. Adam rolls his, and I have to bite back a smile, knowing that this is another conversation Adam and I have already had.

"No, her office is across from mine so that I can see her lights on all night. She's exhausted because she refuses to go to sleep at a reasonable hour."

Something in my mind pings, and I turn to him. "You're also up, you know."

"But that's because I'm doing work for *myself*, not favors for other people."

I purse my lips in defeat, then watch the grin spread over his face. That's when Hallie turns her ire on me.

"What were you working on?"

I sigh. God, now Hallie is never going to let me live in peace.

"Last night I was working on decorations for the holiday party."

"Wren," she says, giving me a disapproving look. "That's not your job. You took over the Thanksgiving decorations!"

"I know, I know, but I offered to do it because Grace just got a puppy and it's keeping her up all night and—"

Hallie's face goes into full-on frustration before she throws her hands in the air, turning her body fully toward me. "Willingly! She *willingly* got a puppy, Wren. What does her getting a puppy have to do with you losing sleep?"

I shake my head, tired of this conversation already. "It's for work, Hal."

"Are you getting paid for it?" she asks, raising an eyebrow. I don't respond because we both know that answer. The standoff lasts a few moments before it's interrupted.

"What is work, by the way?" Adam asks, and we turn to him, having almost forgotten he was there.

Almost.

"What?" I ask, confused by the question.

"You're up late every night, and you leave at the crack of dawn. What kind of work could require that?"

"She's a second-grade teacher," Hallie says with exasperation before I can respond. "But she volunteers to monitor before-care and always ends up staying late to help someone with something because she doesn't know how to prioritize *herself*."

"That's not fair—"

She cuts me off before I can complete my argument, crossing her arms on her chest. "When was the last time you did something for yourself?"

"I'm manning the decorating committee for me," I counter, and even though she doesn't say anything, she gives me a pitying look, telling me she doesn't actually think that's being done for *me*. I'm relieved that she doesn't call me out on that in front of Adam. He already has his suspicions, and I don't need two people on my case about it.

"I'm changing my demands," he says, knocking Hallie and me out of our staredown. We both turn to look at Adam, but his focus is only on me. A wave of heat moves through me with the fierce look.

"What?" I ask skeptically. I don't think I'm going to like where this is going.

"I'm changing my demands. If you go to bed on time tonight, you'll get your nutcracker back."

I stare for a moment, blinking at him. "Excuse me?"

"You heard me. Go to bed at a reasonable hour, and I'll give you back your nutcracker."

"Oh, this is getting good," Hallie says.

I ignore her, keeping my eyes locked on my neighbor. "Are you serious right now?"

"Yes. If you go to sleep at a normal hour—" I open my mouth to argue, then he corrects himself. "*Before ten p.m.*, I will give you back your nutcracker."

"Ten p.m.? That's ridiculous, I—"

He keeps talking as if I didn't say a word.

"Until you take care of yourself, I'm going to be taking care of your nutcracker."

I stare at him for long moments before huffing out a disbelieving laugh. "And you'll keep the decorations up?"

"I never said that."

"Then what do I get out of this?"

"Your nutcracker? Sleep that your body clearly needs?" I speak before I think about the words I'm about to say.

"What do you know about what my body needs?" Silence fills the room, and my heart pounds as Adam's eyes rake over my body. My breaths come a bit quicker as the silence spans, and the edges of his lips tip up.

He doesn't say anything at all.

He doesn't have to. His look says it all.

I'm scrambling to think of some kind of reply, but Hallie beats me to it, breaking the tension with a well-timed Hallie quip.

"Oh my god, this is so hot," she murmurs, and when I turn to her, she waves a hand at her face as if she's genuinely overheating. I roll my eyes at her, but it's the distraction I need to come to my senses.

I need to get out of here, and I need to do it before I say something incredibly stupid.

"Come on. I have cookies to make," I grumble to the woman I thought was my best friend, tipping my head toward the door we both came in through.

"And you have to finish everything up so you can get to bed on time," Adam says.

I don't have to look at him to know he's smiling, and I don't respond; instead, I walk out of his house without a second look behind me.

"I'm kind of thinking you should stay up extra late," Hallie says as she steps outside. "See just how far you can push him." Adam lets out a grunt from behind me, but I continue, moving down the steps to his deck, then through his backyard into mine.

But as I enter my own house, I can't help but wonder...just what *would* he do?

TEN

ADAM

Saturday night, I'm not even bothering to try and write. I'm just watching the woman next door stay up well into the night. Yesterday, I saw her leave her back door from this window and watched with curiosity. I never would have guessed she would have gone across the backyard and broken into my house, but when I tiptoed down the stairs after I heard the back door open, I spotted her.

I should have called out her name, but some baser part of me, who has wanted to be closer to her since the first time she showed up on my front step, moved before I could think. In a moment, I had her pinned against the wall, and I have a feeling that if her friend hadn't interrupted, something would have happened.

I probably could have offered to trade a kiss for the nutcracker, and I was heavily contemplating it, knowing that she was about to offer it. But then I really took a look at her and saw just how damn tired she was, and decided to change my demands. I waited all night in my office to see if she would take me up on my offer, ready to return the nutcracker to its rightful place first thing in the morning, but when I saw the light in her kitchen go off and then the one in her office go on, I knew her stubborn ass wasn't biting.

Despite my new offer, she stayed up late, the light not flicking off until one a.m. on the dot, as if she was trying to prove a point. Her car was out of her drive before I even woke up, and there were no new decorations on my lawn this morning. Even though I would deny it if asked, I felt the loss of that deep in my chest.

Tonight, she seems to be stringing little white balls on a string, making some kind of garland, and honestly, she looks like she could pass out from exhaustion right then and there.

I thought offering to give her back her nutcracker if she went to bed on time would do the trick, but it would end this little game of ours, something I don't want to do just yet.

Scanning my desk, I spot the sign I made a few days ago, reach for it, and then knock on the window. Her head lifts, and she gives me a small, tired smile, lifting her project and shrugging as if to say *I can't yet*. I shake my head in disappointment, then sit back, crossing my arms on my chest. It's twelve thirty, and while I don't have anything pressing in the morning, I now know she has to endure a classroom full of little kids.

I don't know what's spawned this new urge to make sure she takes care of herself, but I'm not looking at it too closely. It's probably some new fucked-up version of procrastination. Perhaps if I help her solve her problems, my own will magically resolve themselves.

But when I watch her prick herself with the needle, wince in pain, and then look at her finger forlornly before a heavy, defeated sigh lifts her chest, something in me snaps.

I stand, then make my way down the stairs and out my back door. Before a single brain cell pipes up to tell me what a terrible idea this is, I'm moving across the yard and up her deck and opening her back door, which, I absentmindedly note, isn't locked despite it being after midnight and her being a woman who lives alone. When I enter, I realize the layout is the same as my house but mirrored, so I storm up the stairs and toward the room she's in with ease.

"Oh my god, what the fuck?" Wren shouts, standing from her chair as I enter the office. A bowl of popcorn sits on the desk, nearly empty, and long popcorn garlands that could be from some idyllic movie trail along the floor.

I cross my arms on my chest and stare down at her.

"Go to bed," I say, staring at her. She looked tired through the window, but now that she's closer, she looks utterly exhausted. I think I can even make out a tear track or two on her cheeks, which pinches something in my chest.

She's fucking *drained,* and it seems she's doing this to herself. She buries that exhaustion, though, in exchange for looking annoyed.

"You can't be in here! You can't just break into my house! That's illegal!"

"You're one to speak."

She doesn't have a cute retort for that one, so she asks me a different question. "How did you even get in here?"

"The door was unlocked, which is a conversation for another day. But for now, it's time for you to go to bed."

She lifts an eyebrow at me, crossing her arms on her chest and glaring at me. A tired glare, but a glare all the same. I thought this was her signature, but the more I learn about the woman, the more I realize this might be something she saves just for me, some kind of personality trait only I pull out of her.

I want to see more of it.

"What?"

"Go. To. Bed. You're exhausted, Wren. You're going to hurt yourself or get really sick. This isn't important enough to risk your health."

"You're being dramatic, Adam."

"I'm not. Even your friend said you were doing too much."

"And what neither of you seems to understand is that all of these things need to get done before the Christmas festival. It needs to be the best year yet!" There's panic in her words, and I try to soften my tone in response.

"Are you the only one with hands?" I ask.

"What?"

"Are you the only one with hands, Wren? Because I can't seem to find any reason why you're the only person who can do all of this." Her jaw goes tight, but I continue. "Hallie said you're taking on other people's jobs. I've watched you offer to do favors for people in this neighborhood over and over again, but who is helping you?"

"I don't need any help," she says so quickly, I don't think even she's buying it. But I can tell that's not the fight to pick, not right now. Right now, I have to get her to bed.

"You can't do all of the things you want to do to help everyone if you're too tired to function, Wren."

"And you can't tell me what to do, *Adam*. I'm an adult." I stare at her for long moments as she looks at me with that admittedly cute, indignant look on her face. She's not going to take care of herself or prioritize herself, it seems.

"Fine," I say.

"Fine?" I nod, and she relaxes, as if she thinks I'm going to turn around and leave. Instead, I take a few steps toward her and bend down, putting a shoulder into her belly and hefting her up and over my shoulder.

"Adam! What the fuck!"

"Which bedroom is yours?" I ask, ignoring the way her hand slaps at my back. It's barely a tap, and I can't decide if it's just incredibly half-hearted or if she is genuinely so tired she doesn't have the energy.

I step into the hallway, hitting the light in her office on my way out.

"Why on earth would I tell you that?"

"Fine, I'll figure it out myself," I say with a sigh, heading toward where my room is in my home, my gut telling me the rest of the layout is the same as mine. Triumph fills me as I push the door open and see the girliest room known to man, but I pause when I realize it's an exact replica of mine, with the furniture all in the same places. The bed is exactly where mine is, though it's probably a queen rather than a king. Instead of basic gray bedding in a twisted mess, hers is perfectly made with a lacy white duvet and more toss pillows in various shades of pink, red, and green than any one person should have. There are photos along the walls, including some landscapes and some family photos, and a small bookshelf sits in one corner. There are also small knick-knacks scattered about, along with various Christmas decorations.

It screams home. It screams lived in. It screams comfortable and cozy and safe. It screams *Wren*.

I realize my own home looks and feels empty in contrast to hers.

I shove that thought down as Wren continues to argue with my back before I toss her onto her bed.

"I can't believe you—"

"Bed. Now," I say, unable to get out complete sentences as I take her in, sprawled on her sweet-looking bed. She's wearing a loose, oversized sweatshirt and shorts, and a pair of fuzzy, warm-looking pink and green Christmas socks. She looks fucking delectable, and for the tiniest, most insane moment of my life, I contemplate climbing in there with her and pulling her against my chest.

"You can't tell me—"

The words leave my lips before I can even think to stop them from spilling out, before I can run them through some kind of filter. "Go to bed, or I'm getting in there with you and making sure you don't leave."

That's when I see it cross her face.

The barest hint of hesitation.

Fuck.

Fuck.

I would do almost anything to see that hesitation out, but I also know she needs to sleep. If I lay in that bed with her, I'm not sure I could convince myself to just go to sleep.

"Get out," she says finally, making the choice easier.

"You'll go to sleep?"

She gives me an exaggerated eye roll.

"Will you storm the castle again if I don't?"

"Over and over, sweetness." I don't miss the light blush that comes over her cheeks before she sighs once more.

"Then yes. I'll go to bed."

I nod, then turn around, making my way back through the house, successfully resisting the utterly wack urge to tuck her in.

I leave through the back door, lift an empty flowerpot onto the porch railing, and find the key instantly. I shake my head with irritation that the woman cares about everyone else—but clearly not her own safety—before using it to lock the back door. Before I can stop myself, I slide the golden key into my pocket.

If she doesn't go to bed at a reasonable hour tomorrow, maybe I'll have to do this again.

I'm smiling to myself as I enter my house, lock up, and turn all the lights off. I get ready for bed, then check to make sure the light in her office is still off.

It is, along with all the lights in her home.

And even though she seemed pissed, she must have actually listened to me, because despite her bedroom light turning back on for a minute or two, it went off not long after, telling me she heeded my warning and went to bed.

I would know. I was watching.

ELEVEN

Wren

I ignored Adam for the next two days after he broke into my house. Even though the bucket of decorations in my dining room stares at me each time I walk past it, I don't add any to his yard. Each day when I leave, I keep my head down, just in case he steps out for his morning run at the same time. (He doesn't, something that unfortunately doesn't go unnoticed by me.)

I also haven't received any new ransom notes, though when I gather the courage to look, I note that the nutcracker is still in the window.

I've also stopped working in my office at night and now do my projects at the kitchen table, though that has absolutely *nothing* to do with Adam. Of course not. Although my stubborn streak prevents me from adhering to his ten p.m. bedtime, I find myself going to bed by midnight each night.

Again, that has nothing to do with Adam. I'm just...tired.

Though I'm regretting not getting more sleep right now as I teeter precariously on a ladder before I have to head to work, fingers frozen from the cold as I work on hanging Mr. and Mrs. Campbell's lights.

Maybe if I weren't so exhausted, I would have been smart enough to keep my mouth shut instead of offering to help.

Yesterday, I went around the neighborhood to check in and make sure everyone was doing okay with their holiday lights and decorations. I also dropped off pamphlets about the toy and food drives we were still collecting for, just like my grandmother always did, skipping over Adam, obviously. When I stopped at the Campbells' house on the other side of Adam, Mr. Campbell told me he was getting to it, but he was working late nights, so he hadn't been able to get to it yet. A silence lapsed, and I *should* have just nodded and moved along, but I didn't.

Instead, I did what I always do: I offered to help, telling him I could probably help him hang the lights before work one of these days. What I *meant* was more along the lines of *many hands make light work*, but he interpreted it to mean I would completely handle the project on my own, hence me hanging up a few hundred feet of lights this morning before I get to work.

I'm reminded why I hang my actual lights up right after Halloween when we inevitably get one strangely warm day. It's fucking *cold* right now, and the thin layer of ice from the recent rainstorm that froze makes everything slippery and, if I'm being honest, a bit dangerous.

I'm almost done, and the timer I set on my phone for the absolute latest I could leave is counting down with less than ten minutes to go when I hear it.

"What are you doing?" a voice calls, and I don't miss that it sounds annoyed, as usual.

"Give me a second, Adam, and I'll give you the attention you're looking for," I say, reaching to snap another light clip onto the gutter.

"Excuse me?" he asks, annoyed. If I weren't concentrating, I'd look over my shoulder to catch his inevitable irritated look.

"One second, Adam, my god," I grumble, trying to snap a light into the little figure. My fingers are nearly frozen, and I'm having a harder and harder time locking each bulb into place, but I'm almost done with this side. I've already resigned myself to the fact that I'll have to find time to finish the job tomorrow morning. But right now, I have just five or so more lights to install on this ledge. Then I can sit in my car and crank the heat as high as it will feasibly go on the five-minute drive to school, hoping the feeling comes back to my fingers quickly.

"You're going to freeze out here, Wren. And that entire gutter is covered in ice. Why not just wait for the sun to thaw it?"

I huff at him, but otherwise don't reply. I hear his feet brushing along the ice-frozen grass, edging nearer, and I groan. As much as I enjoy this back-and-forth between us, I don't have the energy for it today.

"I have school today," I say through gritted teeth, the twist ties I'm using to hang the lights between my teeth. "And I'm working late." Silence fills the space as I snap another holder onto the gutter, my fingers stinging as I do.

"Is it really necessary for you to do it right now? Or for you to do it instead of the actual homeowners?"

I ignore him, of course; he wouldn't understand. Three more to go.

"Wren, come on. Your fingers are purple." There's a new softness to his words that I'm not sure how to respond to, though I decide brushing it off is the best option.

"I'm fine, Adam; go away," I instruct, eyes not leaving my work, even though I'm secretly wondering what his face looks like when he talks softly like that.

I'm down to one more light, though I'll have to stretch to get it or climb down and move the ladder over. It's not the widest stretch I've ever had to make, so I decide to go for it. I need to be in my car and on my way in under four minutes. Stretching, I almost get it, but then my hands slip, throwing my center of balance off, and I lose my step.

I shriek as I begin to fall, closing my eyes tight to avoid watching the ground get closer as I fall to my death.

Okay, it's not so high that I'll die, but I'm definitely going to get hurt.

When I fall, though, it's over much faster than I anticipated. My eyes are still squeezed shut when my body stops moving and warmth takes over my side. Is it blood? Am I lying in a puddle of my own blood, and that's why I don't feel pain? Maybe I actually *am* dying. Maybe—

"Jesus Christ, Wren, what the fuck?" a deep voice asks, cutting through my own panic.

That's when I realize I'm not in a bloody heap on the frozen ground.

I'm in Adam Porter's arms.

And he's moving me across the yard.

"What the heck?" I murmur. My legs are slung over one arm, my back cradled by his other.

"Do you have a death wish?" Adam asks through gritted teeth.

"What—"

"What are you doing out there?" he grinds out. Finally, I shift so I can see his face, and I notice his jaw is tight. He's *mad*. I figured he was annoyed or stressed, but the look on his face is definitely anger.

"Hanging decorations, obviously."

"Everything is coated in ice. You're lucky I was there, or else you would have snapped your neck." I roll my eyes.

"You're being dramatic, I wouldn't have snapped my neck," I say, even though I was convinced I was dead just moments ago. We're moving, but from this angle, I can't really tell where to, but I need to finish those lights and get on my way. I shift, but he holds me tighter. "Put me down, Adam."

"No." There's finality in the word, and I pull my head back to look at him, blinking slowly. His eyes continue to look forward, jaw tight.

"What?"

"If I put you down, you're going to just climb right up that ladder again," he explains. I realize now he's moving us across his yard and toward mine.

"Yes, because I have something to do." I can't move well because he's holding me still, so I can't reach my phone in my pocket to check the time, but I can't imagine I have much more time before my timer runs out.

"No, you don't."

"*Excuse* me?"

"You need to take care of yourself, Wren. You're going to kill yourself if you don't. I tried being nice, but it seems the only way I can get through to you is if I fucking manhandle you."

"I can't believe this!" I pull a hand back and hit his chest, though it's hard, and my hit is more like a swat against him. Still, frustration is brewing in my veins. "You don't know me at all, Adam, much less well enough to be making decisions about what I should or shouldn't be doing. This is crazy!"

"Well, the people who know you well clearly aren't getting on your case enough about it if you're falling off ladders at seven a.m. Why are you putting up their lights?" We're on my lawn now, and his steps are slowing as he moves up my walkway.

"Mr. Campbell doesn't have the time. I'm helping him."

"His car is out front," Adam growls, frustration clear in the words. I look over his shoulder and confirm that Jed's car is in fact out front.

I shake my head. "He's probably still asleep. He works nights."

"So do you, apparently," he grumbles, moving up my front steps.

"He *actually* works nights. He needs the help, so I gave it to him."

Adam shakes his head, and when he does, the scruff of his light beard scratches at my temple, sending tingling warmth through me.

Well, *that's* new.

"You give people too much fucking credit, Wren, and it allows everyone to take advantage of you." I don't like the way his words settle within me. The way they stick a little too close to thoughts and feelings I've been burying, the way they too closely align with what Hallie's been saying, the way they sit sour in my stomach.

But no one is taking advantage of me. If I needed help, everyone would help me just the same. I have the time to help, so I am, just like Grandma taught. His inability to see that and the way he's twisting up my thoughts turns that sour feeling into anger once more.

With it, I push on his shoulder with both hands now. Again, it does nothing. "Put me *down*, Adam!" I shout in frustration. I don't expect him actually to do it, though, so when my legs move to touch ground, they wobble, causing Adam to hold my waist with a firm, warm hand while I steady myself. I push aside how nice that feels, then try to push at his chest, trying to get him out of my way.

But he doesn't move.

"Adam, move. I have to go finish the lights before work." His eyes bore into mine, and I'm stuck in his gaze, unable to look away.

"Why?" The words are spoken so softly, I almost think I'm imagining them.

"What?" I whisper.

"Why are you doing this? Why do *you* have to do this?"

I pause, brow furrowed.

"Because they need help, and I'm Wren. I have to help." The words slip out without my thinking them through, and with them, Adam's eyes widen.

"You *have* to help?"

I falter, not realizing those are the words I said, before I shake my head.

"No, I mean, I *like* to help. I'm helpful." He stares at me like he's waiting for me to finish, so I do in one long breath that takes a weight off my chest. "I have to hang up the lights for Mr. Campbell, and then I have to get to work where I have to be cheery and also firm for two dozen second graders and also fit in doing their trimester reports, and I have to do this this morning because tonight I have parent-teacher conferences and I might make questionable choices, but I'm not hanging lights in the dark."

I take a breath, and the strangest mix of clawing anxiety settling in and a weight being removed from my shoulders fills me as I get all of this off my chest.

"I can't do it tomorrow after school because I have to go to the fundraiser at the bar, and now that I'm thinking about it, I promised Nat I'd assemble the raffle baskets and make them look all pretty, but I have to get these stupid *lights* up because it's *tradition* for the entire town to be lit up, and this is *my year* and the entire town is relying on me to make everything festive and perfect just like my grandmother would do and—"

I have about a million more things to add to that list, but I've stopped.

I'm stopped because Adam is in my space, chest against mine once more in a way that is so reminiscent of what happened in his house the other day. His fingers tighten on my waist a bit more, his other hand resting on the door behind me beside my head and effectively caging me in place in an all-too familiar position.

"What do you need, Wren?" he asks, so low and sweet.

"I *need* to get you out of my way so I can go finish hanging those lights."

He shakes his head. "No, no. That's not what you need."

The hand on the door shifts, pushing a piece of hair back gently, almost reverently, before moving back to the door. My chin tips up without my mind even directing the action, and my eyes go wide as I take him in, all dark eyebrows and long lashes and high cheekbones. His constant brooding has left a permanent crease between his eyebrows, which some people might see as a flaw, but on him, it just adds to the overall package.

And just like in his house the other day, I want Adam to kiss me.

In fact, it's beginning to feel like a need. For some strange reason, I think if he kissed me, everything in the world would be right, if only for a moment.

"Tell me what you want right now, Wren," he whispers, breath coasting along my lips. "For once in your life, ask for what *you* want."

"Adam," I whisper, unsure of what to say, but the word parts my lips, and my body shifts closer to his, pressing my chest further into his. He lets out the smallest groan, one I feel more than hear, and liquid heat moves through me.

"Ask me to kiss you," he says.

My eyes go wide as I feel *everything* right now. The warmth of his body before mine, the cold wood of my front door on my back. My pulse pounding against my neck, the excitement coursing through my veins as I have him so close, my breath leaving my lips, and his coasting along my skin. It's as if my mind is trying to capture everything, every moment and feeling, for later.

"What?"

"Tell me to kiss you. Ask for what you need, baby."

I stare up at him, a mix of awe and confusion and, shockingly enough, *arousal* clouding my mind.

But mostly, confusion.

I've never had to *ask* for a kiss.

"You want me to *ask* for a kiss?"

"Hell, yeah, I do. You don't ask for anything from anyone, but you're going to ask for this. When I finally kiss you, it will be because you wanted it. Because you initiated it. My sweet little people pleaser is going to demand what she needs."

My jaw is slack with his words, and even though frustration courses through me, heat moves through me as well, settling between my legs.

My sweet little people pleaser is going to demand what she needs. That should *not* be hot, right?

A million responses go through my mind, but only one leaves my lips. "*When* you kiss me?"

His smile goes lazy in a sexy way I've never seen before, and suddenly, I understand what they mean in books when they say a *panty-dropping smile.*

"Oh, you and me kissing is a foregone conclusion, sweetness. Just say the word."

My breath hitches, and I open my mouth to respond, though I

don't know what I'm going to say. Turns out, I don't have to think of an answer because my phone alarm goes off.

"That's my alarm. I have to go."

Disappointment flashes over his face, and I wonder if he can see the same reflected on mine. In a heartbeat, his is chased away by determination and a confident smirk, and he steps away.

Without even looking back at him, I stomp toward my car, grateful I threw everything in there already before heading to hang the lights, and I drive off.

I definitely don't think about what would have happened if I had told him to kiss me.

When I finally pull onto Bluebird Lane long after nine p.m., I'm stunned to see the lights on the Campbells' house are already shining bright. I park my car and stand in my driveway, taking it in. Not only is the side I started done, but the entire house has strands of cheery lights. It's done well, too, perfectly straight with the lights hooked into the gutters every three bulbs, exactly the way I would have done it. It even goes up onto the roof, following the lines perfectly.

Jed Campbell definitely did not do that.

I'm still staring, admiring *someone's* work, when a familiar voice calls out.

"No more ladders, Wren."

I snap my head toward the source of the voice and see Adam standing on his front porch, arms crossed over his chest, jaw firm, staring at me intensely. My mind races, trying to put the pieces together before I respond.

"Did you..." My words trail off because they make no sense. Adam couldn't have hung them because he hates everything Christmas. He hates decorations, and he hates lights, and he hates... well, I thought he might hate me, just a little, until recently.

"I hung them up," he answers for me.

"Why?" I ask, taking a few steps toward him.

"It was purely selfish." It seems to be a familiar refrain from him, but I'm distracted from that when he continues. "I don't need the sight of your broken body burned in my mind for the rest of my life if and when you inevitably fall off that thing."

I stare at him, trying to read past the thick wall he has up all the time, but it's like a fortress, unscalable. Still, his actions speak for themselves.

"You're such a liar," I say with a small smile. "I think you did it because you care about me."

"Well, someone has to. You sure aren't going to," he says. The words stick around me, swirling around me like happy, floating snowflakes.

"I've been going to bed by midnight, you know," I say. I don't know why I say it, but I do anyway.

He looks over my shoulder. "I've noticed. Far stretch from reasonable, but it's an improvement."

We both stand there, staring at each other, neither of us speaking out loud about what that really means.

"Good night, Wren." And then he turns and walks back into his house, leaving me baffled.

I almost went to bed early that night, climbing into bed by ten thirty despite having a pile of other things to do. Adam's words of *someone has to* are still swirling around me, and when I wake to see the nutcracker on my front step, I can't seem to decide if it makes me happy or not.

TWELVE

Wren

"Go home, I've got this covered," I say. Carrie, who is manning the raffle table alongside me, turns to me, exhaustion clear on her face. She's getting over the cold that's been going through town, and two days ago, she was fully down for the count. Tonight she's at our friend Nat's fundraiser at The Mill.

"No, no, I promised I'd help! I'm fine."

I give her the same look my mom used to give me when I told bold-faced lies.

"Carrie. Go. I've got it, seriously." She bites her lip, and I realize she's about to cave, so I keep going. "You want to make sure you're all good for Gracie's first Christmas, don't you?" I helped my mom coordinate the community meal train after Carrie and Joe welcomed their baby girl into the world last spring, and I know she's so excited for their first holiday season as a family. Her hesitation is clear, and I jump on it. "Go, sleep."

Relief washes over her face, and she nods. "You're an angel, Wren."

"Just make sure you give that little nugget a big hug for me."

She gives me a grateful look, then grabs her things and makes her way out the door. I sit on the stool where she was, purposefully avoiding Hallie's eye from beside me.

"Oh, so you *can* see when people are too tired and should get some rest. Interesting," my best friend muses.

"A blind person could see that she was exhausted and needed rest, Hal. I was just sitting here, might as well let her get some sleep."

"Or, call me crazy, you could have let her handle her own issue like an adult and gone home yourself and gotten some sleep." I roll my eyes at her dramatics, but her face isn't joking. "I'm serious, Wren. You look completely shot."

"Gee, thanks," I deflect, but the truth of the matter is, I *am* exhausted. The kind of exhausted that's bone deep, the kind where when you wake up, you don't even feel a little better, the kind that you just know will take a week of solid sleep to get over.

Unfortunately, I have so much to do that I can't afford to indulge in the luxury. Today, after school, I spent hours organizing and categorizing the gifts we currently have for the Angel Tree, and then I made a list of what still needed to be purchased using the cash donations we'd received. Celine helped me for the first hour, but then she got a call from her sitter that her youngest had a fever. I told her to head out, and I'd finish myself, but it meant I barely had thirty minutes between getting home and Hallie picking me up to unwind and eat a quick dinner. Then I was back out the door to help Natalie decorate for her fundraiser as I'd promised.

Hallie has been giving me the side-eye since she picked me up, so I've been trying to avoid her and another lecture about taking care of myself. Partly because I don't want to hear it, and partly because it reminds me of a different situation involving Adam and the mixed feelings I've had over the past few days.

I went to bed almost *early* the night Adam hung the lights, but the next two nights, I stayed up late getting more items off my to-do list. I told myself it was because I had work to do, and it was true, of course. I finished the decorations and began prepping for the school holiday party, then moved on to organizing my own shopping list and completing a few gifts.

But if I'm being honest, a part of me kind of wanted to see if Adam would do anything if he saw me up late again. If he'd storm into my house again, throw me over his shoulder, and toss me into my bed.

What would happen if I did tell him to kiss me?

Or even more curious, what would happen if I asked him to curl up in my bed with me?

Fortunately—or unfortunately, depending on how delusional I'm being at that moment—I haven't had to deal with any of those what-ifs, because I haven't seen him since that night he hung up those lights. Clearly, I haven't been on his mind at all, though he has been on mine. In fact, when I do finally lie down in bed, I've been finding it hard to sleep, my mind continually running through that almost-kiss, the way he felt pressed up against me, the way he seemed so sure we *would* at some point kiss.

Except then he ignored me.

Stupid, hot, frustrating Scrooge of a neighbor.

"It's Nat's fundraiser. I have to be here."

Hallie rolls her eyes at my excuse.

"Yes, and you helped set up and handled the donations for and assembled all of the raffle gift baskets. Now you can go home." She moves, sitting on the stool beside me behind the raffle table. "I'll handle this. Get some sleep."

I shake my head. "I'll be fine. Plus, when I head home, I have to finish that quilt." I'd been putting off finishing the binding since it's so time-consuming and boring, but once I do, it will be one more thing off my list.

"A quilt?" she asks with wide eyes.

I sigh, remembering I didn't tell Hallie about that one.

"It's a favor for my mom," I say, picking at the cocktail napkin that came with my Shirley Temple. Even though a real drink would take some of my anxious edge off, I have far too much to do to risk the potential sleepiness.

"Are you kidding me?" She turns fully toward me, and the genuine concern on her face makes me suddenly concerned for how bad I must *actually* look. "Wren, you can't keep this up. I know this is kind of your thing, stretching yourself too thin for everyone around you, but this is next level."

She's right, though I won't tell her that. What good will it do? Even though I have more on my plate than I can handle right now, there's no fixing it. Things have to get done, decorations have to be made, lights have to go up, and I have to help everyone. It's what I do.

"I just need to get through the holidays," I say, trying to put on what I hope is a cheerful voice. "Once the holidays are over, I'll be able to relax. It's temporary."

She looks over my face, a hint of disappointment flashing there. Her voice lowers before she speaks. "You know, this used to be your favorite time of year."

Her words settle in my gut, but my brow furrows in confusion.

"What are you talking about? It still is." She tips her head, giving me a look, and I shake my head in denial. "My favorite time of year is Christmas, you know that. That hasn't changed. I love it. It's magical; you know that. I'm having fun."

"Is it? Because you look and sound miserable."

"No, I don't." She raises an eyebrow. "I don't! I'm just..." I take in a deep breath and look around to ensure no one is watching us before whispering my confession. "I'm a little overwhelmed. It's a lot. I don't know how my grandmother did all of this on her own.'

"Well, she didn't do it on her own, for one." I purse my lips, wanting to argue but knowing it's no good. "And I doubt she jumped right into it all her first year. You were handed the torch, yes, but many people would love to help."

"Yes, everyone is so eager to help with everything that they keep giving me more and more to do," I murmur without thinking. Instantly, I regret saying the words aloud, and guilt floods me.

"That's because you always say yes. Why do something yourself? Look for someone who has time and energy, and you know that Wren King will say yes, even if it means she has to stay up all night Googling or baking or sewing to do it."

"I can't just say no if someone needs help, Hallie," I say softly.

"Oh, I promise you can. I do it all the time. In fact, Madden asked if I could stay late tonight. I looked him in the eye and said, 'No, I'm busy.' And you know what? The world didn't implode. I didn't lose my job."

"But what if he really needed you, and you were his only option?"

Her eyes go soft in a way they rarely do, and she reaches across the table to grab my hand, squeezing it once.

"That's not my problem, Wren. That's his. And if he's in that kind of situation, he could express it, and I would be able to decide if I could intervene on his behalf or find some other solution that doesn't require my personal time and energy. But no one expects that of me right off the bat. I've set boundaries and expectations, and no one pushes them because I keep them firm." Her eyes lock on me, knowingly. "And everybody knows that."

I stare at her for a moment before a question I've been harboring for days spills from my lips. "Do you think people take advantage of me?"

Guilt curls in my stomach, even bothering to say the silly question out loud. But my gut churns even more when I turn back to look at my best friend since preschool. The look on her face tells me everything I need to know. After a long moment where she is clearly trying to choose her words perfectly, she tips her head to the side and gives me a heavy sigh.

"Do I think people take advantage of you? Probably not. That's probably too strong a word. But I think people see a woman who is so kind, caring, and giving, and they realize they can ask her to shoulder more of their stress than they should. And I think that, while you are the kindest, most caring, and most giving person I've ever met, it's to a fault. I think you're so hell-bent on being the person people can rely on, can turn to when they need help, that you never bother to question people or their motivations."

My stomach sinks the way it has since the day Adam hung up the lights, when he told me Jed Campbell took up my offer not because it was his only choice, but because of laziness. I wanted to believe he was lying to get under my skin, but when I stood back and looked at the whole picture, I knew it was the truth.

"I also think you've put so much of the pressure of this holiday festival and traditions on your shoulders that you're casting your own wants and, more importantly, *needs* aside in order to make everyone else happy."

"I don't want to disappoint anyone!" The pressure that's been gripping my chest for the past six weeks tightens, and I say that part far too loud to be comfortable. I glance around, trying to ensure no one has overheard and is staring. Thankfully, everyone around us is lost in their own conversations. Taking in a deep breath, I force myself to seem normal, if only to ease Hallie's nerves. I'm sure a professional would have a lot to say about my trying to ease my own anxiety only to ease Hallie's, but we're not touching that one. Not today. "I just...I want it all to be perfect. The festival. The lights, the magic. All of it. And I want everyone to be able to enjoy it. Just like my grandma did."

"No matter how much or how little you do, it will be amazing, Wren. But if you're dead on your feet, you won't be able to experience that magic yourself. And you know that, at the end of the day, she did all of this so that you and the rest of your family could feel that magic. The rest of the town just benefited from it."

"Hallie, I have to—" I start trying to justify, to explain, but she stops me.

"I know," she says, softness and genuine understanding in her eyes. "Trust me, babe, I know. But she'd be mad as hell that you're looking this worn out. She's telling you to get into your bed, to go home, to say *no* occasionally."

I scrunch up my nose in irritation, mainly because the words strike true.

"Where is this coming from?"

I shrug but don't tell her the whole truth. Instead, I give her a crumb of it.

"I've just been thinking, you know?" I definitely *don't* tell her that the thinking has been spurred by my neighbors' cutting words and potentially painful honesty. "I like helping, but I just sometimes wonder if I'm helping people who just don't *want* to do something rather than *can't* do it, you know."

She nods. "I know. And I love that you're so kind and empathetic, but I won't lie. I've been worried about you. You're always running on empty these days, and you have lost the spark of cheer you normally have this time of year. I hope this is a moment of epiphany for you, and that by asking, you're taking the first step toward prioritizing yourself more. Get some rest. Go to bed before midnight." She gives me a gentle look, then reaches over and grabs my hand. "Seriously, Wren. I'm worried about you."

Guilt churns in my gut as I realize that I may have been inadvertently adding more stress to her plate in the form of concern for me, but it also almost feels like the kind of permission I need to do what feels selfish and prioritize myself in a silly way. I open my mouth to tell her that I'll try my best not to take on more and to prioritize myself a bit more, but I'm stopped when I hear my most dreaded words as of late from a conversation somewhere beside me.

"You should ask Wren! I'm sure she would do it!"

I don't even know who says it since they're out of sight, but my shoulders tense up all the same. Hallie must not hear it, but she catches my shift in mood, and her brows furrow.

"Remember last summer, my mom's dog had puppies, and she let me keep them at her place for a bit so my kids wouldn't get attached? She even found homes for all of them."

That's when I pinpoint the voice to belong to Molly Paulson, one of the PTO moms.

I, of course, remember the incident she's speaking of because I had planned to spend a few days at Seaside Point during summer break to get away, but the dogs required constant attention, so when I agreed to help out, that went out the window. Molly's mother is older, and we all decided—and by we, I mean Molly and her mother —that it would be best if I kept the mom and all four puppies at my place before we shipped them off to their new homes.

It was a fun summer filled with unlimited puppy snuggles, and I was happy to help out as well as find new homes for the puppies, but it ruined any chance I may have had to spend some lazy days on the beach over my summer break.

"Oh, you're so right! She always helps. She's right there, I should go ask now."

From the look on her face, Hallie has heard them and quickly understands what is happening. She looks at me with wide, expectant eyes, and I hold my breath, hoping maybe I imagined it. Or maybe I'll become invisible, and they won't see me. Or maybe—

Not a single one of my hopes is met.

"Hey, Wren, Hallie," Linda says, standing across the raffle table from me.

"Hey, Linda, hey Molly, how's it going?" I ask, my friendliest and fakest smile on my lips.

Please don't ask me for anything, please, please, please.

Because, despite running on fumes right now and despite not having even the tiniest bit of time to shower in peace, I know if she asks me outright to help her out with whatever issue she's juggling, I won't be able to find it within myself to say no.

I'm Wren King, after all.

The town sweetheart, the one who always says yes, who is always willing to lend a helping hand. The one who always has it covered.

"Good! I was just talking about you, actually. Found four baby kittens behind the bar this morning," Linda states. My stomach drops as she looks at me with an expectant look.

"Oh, no! Were they from a stray?" I ask, trying to drag out this conversation. Perhaps if we don't reach the point of her conversation, it will never happen. Maybe we'll get interrupted, and I'll have to step away before she can manage to ask me.

"We don't know—the mom was nowhere to be found. We're trying to find someone willing to foster them for a bit. They need round-the-clock care, and with the kids and everything, I just don't have the time, you know?"

I give her a look that's probably closer to a grimace than a smile.

"Mm-hmm," I say with a nod.

"Anyways, so I was talking to Molly about my predicament, you know, and she reminded me about how you took in her mom's puppies that one time. I think you'd be the perfect person to watch them, you know?"

The blood drains from my face.

I look across the table to my best friend, and Hallie's eyes are wide, and she's mouthing *hell no* to me. Then her eyes move over my shoulder, brows furrowing before a pleased look takes over her face, but I can't focus on that. Instead, I'm stuck in my current predicament.

I want to cry.

I want to scream.

But I don't.

I'm Wren King—the youngest King, the town's sweetheart, the one who always jumps in when someone needs help.

It's an honor to be the person everyone can rely on. It's a point of pride for me. Being the one who helps is as much a part of who I am as being Dottie's granddaughter or being a teacher.

Who am I if not the person everyone can rely on?

And let's be honest, I'll probably be up anyway. What will it hurt to feed a couple of kittens through the night?

So I suck it up and plaster a pleasant face on. "I guess I could—"

Except the words don't come out as I planned because a warm chest is to my back and a calloused hand is to my mouth, stopping them.

THIRTEEN

ADAM

UNKNOWN

Come to the bar.

I stare at my phone for a while, trying to figure out what is happening. After my number got leaked almost a year ago, I got a new one and have given it to very few people, much less anyone who would invite me to a bar on a random Wednesday.

Who is this?

The reply comes back quickly.

Colton. Come to the bar tonight.

The tiniest spark of strange warmth flares in my chest, and despite having no interest in going and sitting at a bar again, I find myself fighting back a small smile. The last time I came to the bar, I enjoyed myself, even if I mostly sat alone and chatted with Colton.

I've never had someone who wanted to spend time or talk to me for no reason other than shooting the shit.

I got into the music business young, Midnight Ash hitting it big when I was barely eighteen, so almost all of my formative years were spent with people kissing my ass, friendliness always coming with some kind of ulterior motive or trying to get something from me. But to everyone in this town, I'm just some persnickety new resident, so it would seem Colton simply wanted to chat and get to know me genuinely.

Still, accepting his offer feels far too strange and out of character for me, so I decline.

> No thanks.

His response comes back quickly and is confusing.

> lol

Confusing, that is, until he sends his next text:

> Your little bird will be there.

Wren.

Wren, who hasn't put a decoration on my lawn in days, a torture I'm realizing I may have actually started to enjoy.

Wren, who, despite going to bed early one night, started staying up late the very next day.

Wren, whom I wanted to kiss so fucking badly, my body ached with restraint. I've come to realize that everyone tells Wren what they want from her and what they need from her, but I don't think anyone ever asks her what she wants or needs. I'm determined to be the first to get that out of her.

I look at the blank notebook before me, random words scribbled in the margins as if they're going to spark some creativity and pull me

out of my rut, but nothing seems to be working. Despite being in
Holly Ridge for almost a month, I still haven't been able to write a
single lyric.

My gaze shifts back to my phone and Colt's text. Maybe I just
need to experience some normalcy. Maybe a normal night out in a
small-town bar will spark something. After all, the best songs are
about normal, relatable human experiences.

The next thing I know, I'm in my car, headed to the bar.

It's about trying new things to get inspired, though. My quick
decision had nothing to do with the last text I received. Of course not.

"You know, I didn't think it would work," Colton says, after I sit
down in the same spot I sat in last time.

"I don't know what you're talking about," I lie.

He shakes his head, thoroughly entertained by my denial. "You
weren't going to come before I told you Wren would be here."

"I decided I needed to get out of the house. I was just kidding
when I said no." He looks at me with a disbelieving look, and I shrug
as if it doesn't matter to me.

But I didn't come here for Wren. I came here because after
declining his offer, I realized I had nothing else to look forward to for
the night other than staring at yet another blank piece of paper. I
enjoyed myself last time I came, so maybe if I continued, the inspiration would spark.

Definitely *not* Wren.

Unfortunately, the second I walked in, I regretted agreeing to it. I
thought it would be a low-key night since it was a goddamn Tuesday,
but I should have known that nothing in this town is low-key.

Instead, seemingly every adult in this town is here tonight, every
table is full, and the volume is louder than it was last time. Christmas
music is playing over the speakers, which means at some point, "All
Lit Up" is probably going to play and make me want to leave. There
seems to be a fundraiser happening, with raffle baskets along the back
wall, along with a high-top table with two stools beside it, one where
Hallie sits, the other where Wren is, her pretty red bow having some

kind of sparkles on it today that are gleaming in the low light of the bar.

Not that I'm watching.

When I turn back, Colton is watching me with a self-satisfied grin and lets out a small laugh.

Ten or so minutes later, after a good amount of small talk that surprisingly doesn't feel tedious, Colton slides two drinks over time, one bright red and one a dark brown soda.

"Mind taking this to them?" he asks, tipping his chin. Without having to check, I know he means his sister and Wren.

"What the fuck do you think I am? Your employee?"

"You're not doing anything better." I glare at him, prepared to tell him to go fuck himself, before he lets out a loud laugh and shakes his head. "You'd be doing me a favor, man. Please. It's for my sister."

I glare at him.

"Did you hear your sister and her friend broke into my house the other day?"

He doesn't miss a beat, nodding. "She didn't tell me, but that sounds like something Hallie would do."

I blink at him, and the fact that he doesn't look shocked at all, nor does he ask any questions.

"This town is fucked, you know that?" I say with a shake of my head. Still, I stand, grabbing the drink and watching the smile on his lips spread wider with satisfaction.

"Seems you'll fit in just fine, then."

I turn toward where Hallie and Wren are, lifting a hand and flipping off Colton as I move toward the small table. As I approach, two other women move over to where Wren is, and they start chatting. Slowing my steps so I don't interrupt at an inconvenient time, I catch snippets of their conversation.

Kittens, apparently. The woman talking to Wren either has kittens or has found some and is looking for someone to care for them.

Inevitably, it seems, the best person for that is Wren.

The fuck it is.

I speed up my steps, and Hallie's gaze catches on me directly after she's given Wren a don't *you dare* kind of look. It seems she's of the same mind I am, suddenly concerned the sweet woman will say yes in her effort to make everyone happy. I can't see Wren's face, but I can picture the deer-in-the-headlights look there. Then Hallie's face morphs, a triumphant look taking over her face as I close the gap between us.

"Here," I say low, handing the nearly forgotten glasses to Hallie, who accepts them almost giddily, but I can't focus on that, not when Wren's voice speaks up.

"I guess I could—"

I don't know what comes over me.

I'm not sure what I'm thinking, except that I need to stop her from accepting another task to add to her endless list of things to do, and I need to stop her now.

My hand lifts, covering her mouth and pulling her entire body back into my chest. Her body goes stiff beneath mine, and her head turns back to look at me. That look in her eye shifts from anxious to alarmed to annoyed in the blink of an eye, but I ignore it, too, nodding at the woman in front of me who is staring at me with shock.

"Unfortunately, Wren is incredibly busy this month, and as much as she would love to help you with this issue, she can't."

I'm sure that Wren is going to be pissed, but really, she should be grateful that I stopped her from saying yes to waking up every two hours to bottle-feed fucking *kittens*. I don't know the woman that well, but even I know she can't be the most qualified person in town to take that on.

I'm tired of Wren taking on everything for everyone. She won't stick up for herself, and she surely won't ask for what she needs, much less *wants*, so I'm taking it upon myself to do just that.

"Oh," the woman says, looking me over. Then she shrugs as if it's no big deal. "No worries, we'll call up the animal hospital and see if they can take them in." Then she acts as if nothing happened at all, turning away to return to her group.

I turn to Hallie after I drop my hand from Wren's mouth with indignation.

"You mean to tell me that she didn't even ask the *vet* to take the kittens before resorting to her?" I direct my question to Wren's friend, knowing Wren will give some fucked-up excuse.

Hallie beams, as if the situation thoroughly entertains her. "Why ask someone who might tell you to handle it yourself for a few days or cost money when you can just ask the town sweetheart who doesn't know how to say no?"

Wren's face snaps from me to her friend, with irritation clearly written across her face.

"I know how to say no, I'm just *helpful*. I can't help it that people think I'm a safe person to ask for help," Wren insists.

"Do you know anything about kittens?"

A moment passes, and she bites her lip.

I want to fucking kiss that lip.

It's all I've been able to think about since the moment I pinned her to my living room wall and then her front door.

I came to this town to be alone, to find my inspiration, and to hide away from the constant pressure and distractions of my life as well as the holiday season itself. Instead, I've spent more time with other people in the last three weeks than I have in a year. I can't stop thinking about my annoying neighbor, and I couldn't escape Christmas in Holly Ridge if I tried.

Wren doesn't respond, but Hallie does.

"Well, you know as well as I do, Wren takes on any project someone asks of her."

"That's ending," I say, turning to Wren, whose jaw is tight with frustration. "I'm tired of watching you work yourself to the bone for other people who probably don't appreciate your kindness." I turn to Hallie, who seems to be the only one in this town who sees how Wren is overdoing it. "The other day she fell off a ladder hanging up my neighbor's lights."

Hallie's eyes go wide, and Wren's jaw goes tight.

"Why was she hanging up Jed Campbell's lights? He's fully capable."

I direct my glare to Wren, trying to convey how even her best friend can see the situation is fucked up.

"Seems she offered, and he didn't see a reason not to take her up on it."

I still remember the way I had to bite back a rude response when Jed told me that, instead of giving him what I think may have resembled a smile, but I can't confirm.

"I'm sure you misunderstood," Wren says, and I shake my head.

"I'm sure you give people way more credit than they deserve in your quest to please everyone you come into contact with."

Her jaw goes tight before she opens her mouth to retort, but Hallie cuts in almost gleefully before she can.

"I get what's happening now," Hallie says with a satisfied look directed toward Wren. "Oh, I like him for you!" Wren shoots her friend a deadly look, but Hallie's attention is on me. "You, sit. Tell me all about how my best friend is once again not taking care of herself."

"No! Do not sit! You are not welcome at this table. I can't believe you just interrupted a private conversation like that!" Wren says in the closest thing to a yell I think she has, ignoring her friend and turning to me with fury in her eyes. "*Why* did you do that?"

Her fury is goddamn cute.

It sparks something in me, making me cross my arms on my chest and smile at her. The feeling of it is foreign on my face.

"Are you really gonna argue with me in front of all these people, Birdie?" Hallie lets out a small squeak, but my focus remains on Wren. "Small towns talk, right?"

Her jaw goes tight, a look I like on her, not because I want her angry, but because something else tells me she doesn't allow herself to get angry very often. No, not Wren, the sweet small-town princess who feels an intense urge to help everyone and anyone, even if it means staying up half the night to get it done or nearly falling off a roof.

Wren would rather work herself to the bone than disappoint those around her or mess with the perfect vision she's curated for herself, much less get *angry* at them.

She looks around the bar and probably doesn't miss how a handful of eyes are in fact on us. It's strange, having eyes on me and not feeling the need to hide away, to shy away from them. As I had hoped when I settled in here, it seems no one in this town realizes who I am.

Wren lets out a little huff before standing, then grabs my arm and tugs me toward the back.

"Ooooh, hell yeah, girl!" Hallie says, and Wren snaps her head in her direction, giving her a glare that is meant to quiet her, I'm sure, but instead makes her smile go wider.

"Don't listen to anything she says, Adam. She wants you, and she needs someone to help her stop saying yes," Hallie calls after us.

I let out a laugh as Wren pulls me toward a somewhat secluded area in the bar, which seems to be a coat hallway on one side and a collage of photos on the other, featuring everything from Little League photos to newspaper clippings of township accomplishments.

"Why did you do that?" she asks through gritted teeth, eyes flaring with anger, hands on her hips. I know it's not the right time to smile, and surely not the right time to tell her how fucking cute she is, so I have to fight back both reactions.

"You can't stay up all night for some undisclosed timeline feeding kittens that are not your responsibility, Wren. That's too far, even for you. You have to know that." There's a flash of something, maybe understanding or agreement, in her eyes before it's gone, stubbornness taking its place.

"You don't get to tell me what I can and can't do, Adam," she says, crossing her arms on her chest and turning fully to me, her back to the collage wall.

I shrug. "Someone has to."

She gives me a disbelieving look. It's cute. Again.

"No, they do not."

"You're surely not going to value your own time, energy, or health. Who else is going to do it?" She looks like she wants to argue my point, but decides it's not worth it.

"God, you are just so frustrating!"

I lift an eyebrow at her. "Why, because I'm the first person to challenge your idea that you have to be everything to everyone?"

She sputters before shaking her head in disagreement. "No! Because you are the absolute worst! You refuse to decorate to participate in a town tradition. You stole my freaking nutcracker—"

"I gave that back," I cut in, but she's on a roll, clearly rambling on and not stopping any time soon.

"And you are stalking me, watching what time I go to sleep—"

"Someone has to."

"And you keep giving me shit for helping people as if I'm *hurting* people! There's nothing wrong with wanting to get help from people!"

"If you're hurting yourself along the way, there is," I say softly.

"You give me all this shit, tell me I can't help put up lights, and manhandle me, then press me to my door and look at me like..." She pauses, trying to find the words, but shakes her head. "Like you did. And then you won't even *kiss* me! You stand there all grumpy, save my life, and you tell me I have to *tell you* to kiss me. But everyone knows that's the man's job! God, if a woman is staring up at you all goo-goo-eyed and parted lips and bated breaths, you fucking kiss her, Adam! You don't make her—"

That sounds like as much of an outright request as I'm ever going to get from her, and considering I don't need much to convince me to kiss her once and for all, I give her exactly what she seems to be asking for.

I press my lips to hers, shifting my body and hers until her back is to the wall and my body is towering over her, shielding her from anyone who might walk past. There's a split second when her body tightens, but just as quickly, the resistance melts away, her body going lax in my arms, her lips parting gently so that mine fit perfectly between them. My hips move, pressing her into the wall, and she gasps. I use the opportunity to slip my tongue between her lips, brushing against hers. The tiniest, sweetest sound leaves her as I taste her for the first time, and I groan, deepening the kiss.

I shouldn't be surprised that Wren matches my energy, devouring me the same way I'm inhaling her, but I am all the same.

It's hot.

It's intense.

It's so much fucking more than I ever thought a kiss could be, not just with her, but in general. I've kissed my fair share of women in my life, but it's never been like this. And I know down to my gut it's because it's *Wren*.

And in that moment, I decided that Wren King was mine.

FOURTEEN

ADAM

The realization hits me like a train, but I can't really say it isn't one I didn't see coming, even if it was subconsciously. But now that she's staring up at me, panting with wide eyes, lips kiss-swollen from mine, it's something I can no longer ignore.

"Is that what you wanted, Birdie? You wanted me to kiss you? All you had to do was ask," I say, and a smile tips at the edges of my lips. She blinks up at me with dazed eyes, eyes unfortunately lined in exhausted circles, but then there's a flash of irritation, and her hands move up to the back of my neck, pulling me down to her once more.

"You're such an ass," she grumbles right before she pulls my lips down to hers. I laugh into the kiss, feeling lighter than I think I ever have, but she simply pulls me closer as if she feels the same all-consuming urge to get as close as humanly possible to me. Her body is shifting, squirming, grinding as she kisses me, and I wonder...

I shift her, eager to do the same, and shift my legs so my thigh rests between hers, her sweet, uncovered thighs nearly straddling me. My hand moves to her hip, and I pull her closer, and a squeak falls from her lips, swallowed quickly by mine when it turns into a moan.

A moan as she grinds herself onto my thigh, my lips on hers.

Fuck.

Her breathing goes a bit frantic, her hips moving in a steady pattern, and my cock hardens in response.

I wonder for a moment if she could come just like this, my leg between hers, fully clothed, my kisses the only skin-on-skin contact we have.

Unfortunately, we're both reminded of *where* we are when a door closes not far from us, and her body goes tight again, like she's been snapped back into her common sense. Even though I don't want to, I break the kiss, moving to press my forehead to hers and gaze down at her. Her chest is rising and falling rapidly, little pants coming from her lips, and her eyes are hooded with fleeting desire when they finally meet mine, fire blazing there.

She's pinned to the wall, my leg between hers, her hips still shifting against it like she desperately wants more, breaths panting from her lips.

I'm going to take her home.

I'm going to strip her out of her sweet little outfit and kiss every inch of her body, make her feel so fucking good until she forgets about everything and everyone. She forgets about responsibilities and promises and favors, only focusing on what she wants, what feels good, and the pleasure I can bring her.

More importantly, I'm going to make her beg for each and every touch until it's deeply ingrained in her mind that she has to ask for what she wants, that she has to speak up for herself.

That's my plan—that is, until her lips purse and her eyes squeeze shut as she fights back a yawn.

With it, my plan changes instantly.

"We're going home."

Those bright blue eyes go wide with panic and confusion. "What?"

"I'm taking you home. I'm going to get you out of here before you agree to more insane things that will eat at the very few hours you let yourself have to yourself, and you're going to get to bed at a reasonable fucking hour." I step back, reaching for her hand to move her, but her feet stay cemented where they are, her jaw adorably tight. Instead of her dazed, turned-on look or her sweet, tired one, I realize I have stubborn Wren on my hands once again.

"No, I'm not."

"You're exhausted, Wren. If I'm kissing you the way I just did and you're responding the way you just did, and you're yawning after it, something is very wrong. You're going home, and you're going to bed."

"Maybe it just wasn't that good," she says, looking at me with all the attitude she can muster.

"Feel free to tell yourself that, Wren, but we both know the truth. Now come on. We're going home."

"I am an adult, Adam. I don't need you telling me when my bedtime is or that I need to go home."

I raise an eyebrow at her, and despite myself, my irritation starts to grow. She so badly wants to prove herself, but she's missing the most important part: taking care of *Wren*.

"Then act like one and take care of yourself. You keep this up, you're going to send yourself into an early grave."

"You're being dramatic."

"You almost fell off a ladder the other day," I remind her.

"That wasn't because I was tired. It was because it was icy and cold."

I stare at her, trying to make her see that she's simply proving my point. "Just another situation where you weren't worried about your health or safety."

She rolls her eyes, and the movement goes straight to my cock. I reduce the space between us once more and pin her to the wall.

"Roll your eyes like that again, and I'm putting you over my knee and spanking your ass until you listen to me."

With my words, I expect a tight jaw.

I expect a flare of anger or some angry response.

Instead, her lips part.

A sharp little inhale comes from her lips.

Her eyes widen in shock.

And then they light up with heat.

Fuck.

My little birdie likes the idea of that, even if she would never admit it.

"Now, you're going to follow me out into the bar, and you're going to say goodbye to our friends. Then you're going to get into your car and drive home, and I'm going to tail you, making sure you don't get into a wreck on the three-mile drive home. Then I'm going to watch you walk into your house, turn off all the lights, and go the fuck to sleep."

A small pink tongue dips out of her mouth, wetting her lips, and I watch it with fascination.

"I came here with Hallie," she says, voice low and conciliatory. "I'm not making her leave just because my asshole neighbor thinks I have a bedtime."

"Even better. I'll drive you home," I say.

"I don't need you to drive me home. I'll wait until my friend is ready to go."

Her irritation is rising once again, and I fight the grin pulling at my lips. God, I really like this push and pull between us.

"No, you won't. You're going home. Now." I step away, motioning for her to follow me again, but she crosses her arms on her chest, glaring at me.

"What are you going to do, drag me? I'm not going to just go with you, Adam."

I let the smile win.

"If that's what it takes."

"You wouldn't." I lift an eyebrow in challenge. "Why—" she starts, but her question turns into a yelp as I bend my knees and put my shoulder into her belly, tossing her over my shoulder as I stand. "Adam!"

I ignore her shriek as I move back the way we came to the bar with her over my shoulder.

"Put me down!" she shouts, slapping my back. I just laugh, feeling freer than I have in months—years, maybe—as I move toward the table she was at to grab her things on our way out. As we approach the loud, populated area, I shift my free hand to the hem of her dress to hold it down and keep it from drifting up.

"Are you feeling me up?" she asks, voice aghast.

"I'm covering your ass, Wren."

"That's essentially the same thing!"

"Do you want the entire bar to see your ass?"

Silence fills the air before her sass kicks in.

"I don't want you touching my behind!"

So goddamn sweet, she doesn't even want to say the word *ass*.

"Trust me, if I were feeling up your ass, Wren, you would know."

She goes silent for a moment as we move toward her friends.

"I'm taking Wren home," I tell Hallie as we approach the table she was sharing with another brunette. Both of them are staring at me with wide eyes, the brunette looking nervous while Hallie looks thoroughly entertained.

"No, he's not! He's kidnapping me! Someone help me!"

"You're making a scene, Birdie," I say over my shoulder.

"No, *you're* making a scene! By kidnapping me!"

I ignore her, shifting my attention to Hallie.

"Is this him? The hot neighbor?" the brunette asks Hallie, and she nods. "Nice." There's a pleased smile on her lips that Hallie returns, all three of us ignoring an arguing Wren. "I'm Nat, Wren and Hallie's friend."

"Adam," I say, then turn to Hallie. "I'm taking her home because she's exhausted and needs to go to bed early."

"You're treating me like a child!" Wren says from behind me.

"You know who else fights a reasonable bedtime? Children." I say, looking at her over my shoulder. Her face is angry and red, and I have to fight not to laugh.

"Oh, I think I like him a lot for you, Wren," Hallie says, and despite myself, I let out a chuckle that I try to hide with a cough. Wren hits my back again. "Make sure she actually goes to bed."

"Plan on it," I say, thinking of the key to her back door. I fought the urge to use it the last few nights while she stayed up late, but I won't be fighting that urge anymore.

"Hallie! You're supposed to be on *my side!*" Wren shouts.

"Oh, I definitely am," Hallie says with a grin.

"And if you saw what we see right now, you'd know we are *definitely trying to get you what you need*," Nat says.

"This is insane," Wren grumbles, but stops arguing.

"See ya, Wren," Nat says with a sweet voice. "You really do need more sleep."

"I'm not talking to either of you for weeks," she says. "You're off my Christmas list, too!" She says it like a threat, but the women just laugh it off.

I wave at them goodbye, then turn, waving at Colton. "Mind if I get you next time?"

"This round's on me. Worth the show!" he says with a laugh. Wren groans, and I give him a nod and a wave before heading for the door.

"Let me walk, Adam!" she says as we walk out into the December chill. I shake my head, reaching in my pocket for my keys and unlocking my truck, but I don't answer. Not as I open the passenger-side door, and not as I place her gently into the seat. Surely not when I lean across the seat to grab the seatbelt, tugging it over her and hearing her breath hitch before buckling her in.

When I jog around the front, I start the engine before closing my door and fight a laugh when I see her sitting there with a scowl, looking straight ahead with her arms crossed on her chest. She's silent the entire five-minute drive back home, but every chance I can, I look over at her, watching the way the lights play along her face and the way her eyes widen with interest when she sees some new decoration she must not have noticed. When she catches me, she rolls her eyes, her jaw going tight again, and I have to look away so I don't laugh.

When I pull into my drive, I cut the engine, then slide out of my seat, slamming my door as I make my way over to her.

"Oh, you're going to let me walk now?" she asks with exaggerated snark as I open the passenger door. I grin widely at her. I can't stop it, not when she's like this, all frustrated and annoyed. Not when I have a feeling I'm the only one who gets her riled up like this.

And surely not when she was mewling into my mouth as she rubbed herself against my thigh ten minutes ago.

"Nowhere for you really to run off to, and I can't see you heading back to the bar." She doesn't respond, and I reach out to help her out of my truck. She sneers at my offered hand like it's poisoned, then shifts her body out, avoiding me completely. I slam the door behind her as she makes her way up to her walkway, then stomp angrily up her front steps.

I follow her, and when she reaches the door, she turns on a heel and glares at me. "Are you also going to follow me inside and make sure I brush my teeth and go right to bed?"

I stare at her, fighting the overwhelming desire to say *yes*.

But if I follow Wren King inside, neither of us will be going to bed anytime soon, and considering the exhaustion written over her face and the clear irritation in her words, I'll have to shelve that idea for a bit.

"I could follow you in, but it wouldn't help with your sleep issue." Her jaw goes a bit slack, and I feel the satisfaction of stunning her in that way, especially when a little blush burns across her cheeks.

"You're a pig," she says under her breath, but the words are lacking conviction.

"Never said I wasn't. But next time you want me to come over, you just have to ask for what you want, and I'll be right there." Her brows furrow at me, masking the flash of desire.

"Why the fuck would I want you to come over?" she asks, hands on her hips and glaring up at me.

"I think you made your feelings clear in the bar, sweetness," I say, lifting a hand and tucking a piece of loose hair behind her ear. "And so did I. But I'm not acting on them until you've gotten some rest." Those pretty eyes roll, and I think that I'd like to make them roll in another way.

Get your head together, Porter. Stick to the plan.

"That is not happening again. It was a lapse of judgment. A tired lapse of judgment."

"Sure it was, sweetness," I say.

"I'm serious! Why would I want *anything* to do with you? You're a jerk who hates Christmas and is constantly manhandling me."

I take a step back and nod.

"Well, when you decide you want to make another lapse of judgment, you come over. But you're going to have to ask for what you want, baby."

"In your dreams."

"Don't you know it?" Her mouth opens as I say it, looking at me with shock as I take a step backward down her porch. "Now go inside and go to bed, Wren."

I stand at the foot of her steps, watching her as she takes me in before she must decide she doesn't want to argue, turns on her heel once more, and heads inside, slamming the door when she does.

And despite what she said, that night I watched her place from my office. Over the next twenty minutes, the lights go out one by one in each room until all lights are off at 10:12.

I'd call that a win any day.

FIFTEEN

Wren

Even though I stare at the small basket of decorations I've compiled for my quest to get Adam to decorate his house every morning, I don't bring a single one over there in the days following our kiss. In fact, I make every attempt to avoid the man whenever possible.

I leave for school earlier than usual, before the time I've determined he goes for his run. I take on extra after-care duty when Mr. Saunders asks if I can cover for him. Even though I tell myself it's just my usual habit of helping, I know in my gut it's not that.

I'm avoiding my house because I'm avoiding Adam. I'm avoiding Adam because he completely scrambles my brain with his desire to push me to put myself first and, of course, that *kiss*.

I'm avoiding him because I don't know what to do about this man who sees past my walls, who continues to pressure me to put myself first, even though he barely even *knows* me.

The worst part is that even though I tell myself that he's an asshole and doesn't understand me or my town, I'm starting to wonder if there's some truth to what he's been trying to show me. Hell, Hallie's been saying it for some time now, just with kid gloves and in her gentle way, so I could easily ignore it.

Of course, I'm stubborn, so instead of slowing down, I've ramped up my schedule, which means I'm even more tired than normal. When I receive an early morning call from the school district telling me that school has been cancelled due to snow, a wave of relief washes over me. I laze about in bed for longer than usual, then make a cup of coffee before drinking it in the living room, watching the snow fall in fat clumps. It quickly piles up on the frozen ground, leaving a thick layer on all of my decorations.

It's so peaceful, and for the first time in a while, I don't feel the gut-wrenching anxiety of my to-do list looming. Instead, I take my time cleaning up the kitchen a bit before heading upstairs to my office, where I put on a show and start binding the quilt, determined to slowly finish it on my unplanned day off. Unfortunately, I've only completed three of the four sides when the power goes out.

The town has tons of trees throughout, so it's not uncommon during a snowstorm like this for a tree branch to get too heavy and fall on a power line. Hopefully, the power will return soon, since my heat is unfortunately electric. Otherwise, I'll have to brave the outside and grab some of the firewood my brother dropped off a few months ago and get the fireplace going.

Ten minutes later, my hope that the power will return quickly is almost completely dashed, and an unknown number texts me.

UNKNOWN

Do you have power?

I squint at my phone, unsure of who could be messaging me. I don't think I've given out my phone number to anyone recently, but maybe it's someone who also lost power and is looking for help. Before I answer, though, the typing bubble pops up once more, followed by a new message.

This is Adam.

My stomach flips a bit at the name on my screen. Why is Adam texting me?

And where did he get my number?

> How did you get my number?

Again, he answers quickly.

> It was in a packet of papers someone dumped on my front door when I moved in.

> Do you have power?

Moving to the front window, I check the street that's now coated in a thick layer of snow to confirm none of the houses are lit up. I think I see a light on in Adam's house, but the rest are mostly dark except for a few that I know have generators. Many houses on this street have gas heat, something my house was never converted to, so I'm not worried about anyone freezing to death.

Except, maybe, for me.

> No, I think the entire street is out.

> I meant a generator. Do you have a generator?

I don't respond.

My oldest brother, Jesse, has been bugging me since I moved in that I needed to get a generator for the house, but I kept waving it off. I had no time or energy to shop for a boring generator. Especially not when there were many more fun things to get for the house, like decorations and paint. Generators are pretty common around here, and we had a giant one at the farm I grew up on. Grandma never needed one because any time there was a forecast for even the smallest bit of snow, my dad would insist on picking her up and taking her to the farm for the night.

I know Madden and Jesse are totally going to get on me about it.

> Wren?

And it seems my grumpy neighbor is *also* going to be on me about it. I don't respond, knowing he will probably have just as many opinions about my lack of storm preparedness as my brothers. Honestly, I was having a pretty peaceful day.

> Wren.

> Is your phone charged? Or did it die?

I shake my head at his overprotectiveness, noting that I have an eighty-five percent charge, a small miracle since I never remember to keep my phone charged overnight.

> My phone is charged. I don't have a generator, but I don't want to hear you giving me a hard time about it. I already have two older brothers and a dad; I don't need more.

He doesn't respond right away, something I'm grateful for, before I start looking around my dark house. I glare at the empty fireplace I've never actually used before, knowing that I'll have to go into the shed and get some of the wood there to start a fire.

Or I could wait. Sometimes, the power comes back on relatively quickly.

> Wren, you're going to freeze. I have a generator—just come over here.

I groan at his seeming ability to hear all of my thoughts and second-guessings.

But I am a strong, powerful, *capable* woman. I don't need a man and his stupid gas-powered machine to keep me warm. I can do it all by myself.

> I'm going to start a fire. It will be fine. Leave me alone.

A text bubble pops up, and I can already see his argument impending, so I add on before he can respond.

> I can take care of myself.

Then I throw my phone onto the couch and start bundling up. As much as I'd like to think things will just fix themselves, I also know I should get a fire going before the house *actually* gets cold. I slide a hat over my head, pull on my jacket and a pair of boots, and resolve to throw my soon-to-be-wet pajamas in the wash and put on warm, dry clothes when I'm done. Then I trudge outside in my pink puffy jacket and my pajama pants with little polar bears wearing tutus that Hallie got me for Christmas last year.

Unfortunately, since I never actually checked the wood storage delivered directly to my storage, I didn't have nice, neat little logs perfect for starting a fire. Instead, I had large chunks that I'm pretty sure would be too big for my fireplace. That was when I remembered that each fall, without her having to ask, my dad or one of my brothers would come to my grandmother's house and chop wood for her to make sure she had what she needed for the winter, since she loved having a fire in her fireplace when she was home.

It seems they didn't realize I would need the same assistance, or I suppose I should have checked earlier.

When I walked into the woodshed, I found it empty of anything other than some sticks and things to use as tinder, so I gathered up a pile of that and set it aside before I went over to where Jesse and Madden had stacked up the cured wood for me. The rounds are small enough for me to lift, though I won't deny they wind me with their size and weight. Now I'm staring at the full rounds of wood, the stump I cleared of snow that is quickly piling up again, and the axe in my hands.

I've watched my dad and brothers do this for as long as I can remember. I roll my shoulders back, slide my cutesy pink gloves back on, and set the log in place to thwack it a few times until it's in manageable pieces. I mean, how hard could it really be?

After the third time of hitting the log I'm trying to split and getting nowhere, I realize the answer is *very hard*. Just a few hits in and everything already hurts, and I haven't even split a single piece of wood. I groan into the snowy sky as the axe gets stuck, and I have to try once again to pry it free.

"You need to go higher," a familiar voice calls. My back stiffens, and I try not to let it show, but my eyes close, and I pray to anyone who will listen that I imagined the words.

Maybe it's just a cold-induced dream, maybe it's—

"You aren't getting enough force to actually do the job."

It's Adam.

I know that, but when I turn to look at the back porch of his house, I see him in a sweater and jeans, watching me with an amused smirk. He's leaning on the railing he must have cleared off, and there's a fine layer of white snow on his hair, so I imagine he's been standing there for some time. His smile goes soft after he takes me in. I can only imagine what he sees: me in my puffy jacket, pajama bottoms tucked into soft boots, my nose cold and probably dripping.

Why can't the world give me a *single freaking break*?

"You don't have to do that, Wren. Just come to my place. I won't even bother you; you can sit in the living room, and I'll stay upstairs."

"I'm fine, but thank you for the offer," I say stiffly, then turn back around to face my new enemy. Wiggling the axe until it is free of the log, I bring it up high and drop it harder, the metal splitting the wood right down the middle. I jump and clap excitedly and then look over my shoulder at Adam. He's watching me intently, but there's playfulness in his eyes.

"Now you just gotta do that a dozen more times," he says, ruining my high. I glare at him before turning back around, and he sighs audibly. "You're going to freeze out here, Wren. Just come in where I have heat. You can charge your phone and eat a hot meal."

A warm home and a hot meal sound *so nice*, especially since I didn't bother to wear weatherproof boots outside, instead slipping on ones that are already soaked, but I'm stubborn, so I shake my head.

"I can take care of myself, thank you."

He stares at me, and that flicker of a smirk has melted away. He lets out a breath, then shrugs, though I can tell my lack of agreement is annoying to him.

"Suit yourself."

I watch him for another moment, expecting him to go back inside, but he doesn't. Instead, he gives me a shooing motion with his hand, and I roll my eyes before turning back around.

The next piece takes three hits, the second of which sends fragments flying off the stump, but by the third split, I think I'm getting the hang of it.

I should know better than to get too confident, though.

"Shit!" I shout, grabbing my hand and shaking it as my finger throbs. It was pinched between the handle and the wood because my aim apparently *sucks*, and I can already feel my pulse in it. I hop on one foot as if that's going to help, then shake my hand out. The cold made it even more painful, and I could feel cold tears pooling in my eyes. *Stupid freaking wood. Stupid freaking storm. Stupid* freaking *neighbor watching me.*

"Jesus, Wren," I hear, but barely register it, too lost in my pained dance. But the next thing I know, I'm scooped up into increasingly familiar, strong arms and being moved away from my backyard.

"What are you doing?!" There's no response. In fact, the only sound is the sound of Adam's shoes crunching on the soft snow.

Toward *his* house.

"Take me into my house, Adam. I'm fine!" I shout, slapping at his chest with my good hand.

He doesn't respond.

Instead, he takes the four steps up to his back deck two at a time, despite the inches of snow coating them, until we're at his back door.

"Let me go!" I shout, but he just holds me tighter, somehow managing to open the door without dropping me.

It's impressive, but I'm annoyed.

"I'm serious, Adam. Put me down!"

He listens to me this time, but not the way I want. Instead, he moves through his kitchen, setting my ass on the island, then moving to grab my hand. He knows the exact one, I realize, not because it's obvious, but because he was watching. Gently, with reverence I don't expect, he pulls off my gloves that are wet with melted snow before softly grazing his fingers over the small dent where my finger was pinched. It will bruise, but otherwise should be fine. It's not so bad now that my hands are warming up, to be honest.

"Bend it," he demands.

I glare at him. He glares back.

"I'm serious, Wren. I need to make sure you didn't fucking break your finger."

"If I had a broken finger, you'd know, Adam. I'd be screaming."

"No, you wouldn't, you'd be pretending it doesn't hurt so as not to freak anyone out." I glare at him, and he raises an eyebrow in a challenge I can't fully argue because he's not completely wrong.

I try anyway.

"I'm a baby when it comes to pain. I'd be bawling, trust me. He doesn't break his glare, doesn't smile, so I sigh but do as he asked, carefully bending my injured finger. It's tight, but it doesn't bring any extra pain, which seems like a good sign.

"Not broken," he confirms under his breath, then runs a gentle thumb over the spot I pinched. "You're lucky." He takes both of my hands between his, rubbing to warm them. They get tingly with the warmth, but neither of us says a word until all of the feeling returns to my fingertips. Once they're warm, his hands shift again to look at the finger, turning it to look at other angles before he steps back. Instantly, I miss his warmth.

His hands move to the zipper of my jacket, sliding it down before helping me to shrug off the wet article of clothing and hanging it over one of the stools. Then he picks up my hand once more, staring at it as if the absence of my jacket would change anything.

It doesn't.

"Stay here," he says. I glare, but I nod. Now that I'm in warmth, I don't have the energy to argue with him. My arms are tired, and I know tomorrow they'll ache like I did one of those barre arm workouts Hallie loves to make us do.

After a moment, he returns with a white box that I quickly recognize to be a first aid kit. He digs through it before grabbing out a bandage.

"Adam, I don't need a Band-Aid. It's not bleeding or anything."

"Humor me." His voice is firm, and I shrug because, really, what is a Band-Aid going to hurt? Then I watch his big fingers peel the backing. It looks out of place, his big, calloused hands working on the small bandage. He has laser focus, though, as he gently wraps it around my much smaller finger.

"There," he whispers, brushing a finger over the bandage I didn't need. I give him a gentle look of gratitude, and my heart pounds as he lifts it, pressing his lips to the spot that still throbs quietly. "Was that so hard?"

"Was what hard?" I ask breathlessly.

"Letting someone take care of you."

A million sassy responses fill my mind, but none of them come out. Instead, the truth fills the space between us.

"I don't think it's that hard when you're the one doing it."

His eyes go soft, and it's clear that he really freaking liked that answer. It's even more obvious when his hand lifts and moves behind my neck, fingers ghosting along the skin there before sinking into my hair as he steps closer, taking up all of the space between my legs. There are still snowflakes in his hair and quickly melting on his shoulder, but I can only focus on his face. On the awe and desire written so clearly there.

"I'm gonna kiss you now, Wren," he whispers, lips just an inch or so from mine. I can't help but let a smile ghost along mine.

"Oh, you're not going to make me beg for it?" I whisper in return. Our lips brush gently with the movements, and I breathe in his air. He smiles then, something I can feel more than see with him.

"Not this time. Not for this. We can save begging for later in the night," he murmurs against my lips, and I gasp, ready to argue, but just then, Adam leans in fully, and his lips are on mine, cutting off any other thought.

SIXTEEN

Wren

It's nothing like the last time we were like this, none of the frustration or anger in the press of his lips to mine.

It's rough and filled with a need I've never felt before in my life. It's heady and hot, intoxicating and quickly taking over every aspect of my consciousness. His hands move to rest over my T-shirt on my waist, pulling me closer, stepping closer to reduce any space between us until our bodies are flush, the thin layer of clothes we're each wearing doing nothing to stop me from feeling the heat of his body against mine.

But somehow, it's not enough.

My body shifts, trying to get closer, and a small mewl leaves my lips. Something changes, snapping in Adam. His movements become urgent, his hands moving with purpose. His warm palms slide over my hips, then up under the light T-shirt I slept in, dragging the fabric up as he does. I lift my hands, our lips still moving against one another and only breaking for a moment while he tugs the T-shirt over my head. He tosses it in a corner, but I can't focus on where exactly, not when his hands are sliding over my bare skin, wrapping around to pull me to his chest. I put a hand on his chest between us, though, stopping him. He looks at me with a mix of worried confusion and a smile on his face.

"You too," I whisper, the demand feeling awkward and foreign on my tongue, but I know it was the right move when his grin goes wide and pleased.

"If you ask for it, you get it," he murmurs, then crosses his arms behind his back, grabbing and tugging the long-sleeved tee over his head.

Lean muscles ripple and flex as he does, and I have to bite my lip from making a noise at the sight. The shirt gets tossed in the same direction as mine before his hands move again, pulling me to him. My hands press into his hard chest, and I groan as his lips fall onto mine, sliding up and over his shoulders to twine into the hair at the back of his neck as his tongue dances with mine. His own hands slide up my back, stopping at the clasp of my bra and pausing. I nod into the kiss, and his fingers move deftly as we kiss, undoing then sliding the straps down each arm.

It's frantic and needy and hot, and I want *more*. I whimper with loss when he pulls back, and a cocky grin plays on his lips, but that look turns into something different. Something hotter as his eyes travel down to my breasts.

"Fuck, these are pretty," he says, cupping my breasts and pinching the nipples and making my breath hitch. His lips tip in amusement as he watches my every reaction, repeating the action. My back arches, and my eyes drift shut, and he groans, one hand moving to the back of my head again and pulling my lips to his. He kisses me again, and his tongue mimics the movements of his fingers. My hips shift as need begins to pool in my belly. I brush up against his hard cock, and he moans into my mouth before breaking the kiss once more, both hands moving to my waist and then trailing down to my hips.

"These are cute, Birdie, but they gotta go," he says, fingers moving under the waistband of my pajama pants. I forgot that I had them on, and a blush burns over my cheeks, embarrassed that the hottest man

I've ever seen is before me and I'm wearing...this...but then, when I look at his eyes, I feel that embarrassment melt away.

He looks like he's never seen anyone more gorgeous.

He looks like he needs me in a way I've never experienced.

He looks like he wants to devour me.

I nod in agreement to his unasked question, and a satisfied look spreads over his face. His thumb hooks into my pants and underwear, and without him telling me to, I plant my hands on the counter and lift my ass a bit, and am rewarded with him dragging down my pants. I expect him to push them down and then pull me close, but Adam never truly seems to do what I expect. Instead, as he drags them down, his body lowers *down, down, down,* until my pajama pants are off my dangling feet and I'm towering over him.

Towering, because Adam is on his knees before me, his face right before my pussy, breath coasting along my skin. My own breath is stuck in my lungs, and I try to ignore the discomfort I feel at the imbalance of our positions, both my being completely naked and him being very much not, as well as him being on his knees with me looking down my body at him.

It all disappears, replaced with searing heat and need, when he presses a kiss to the inside of my knee. Moving on instinct, I spread my legs, desperate to feel his kiss elsewhere.

"That's a good girl." He whispers his praise, and he's so close, I feel the scruff of his beard along the inside of my knee. I let out a sigh as I feel the pressure of need curl into my belly. His hands grip both of my legs firmly, further spreading me for his eyes to take in, his thumbs just inches from my pussy.

From where I suddenly need him desperately.

I've never been a very needy person with a partner. The goal of sex has always been simple for me: make my partner feel good. Occasionally, I get to feel those warm flutters from an orgasm along the way, but everyone knows that it's just not something women always feel. I've had an ex put his head between my legs, but it was always just something that felt like a chore to be checked off a list. When it became increasingly clear that my ex didn't get joy or pleasure out of it, I never pushed for it again.

But right now, the look in Adam's eyes is telling me he very much wants to put his mouth between my legs, and honestly, I want nothing more than to *let* him. My fingers itch to move through the hair on his head, to push him against me, to beg him to eat me out until I come on his face.

But that would be crude and probably a little bit rude, so I don't. Though when he looks up at me, his eyes wide and heated and his full lips parted, my restraint crumbles just a bit.

"You are so fucking beautiful, Wren."

I blink at him, confused. "What?"

"Every goddamn part of you, gorgeous. Perfect. I should have known, you being my own personal wet dream brought to life, but fuck, you're more perfect than I could have imagined." A blush blooms over my cheeks. "I especially like it when I say something like that, and the pretty blush on your face moves down your neck." He gives me a wicked grin. "Do you know how long I've been wondering how far it goes?"

One hand leaves my thigh, and I almost whimper at the loss of his warmth, but then his hand is cupping my breast, lifting it, and stroking a thumb over the nipple. My breath hitches at the caress.

"If it would go down your chest and turn these that same pretty pink?" His fingers meet, pinching and rolling my nipple, and I moan. "Happy to report it does," he adds. The hand moves to my other nipple, giving it the same treatment. I want to tip my head back, close my eyes, and revel in the pleasure his simple touch is giving me, but I want to remember this moment in vivid detail. He seems to be taking his sweet time, alternating nipples all the while the thumb of his other hand swipes lazily against the sensitive skin of my inner thigh. I tighten, my body desperate for more, for release, and the words tumble from my lips.

"Please, Adam."

With them, his eyes snap to mine, a teasing grin on his face.

"Please what, baby?" he asks. His hand slides up half an inch, and I whimper. I bite my lip, looking down, not sure of how to respond. I want so much right now, but I don't know what he is comfortable with. But most of all, I just want his hands on me. I want this neediness to be abated in any way he can.

I take in a breath, trying to steady myself as I look into his eyes and make my request. "Please touch me."

A small, almost inaudible groan leaves his lips, and his hand leaves my breast to trail down my belly, over my hip, and to my thigh, mirroring where his other hand is. Both shift higher, his thumbs grazing along the crease where my thigh meets my center.

"Where do you want me to touch you, sweetness? Here?" His thumbs are swift, grazing along the close-cut curls, and I nod.

"Yes, yes." The words are frantic, and he smiles again, but I can't concentrate on what it might mean, not when his thumbs are moving again, hands sliding up, and he's urging the digits to tug my folds open, exposing my most intimate parts to his eyes.

"Is this where you want me to touch?" His eyes leave my center for just a moment to lock on mine.

"Yes, please," I whisper. His look goes almost catlike before he looks straight ahead again. I take in the visual I have as well. This angle is absolute perfection, and I hold my breath for his next move. He's kneeling on the ground, my legs framing his head, his hands holding me wide, thumbs holding my pussy open for his inspection. I should feel self-conscious— hell, in any other situation with any other man, *I would*. But the way he groans when the fingers of one hand shift so his thumb can graze over my center, barely even whispering to me, I can't seem to find it in me.

"Oh, what I want to fucking do to this," he murmurs. I clench at the tone of his voice and his words, and a groan leaves his lips again. He must have fucking *seen* it.

Again, I shouldn't be embarrassed by that.

Again, I'm very much not.

"Yes, please," I whisper.

Again, he looks up at me.

Again, he smiles, but this time, it's not a kind smile, not a loving smile, not even the smile of a man who knows he's about to make me come like a freight train. Instead, it's one of a man who knows he's about to drive a woman crazy.

"Tell me what you want, Wren."

The breath stops in my chest, and my brows furrow even though my gut knows where this is going.

"What?"

"Tell me what you want. What will make you feel good?"

I lick my suddenly dry lips and stare at him in feigned confusion. I can *feel* a deep blush burning my cheeks and moving down my chest, just as he described minutes ago.

"I...I don't—" I suck in a sharp breath as his thumb grazes over my clit. "That," I say, nodding quickly. "Do that. Do that again."

"Do what?" He's clearly entertained by this game, though I am not. I am becoming quickly frustrated, not just sexually, but also mentally. Why does *everything* with us have to be a battle?

Because you like it that way, the voice in my head whispers. I bat her away.

"Whatever you just did! I don't know, Adam. Just make me feel good. Whatever you wanted to do before, do that. Whatever you want, Adam."

He shakes his head, and I groan with frustration.

"Mmm, not this time." His words feel like a threat and a promise, and I tighten, something that he must see if the deep groan he lets out means anything. "I told you, Wren. You don't ask for what you want enough. So I'm making it my mission that you learn to demand what you want." He moves his thumb, grazing along my clit, and I gasp at the graze. "Starting here and now."

"Adam," I whisper.

"Fuck," he groans, 'and I wonder if that's his resolve cracking. "Fuck, if my name on your lips like that doesn't make me want to throw this fucking plan out the window." The tip of his thumb moves down, barely entering me, and I nod fervently.

"Yes, yes."

But then his eyes shift from my entrance to my face, and an amused grin spreads over his lips.

"Tell me. Tell me what you want."

He purses his lips and blows cool air along my wet cunt, and I cry out. I'm so turned on, more turned on than I've ever been in my entire life, and this man has barely even touched me.

"Adam!"

"Tell me what you want, Wren," he demands through gritted teeth as if this is paining him just as much.

"I don't care—"

He cuts me off, his gaze leaving my center to stare at me, eyes suddenly fierce and serious.

"Don't play that game with me. With everyone else, you can tell them you don't care or that you don't know. But not with me. You demand what you want when you're with me, Wren."

His words move through me, searing and sending sparks of need through me, and I realize that I'm not getting anything if I don't ask for it. He wants me to feel this pleasure, to be the one to give it to me, and I realize in some strange way, he's going to get satisfaction out of me getting that. It appeases the version of me that hates feeling selfish, that is uncomfortable with putting my own wants and needs first.

I take a deep, unsteady breath, then hold his gaze when I finally speak. "Finger me."

He groans loudly, like the two words bring him both immense pleasure and pain, but he obliges all the same. Adam slides two thick fingers into me, stretching me as they fill me. I lean back a bit on my hands that are planted on the counter, staring down at my body to watch where his fingers are disappearing into me.

"Oh god," I groan, tightening not just at the fullness or the immediate pleasure it gives me, but the visual of him. His grin is wide as he pulls out and then slides back in, crooking his fingers to brush against an extra-sensitive spot at the front of me.

"Fuck, you're so wet, Wren," he groans, and I tighten around him at not just his words but the tone, at the sound of pure rapture in them, and the way his eyes are locked on my center, his fingers disappearing into me. "Look at you." He pulls his fingers out, and the light catches on them, glinting on the wetness on his fingers.

I want to blush, but I can't seem to find it in me, not when he's looking at me like that. Now, my body is on fire with need, and without him, I feel empty.

"More," I whisper, my hips lifting.

"That's my good girl."

I whimper at his words, the sounds morphing into a moan when he slides three thick fingers into me. The stretch is exquisite, though not surprising considering I can't tell you the last time someone had me in this way.

Adam must be reading my mind when he comments on it. "You look so fucking pretty stretched around my fingers like this, baby. So pretty. I can't wait to see you like this around my cock."

I groan, then nod vigorously. "Yes, yes. That."

He lets out a low, teasing chuckle before shaking his head. "No, no. You're going to come like this before you get anything more. I want to watch."

I let out a defeated sound, and his laugh fills the quiet room again, but then his thumb curls up to my clit, circling me there as he finger fucks me, and all thoughts of disappointment melt away.

Somehow, I'm already close to the edge.

I normally take a while, if I find it at all, when I'm with someone else. I often find myself preoccupied with ensuring my partner's enjoyment, putting my own pleasure and enjoyment on the back burner.

In fact, I don't think I've ever had someone like Adam, someone so tuned in and locked onto my pleasure and needs. So determined to watch me take that pleasure for myself,

Honestly, though, I should have known he would challenge me in this way—he does with everything else, after all.

"I'm close," I whisper without meaning to. A blush burns on my cheeks, but when I see the look of adoration and determination on Adam's face, it melts away as quickly as it came.

"What else do you want, Wren?" he asks, and my breathing catches in my throat. "What do you need?"

"I—" I start, but the words fall away as he continues to finger fuck me, the rhythm speeding up and taking my breath away. My eyes try to drift shut with the building pleasure, but I force them open. I'm not missing a single moment of this, not willing to risk not seeing Adam kneeling between my legs like this.

"Hmm?" he asks. I try to respond, really, I do, but his fingers are expertly working me, and words don't seem to want to work. "I'm sure there are more things in that pretty little head of yours besides my fingers fucking you."

The image of his head between my legs, my fingers twining between the thick strands of his hair, holding his face to me as I come, flashes in my mind, but I shake my head to remove it.

I'm happy with this.

Guys don't like that, so they put their mouth there. Right?

He stares at me, and then a slow, mischievous smile spreads over his handsome face, as if he's seen what went through my mind on a Jumbotron over my head.

"Now, if we were talking about what I want," he says, almost casually as he finger fucks me, slowing his thrusts. My breathing is heavy, and a whimper leaves my lips as he adds just a hair more pressure to my clit. "If we were talking about my desires, I'd say I want little more on this earth right now than to eat this pretty pussy. Lick it clean, suck on your pretty little clit." He groans when I tighten around his fingers, then looks up at me knowingly. "What do you think about that?"

I nod.

God, I want that.

I just know this man with his filthy mouth and his expert fingers will be absolutely ground-shaking if he gets his mouth on me in that way.

"Words, Wren. You have to ask for what you want," he says.

Irritation flares, but when his fingers shift, pressing on some new sweet spot inside of me, it's replaced with need.

Some new version of me takes over, some version I've never met, but I'm grateful it exists. My hand lifts, running through his thick hair and staring down at him. "I want you to—" My breath hitches as he fucks me harder with his fingers, like he can't stop himself. "I want you to eat my pussy, Adam."

A deep groan fills the room, and I moan in response, though I whimper when I feel the loss of his fingers.

"Feet on the counter," Adam says firmly.

My lust-filled gaze meets his with confusion. "What?"

"Put your feet on the fucking counter, Wren. Spread wide for me so I can feast."

My hesitation only lasts a moment, quickly washed away by the fierce look on his face before I oblige, lifting first my left, then my right foot and resting it on the corner of the kitchen counter. It crosses my mind for a single heartbeat to be embarrassed, spread wide and on display like this for him, but Adam lets out a soul-deep noise of appreciation before his fingers slide into me again.

"Fuck...look at how pretty you are. All spread out for me. So fucking wet for me." He stares at me in awe before his eyes move up to mine. "Who is all of this for, Wren?"

My tongue moves out, wetting my lips before answering without thinking.

"It's all for you, honey," I murmur, my eyes locked on his.

"Fuck, yeah, it is," he groans low, then his mouth moves, lips wrapping around my clit and sucking hard.

I scream.

It felt good before, his fingers fucking me and his thumb on my clit, but this is something so new and exquisite, I know he's ruining me in this moment for any other man.

His mouth moves over me, tongue licking, fingers fucking, and all I can do is sit there and take it. All I can do is watch this man on his knees, serving me.

I don't have to tell him what I like, what I need, and I surely don't have to pretend I'm enjoying it.

It doesn't take long at all before I'm close, teetering on the brink of the most glorious orgasm of my life.

I need a bit more, and my hand moves from the counter with a mind of its own and shifts to hover over his head, pausing as I realize what I almost did. Adam's eyes snap up to my face, probably sensing my hesitation in a way only he can, then they move to my hand.

The noise that comes from him is nearly feral and vibrates through me before his hand leaves my thigh, grips my wrist, and slams my hand into his hair. The move presses his face between my legs harder and ratchets up my need, pushing me closer, and I snap.

My fingers grip his hair, pulling him into me more fiercely as I shift him and my own hips to get what I need where I need it.

And then I come.

I come and I come, screaming Adam's name, my body quaking as the most intense pleasure racks my body in seemingly unending waves as his fingers continue to move inside of me, as his tongue and lips and even a graze of his teeth work my clit. Finally, it begins to ease, and my fingers begin to loosen in his hair as his fingers slide out and his tongue licks me clean. But when he groans in undisguised satisfaction right into me, another smaller orgasm moves through me, sweeter and softer but no less pleasurable than before.

Finally, he pulls back, wet glinting over his lips, grinning at me before he stands.

"That was fucking spectacular, Wren," he says, then buries his hands in my hair, pulling my mouth to his.

SEVENTEEN

ADAM

As I press my lips to Wren's, I am once again taken by surprise when she doesn't hesitate to slide her tongue into my mouth, kissing me deep, even though I still have her taste on mine.

I have never experienced anything hotter than Wren King moaning my name as she comes, except maybe for when she tightened her hand in my hair and pulled me closer to her pussy to take what she wanted. My hard cock throbs at the memory, confirming that Wren taking what she wanted was *definitely* the hottest thing I've ever seen.

"Your room," she murmurs when I pull back. "Your room, now."

I grin, then press my lips to her neck. "Your wish is my command, Birdie. Wrap your legs around my hips."

"Wha—"

I lift her with an arm around her waist, the other moving to her ass, before she wraps her legs around my hips and her arms around my neck on instinct.

"Atta girl," I say, and she lets out a little mewl. I curse under my breath because, of course, Wren likes to be praised.

As much as I need to hear her upstairs, I take a few steps, then press her to the wall before I press my lips to hers. Her hips move against my lower stomach, and I feel her wetness there. For a moment, I think about just pulling out my cock and fucking her here, but not for our first time. Instead, I break the kiss and make my way up the stairs with Wren in my arms. Her mouth begins its own exploration, pressing wet licks and nibbles to my cheek, my jaw, and my neck.

Finally, we get to the top of the stairs, and I take long strides to my room, trying to block out the small mewls and breathy moans as she grinds herself against me and kisses any bare skin she can reach. As I enter my room, I toss her onto my unmade bed and take a moment to marvel at the sight of her—her skin smooth, legs spread, lips puffy, and eyes dazed.

"Fuck, you're pretty," I murmur. Then, because I can't resist, I slide two fingers into her. She moans, hips rising, and I pull out, chuckling at her whimper before making my way to the bedside table. I grab a condom, then toss it to her before shucking off my jeans and underwear. She already has the condom unwrapped and is on her knees, shifting to where I stand at the edge of the bed. Her small hand reaches out, eyes locked on mine as she bites her lip and wraps it around me. It takes everything in me not to close my eyes and moan at her tentative touch. She strokes me once, twice, three times, and a deep groan falls from my lips. She sighs with satisfaction before she moves, rolling the condom over me.

I've never been so turned on by a fucking condom in my *life*, but Wren makes everything hot, it seems. She moves to her full height on her knees, then wraps her arms around my neck and presses her lips to mine.

I kiss her, then wrap an arm around her waist, moving and tugging and shifting her until I'm on my back and she is straddling my hips, a leg on either side of me. Then I take my cock in hand and slide the tip through her. She's soaked again, and a soft sigh leaves her lips with the move.

I want her like this the first time, not just because I want to watch her sink onto me, which I very much want to watch, but because I want her in control.

We have all the time in the world for me to fulfill the dozens and dozens of fantasies I've created, but this first time, she's going to find it again and again. We're starting this off the way it always should be: with Wren's wants, needs, and most importantly, pleasure coming first.

Literally.

"Please," she whispers, eyes wide with the same need I know is reflected all over my face, and without a word, I notch the head of my cock into her entrance, then put my hands to her hips, helping to lower her. Her eyes flutter shut as I stretch her.

"Fuck, you're big," she murmurs, and I can't help but let a proud, satisfied look spread over my lips. Her eyes snap open, and she rolls those pretty brown eyes, then slaps at my chest. It shifts me inside her, though, leaving her gasping, eyes going wide. I grit my teeth as she tightens around me, and my hands move with a mind of their own, pressing her down until her hips settle on mine, filling her completely.

"Fuck," I groan, forcing myself to keep my eyes open, forcing myself to commit every moment of this to memory.

"Adam," she whispers.

"I know, sweetness, I know. Fuck, it's perfect." She nods, biting her lip when she shifts, grinding her swollen clit against me, and tightening once more. "Okay, baby. You've got to move now. Ride me, Wren."

I want her to be on top, to take what she needs, knowing it's sometimes easier for a woman to find it when she's on top and in control. I'm prepared to sit back and watch her find it. Something flashes across her face, but it's gone before I can really identify it. Then I'm lost in her as she plants her knees into the bed and starts to move, lifting and falling, fucking me.

It's exquisite.

It's perfection.

And the visual is even better, as Wren tips her head back, her hair falling down her back, her hands lifting to cup her breasts, pants coming from parted, full lips.

But despite this being what all of my recent dreams have been made of, something is off.

She's...putting on a show.

A fucking great show, but I'm in tune with her body enough right now to know it's not doing much for her. It might feel good, but it's not driving her crazy.

And I want Wren absolutely out of her mind.

"No, no, no," I say, putting my hand on her hips to stop her from continuing to ride my cock, since if she continues like this, it will be over before I can make her come.

Her eyes go wide. "Was it not good?" she asks with panic in her voice, and I let out a little laugh, one that turns into a groan as it sends me deeper into her.

"Wren, you keep that up, the way you feel, the way you look, and I'm gonna blow in less than a minute. But I want to feel you, too."

She blinks at me for a moment before those pretty brows furrow, and she looks at me, confused.

"Can you not...feel me?"

"Oh, I can feel you fucking my cock, Birdie, trust me. And it feels magnificent. But I want to feel you come around me, and if we keep it up, you won't get yours."

"But—" she starts, but I shake my head, reaching up, putting a hand to the back of her neck, and pulling her down to press my lips to hers. The slide of her along me has her gasping and me smiling.

"And I very much want you to get yours, Wren."

When our eyes meet again, hers are a bit hazier with pleasure, but now a hint of embarrassment has joined them.

"Oh, no," she says, giving me the slightest shake of her head. She tries to sit up, but I hold her there. "I, um, I can't."

"You can't?" This should be a strange conversation to have with her on top of me, my cock deep in her, but it feels natural.

Learning.

Us.

Perfect.

"I can't come like...this." That blush burns over her cheeks, deepening the flush that was already there.

"What do you mean, like this?"

White teeth bite her full, plush lips, and she sits up once more. I bite back a groan of pleasure with the move. She sees it still, and a devious gleam shines in her eyes. Despite my hands on her hips, she lifts a bit, just an inch or two, before filling herself once.

My breath catches, and I have to clear my throat before I can repeat my question. "Answer my question, Wren." She rolls her eyes, and if this weren't the first time I was fucking her, I'd pull her off me, put her over my knee, and spank her.

Maybe next time.

Maybe every time she puts someone else before her own needs, I should spank her.

I'm distracted by my daydream when her response finally comes.

"Penetration," she whispers, the blush returning in full force, and she avoids eye contact with me.

I nod, knowing. "How can you come?"

That blush deepens, moving to the tops of her breasts. I can't resist any longer, moving up a bit, bending to pull a nipple into my mouth. A moan leaves her lips, and I suck on the peak before looking up at her. Her eyes are hooded as she looks down at me, and the flush on her cheeks isn't nervousness or embarrassment anymore; it's pure arousal.

"Like that," she whispers. I move a hand to cup her breast and twist at the nipple with two fingers. Her breath hitches, and she tightens around me.

"You like it when I play with your tits, baby? Is that what you need?" She shakes her head and bites her lip, looking away. I continue working her nipple and lift my hips, pushing in deeper and grinding against her. She moans but still doesn't speak. "Neither of us is getting what we want until you tell me what you need, Wren. Might as well get it over with."

She bites her lip again, weighing her options with nervousness and maybe even a little embarrassment. I tweak her nipple, then encourage her once more, targeting where I know she's weak.

"I'm so hard, baby, and I know you want to make me feel good." She takes in a sharp breath and tightens around me again, confirming my thoughts. "Do it by telling me what you like. Nothing has ever been hotter than you getting off on my kitchen counter. That? That's going into my mental files forever. I'm going to be jacking off to the memory of the first time I made you come until I fucking die." She mewls at my words, and I file that away, too. *Wren likes dirty talk.* "What do you need, baby? Something before felt good. What was it?"

She sighs but finally answers. "My clit," she whispers. "When you moved, it...you know. That's what I need to, uhm, come."

Pride shines through me as I realize what she's saying and that she's using her words to tell me what *she* wants and needs.

"You need your clit rubbed to come, got it." I don't tell her that this is something that we can work on, that I'm about to make it my personal mission to make her come with just my cock, to tease her and drag out her pleasure so that the head of my cock hitting the right spot has her shaking in my arms.

That's too much too quick for my sweet Wren.

Instead, I move, shifting so I'm sitting up on the bed a bit more, Wren in my lap, then put my hands on her hips. Keeping her planted with my cock deep inside her, I shift her back and forth, making sure her clit grinds against my pelvis. Her breath hitches when I do, before a low moan leaves her lips.

"There it is, baby," I groan, feeling her tighten. I repeat the action, then shift her, encouraging her more. Her hips start to rock on their own, and a small moan leaves her lips.

My cock gets harder at the sight.

"Just like that, Wren. Fuck, you're beautiful. Ride me until you come. Take what you need from me."

"But it's not good for you like that," she says breathlessly, pleasure clearly building for her.

I can't help it, I let out a laugh.

God, this woman is so scrambled, it's going to take me a decade to undo all of it.

It's a good thing I have all the time in the world, I suppose.

"Wren, I promise you this, nothing will be better for me than you grinding down and finding it while you're full of my cock. You could sit there, rub that pretty little clit of yours on me until you come over and over again, and never move on me, and it would be fucking phenomenal." That makes her pussy clench around me, and I groan. "That. That right there? Better than anything I've ever felt."

I shift her a bit, using my hands to help her grind her clit against my pelvis, and she lets out a breathy moan. "I like you selfish, Wren. I like it when you take what you need, when you demand it, and when you get what you want. Nothing makes me harder than watching you assert yourself."

Slowly, she starts to shift on her own, and my hands leave her hips, hovering over her. My eyes shift, watching where she sits on me, her swollen clit rubbing against me, then to her breasts, one hand cupping one and tweaking the nipple, then to her face. Her eyes are drifting shut, her head tipped back, her lips parted with panting breaths.

I want this painted on the back of my eyelids.

I want to see it every fucking moment of my life.

"That's it. Be selfish, Birdie. Take what you want." I watch her with near breathless anticipation as she hovers over me. "You can give me a show, baby, but I want that show to be you finding it while you're full of me." I put my hands behind my head and watch, another blush burning on her face, but something about my words— be selfish—makes that determination move across her face again.

She lets out a shaky breath before her hips start to move, grinding and rocking on me.

"Oh god," she whispers, and my cock hardens as she continues to move. "Shit," she moans, and I bite my lip as she speeds up her hips, snapping them back and forth and taking the pleasure she needs.

"Adam," she whimpers, and I start counting beats in my head to distract myself from ending this too early. "More." I lift my hips, shifting her, and she yells out, clearly liking the new angle. "Oh, yes, right there. Just like that." She leans back a bit, hips lifting just a bit as she fucks herself on me, and her hand trails between us, fingers circling her clit. I watch with fascination, cataloging every movement, not just for future memories, but to understand what she likes and needs.

Whoever had Wren before me clearly didn't value her pleasure, and while I'm not shocked, I will make sure that every time she is with me, she knows her pleasure is my biggest concern.

My *only* fucking concern.

"That's it, Wren. God, you're fucking hot," I groan, lifting my hips a bit, helping her take me deeper, grinding her clit against me harder, and then her head snaps back.

"Adam!" she shouts before her body starts to tremble, before her hips move with more fervency than before, and she tightens around my cock like a vise. One hand is on my chest, holding herself there, the other is tweaking her nipple, her head snapped back as she moves and comes on my cock, taking the pleasure she needs and deserves.

I've never seen anything hotter on this fucking planet.

When I see it, I can't hold off either, filling the condom as I come with her.

Wren collapses against my chest, and long, long moments pass as we both catch our breath before she lifts her head, grinning down at me.

"I think I'm seeing the value in asking for what I want now."

I burst into laughter.

EIGHTEEN

ADAM

Wren insists we make a fire in my fireplace, which I do, though when she tries to go next door to get firewood and s'mores materials from her house, I put my foot down. Instead, she stays warm and dry in my place, wearing one of my flannel shirts that is way too big on her and her panties, while I get dressed and go over to her place to get what she needs.

I'm cleaning up after making grilled cheese sandwiches, and Wren is sitting on the kitchen counter once more, chatting away, when suddenly, something comes to me.

A spark that I haven't felt in what feels like forever. The tiniest twinge, a chord progression that probably won't last longer than ten seconds, but it's...something.

I reach for my phone to jot it in my notes, hoping I don't lose it. Then, I look at the woman in my arms and decide I need paper, a pen, and possibly my piano. As it sits on my mind, more gets added, a few lyrics begin to swirl, and I feel that tight excitement in my chest that I haven't felt in far too long.

Here with Wren, I'm finally inspired, and I don't want to ignore it. Instead of the typical dread at the idea of writing, I feel electric, excited. I want to go to my office *now*.

But I want to do it with her by my side.

It would require showing her *me*, and even though I've enjoyed being Adam Porter, her apparently mysterious, grumpy neighbor, if this is going to be something, I can't hide forever.

Even more so, I don't *want* to hide from Wren.

"I want to show you something," I say, drying off my hands and then moving over to her, putting my hands on her waist, lifting her, and setting her on her feet.

"Show me something? What kind of something?"

I stare at her and feel those nervous butterflies in my chest before I push them aside. "Who I am. What I do."

She grins at me again, a teasing look going into her words. "Is it your serial killer room?"

"My serial killer room?"

"I told you, Hallie and I have a list of potential past lives for you. She was very stuck on a serial killer for a while."

I shake my head and laugh, but grab her hand, moving her through the house. "And you came home with me anyway?"

"I didn't say I thought you were a serial killer. Plus, I don't think I had much choice in the whole coming home with you thing. You kind of dragged me in here."

"I did not drag you here," I grumble, but can't seem to fight the slow smirk that accompanies it.

"Sure you didn't, baby," she says, reaching up and patting my cheek. "But we've moved past serial killer."

We hit the stairs, and I start pulling her up them, any hesitancy gone and excitement filling my veins. The small melody is still there, looping in my mind and continuing, adding a note or two every round.

Between the goodness of inspiration and knowing I'm about to show Wren everything, I'm fighting the urge to take two steps at a time.

"No? What were your thoughts?"

"Witness protection." I pause and turn to look down the stairs at her, and she's beaming at me. I let out a laugh. "It would explain why you stayed home and were all boring!" I shake my head, then finish moving up the stairs. "But my favorite theory is your dad is Santa, and you're hiding out here to avoid the family business. It would explain why you hate Christmas."

I turn down the hall, and the door to my office comes into view. Nerves tighten my chest, but I push them aside.

"Not quite. But I guess you can say that I'm in hiding."

She lifts an eyebrow, and I reach the door, my hand touching the knob and twisting. My heart is pounding with anticipation, trying to account for every possible outcome and prepare mentally for it, but I know it's no use.

All I can do is open the door and let her in.

So I do, pushing the door open and then pulling her inside. She stops my hand when she does, stepping to the center of the room and staring at the walls, eyes wide.

"What is this?" she asks, looking around.

I take in the room like I've never been here before and try to see it as she would. There's a piano against a wall, the desk in front of the window with a dozen crumpled pieces of paper, and an unused typewriter on one side. On the desk itself are notebooks and blank sheet music. One wall features two guitars and a bass, hung up but easily accessible. I look around the room, feeling that tension melt away as the Band-Aid is ripped off, and I wave a hand to the room.

"I guess...I guess this is who I am." I look at her and give her a nervous smile, but her eyes widen as she takes in the room, with records, trophies, and instruments lining the walls. She moves to the piano, fingers gently grazing over the top of it as if she's afraid, actually, to touch it.

"I was in a rock band years ago, and now I write and produce. More behind-the-scenes stuff. It's really no big deal, but—"

"No big deal?" she asks, turning to me with wide eyes before waving her arm at the far wall. "Those beg to differ." She's staring at the wall, where all my awards are hung and displayed perfectly. I don't know why I hung them, really, since I hate looking at them. They feel like reminders of what could have been, watching me as I try to write.

A single platinum plaque and four gold ones, each with records, adorn the wall. My biggest accomplishments and my biggest short-comings are there for her to see. A shelf holds awards, and she steps forward, reaching out to touch one of the golden statues before pulling her hand back like she might break it. She moves with wide eyes.

"You...you won all of these?"

I shrug. "It's not much. I haven't ever gotten Song of the Year." I'm almost embarrassed to admit it aloud. Given Greg and Trent's tone and the sad looks I get from colleagues when-ever it comes up in conversation, it's a carefully curated response.

I've written for some artists who have had number one hits that stayed at the top of the charts for weeks and remained in the top 100 for months, although mine have never become singles to top the charts. I've produced fantastic songs, some of which became under-ground fan favorites, but none of them have received any true recognition.

My career has grown stale, and everything in this room seems to be a constant reminder of that. But when I look at Wren, it isn't the generic, pretend-impressed look on her face that I have come to expect when I tell people about my accomplishments. It isn't that look of pity I expect, that one I've seen from so many in the industry before.

It's *awe*.

"Adam, you're out of your mind. This is...wow. This is so wild. I can't believe I didn't know!"

"I don't really talk about it much," I say, suddenly feeling shy.

She turns to me with a wide smile. "You don't say. Gosh." She looks around, taking things in before turning back to me. "So you were in a band?"

I nod, pointing to where most of the awards are. A couple of gold records, along with several Band of the Year, Rock Album of the Year, and Rock Single of the Year trophies.

"A rock band. Midnight Ash." She looks at me like she's combing her mind, trying to place the name, a nervous blush burning over her cheeks when she can't place it. It's so sweet and so Wren, I can't help but laugh, then pull her into my side to press a soft kiss to her hair.

"Not exactly your style, Wren, and you were probably ten years old when we started getting popular."

She scrunches up her nose, then ducks under my arm. "Yeah, because you're so old."

I reach to pull her back into me and possibly spank her for being such a brat, but then she's moving across the room to inspect the different awards.

"My god, you've worked with Willa Stone?" She turns to me with excited eyes, and I try to find the gleam I've come to expect when people learn who I am. The one where someone becomes eager to take advantage of my connections and to meet big stars by dropping my name. The last time I tried to date someone outside the industry was nearly three years ago, and it lasted all of two months. I quickly realized she was playing games, just wanting to meet her music idols and convince me to spend money on her.

But it's...not there.

She's just impressed, and I stare at her in awe, my chest warming with the realization.

"Yeah. She does a lot of her work herself, but I've come in to help out with co-writing a few times. I've produced a few of her songs."

"Adam, I can't believe you aren't screaming from the rooftops about this. This is so cool. You're so talented." When she pauses in front of the plaque that, when the door is open, is hidden, I know it's all going to come out. Not that I was planning to hide it any longer.

My lone platinum record.

"All Lit Up" went platinum last holiday season after spending three years at gold, and even though Greg was elated about it, it was the moment that sent me into my current existential dread.

It's hard not to look at it and feel bitter. That record is my biggest accomplishment, but it's also my own personal failure.

Every time I'm reminded of it, I find myself wondering just how good a musician I could be, given that nothing I've ever done compares to a stupid Christmas song I wrote in twenty minutes. Not the ones that felt ripped from my soul, that I put my blood, sweat, and tears into—the ones I really believed in.

"You wrote 'All Lit Up'?" Wren asks in a breath.

I sigh, then sit on the edge of a desk and run a hand through my hair a few feet away from her, needing space. "Yeah."

She turns to me then, raising an eyebrow at me in determined disbelief that is so Wren, I can't help but let out a chuckle.

"And you hate Christmas?"

"Honestly, it's the reason why," I say with a self-deprecatory shrug. She continues to stare at me as if she doesn't understand, so I explain without further prompting.

"I wrote that song when I was twenty-eight. Midnight Ash had broken up, and I'd sold a few songs since, but nothing to really get my name moving. I wrote it in the middle of the summer after getting high and watching one of those cheesy Christmas in July specials." She lets out a snort of a laugh. "Willa picked it up, and it went crazy. It was number two on the charts all December and went gold the next year."

She smiles at me, and the shame that normally comes with it doesn't feel as deep.

"And then what happened?"

"The next year, all anyone wanted from me was Christmas." She nods, following what I'm saying. "I wrote four more that season." I gesture to where the gold records sit, and she reads the titles with wide eyes.

"Oh my *god*, Adam! You're kidding me! So you're like Christmas music royalty?" I shake my head, grimacing. "Oh, we're not happy about that." She reads me, taking me in, and I let out a sigh. When I explain this to someone not in the industry, it feels...silly. Insignificant.

"If it weren't a Christmas song and had the same kind of growth, it would have made Record of the Year easily. However, everything else since then has basically flopped or performed well enough, but nothing of true note. Now, I receive a yearly reminder that the best work I've ever done was on a generic Christmas song. A song most people hate just because it's an earworm they can't stop singing. It's gotten to the point where most people in the industry think I'm just this idiot who only writes Christmas songs. They don't even *want* to hear my other shit; they just want Christmas. So this year, I told my agent I wouldn't be doing any holiday music." I remember the conversation with Greg, the way he begged me to reconsider, but I knew if I kept going, I'd burn myself and hate writing.

"Unfortunately, he couldn't sell a single one of my normal songs. In past years, it was a mix of what I sold, Christmas, and normal songs. But this year...crickets." She steps forward and sets a hand to my cheek. There's none of the judgment or pity I've been seeing for a year, and I give her my next confession. "It put me into the worst creative rut of my life. I haven't been able to write at all, not in six months."

"Is that long?" she asks, genuinely curious. She's so far out of the industry, she doesn't know what the norm is. It's so refreshing.

"Yes, that's long, especially for me. It's been...painful, not writing. That's why I moved here." I sigh, looking out the window. The street is coated in a thick layer of snow, as the plow still hasn't made it our way. "In LA, everyone looked at me with pity. In New York, it was too...busy. I thought maybe my muse needed some peace and quiet, so I found a random town on the map and moved here. Somewhere small, somewhere no one knew about me or my career."

She gives me a soft smile. "Holly Ridge."

"Holly Ridge."

I return the look, remembering her coming to my door. "I thought I could escape it here, hide away from it all, spend a few months writing and find...something."

"And did you?"

I shake my head, but then I hear it again, playing in my mind, and grin genuinely. I almost forgot, so lost in telling her my story.

"No, not until before, in the kitchen. I brought you up here not to show you who I am, but because I got inspired."

Her eyebrow quirks. "You did?"

Suddenly, nerves fill my belly, and I press a kiss to her lips to assuage it a bit. "Yeah. Seems I may just have found my muse in Holly Ridge after all." A blush burns on her cheeks, and I feel absolutely fucking giddy with inspiration. "I need to jot something down."

Her eyes light up. "Music?"

"I'm not writing a recipe in here."

She rolls those expressive eyes, pushes on my shoulder, and I feel it again—that lightness in my chest. Those chords run through my mind again, another adding to the end, and excitement rushes through me on the heels of that warmth.

"Can I stay and watch? I promise I'll be so quiet," she says, miming zipping her lips.

"Not planning to let you out of my sight for a while, Birdie," I murmur, leaning down to press my lips to hers before I put my hands to her waist and lift her, placing her on the edge of my desk.

I grab a piece of blank sheet music and jot down some notes. In the margins, I jot down words that come to me, then move to the piano and start moving my fingers across the keys. I try not to feel self-conscious, but I find the concern is moot. When I look up at her, she isn't watching me—she's leaning with her back against the wall, eyes closed like she was listening but not watching otherwise. She must feel me looking because her eyes flutter open, a dazed look written across her face.

"Pretend I'm not even here. I'm not watching at all." Then she pauses. "Or I can leave if you want—I promise I won't be offended. Whatever your process is, I'll respect it."

I shake my head. "No, no. It's fine. I'm just not used to having someone here when this happens."

Her face goes soft. "Well, I'm honored to be the first."

And the last, I want to say, but I stuff it down.

Instead, I stand, moving across the room to kiss her once more, quickly and hard, before sitting back at my piano and jotting some notes. Then I move my hands back to the keys, testing them out and making a few adjustments. I move like this, feeling more like myself than I have in some time, before the inspiration fades sometime later. I sit back, grinning at the paper victoriously before I turn to glance over my shoulder. Wren is watching me with wide eyes and rapt attention.

"Wow," she whispers, eyes wide.

"Hmm?" I ask, standing, then moving to put away my paper, notes scribbled in margins, and lyrics for a potential bridge in a corner. It's not a song—far from it—but it's...something. More than I've had in some time, too.

"That was magic," she whispers. I shake my head, then laugh at her awed face. "I'm serious, Adam. I've never seen anything like that."

"It's really nothing. I didn't even finish the chorus."

She shakes her head in disbelief. "I can't even play the recorder, much less a piano. You could have pretended to do things for the last ten minutes, and I would still be impressed."

"You can't play?"

She shakes her head. "And don't even think about asking me to sing. It's not pretty. I can craft, and I can bake, and I can manage a classroom like nobody's business, but music will never be something I'm good at."

"Piano isn't a talent, it's a skill." She stares at me, disbelieving. "I'm serious." That same skepticism is on her face, and I can't help but grin at her. It seems contagious when I'm around her. "Come on, I'll show you."

She looks at me skeptically, but I'm moving, grabbing her, then moving once more. I situate her between my legs on the bench, then place her fingers on the keys, layering my hands over hers. I show her slowly how to play "Twinkle, Twinkle, Little Star," and she giggles when she hits the wrong key. We stay like that for a long time before it sounds normal. I keep moving her hands beneath mine, showing her different songs, but eventually, her hands move out from under mine, then move up, hooking around my neck as she leans into my chest.

"Play something for me," she whispers.

I press a kiss to her temple, then mess around, moving from a few bits of song to song before settling on something I haven't played in years.

"All Lit Up."

As I do, I remember the joy I felt when I wrote it and when I heard Willa in the studio recording it. Not because I ever really loved Christmas, but because I knew people did. I knew people felt this genuine, all-consuming joy that came with the holiday, something I faked just enough until I captured it in this song.

I remember when I was finishing it up, thinking it could be something decent. Never did I think it would be what it became, and I surely never thought that I would hate it one day.

Though with Wren against my chest, humming the tune off-key as I play, I don't know if I hate it nearly as much as I once did.

How could I, when this new memory will now be attached to it?

Eventually, the notes fade and the song ends, and I move, wrapping my arms around her.

"Oh my god, I'm going to have to wrangle you into some events next time I need someone to play music for us." My gut drops, and I turn away, but she reaches up, gripping my chin and turning it back to her. "Hey, I'm joking. You know that, right?"

I stare at her, noticing the honesty on her face, and then I relax just a bit. She shifts, moving until we're face-to-face, and I can see how sincere she is, knowing in my gut that she's right. She was joking, but I have a feeling that if I want to be with Wren, I need to address this sooner rather than later.

"Yeah," I say, then push a strand of hair behind her ear, unable to stop myself from leaning down and pressing my lips to her cheek. "I just...I like being here, not having anyone know who I am. It's nice not having that over my head. People treat me...normal here. I kind of want to keep that as long as I can." I bite my lip, feeling stupid but needing to confess all the same.

"Well, your secret will be yours for however long you want to keep it." There's honestly in her eyes, and I brush hair back from her face.

"It's not that I don't trust you or even the town. It's just that I've been in this industry for so long, I've seen people get used in ways you wouldn't believe. People they thought were friends, lovers, family —fame and money get in people's heads and fuck things up. I don't know the last time I was somewhere where I met people who I knew to my bones didn't have an ulterior motive. It's been nice being here and knowing that no one I meet here wants something from me." I smile then, pressing my lips to hers again. "Except you, of course. You definitely have an ulterior motive to get on my good side."

Her eyes go wide with panic. "What? I don't have ulterior motives! I swear, I didn't know—"

I let out a laugh, feeling a sense of lightness.

"I mean the Christmas lights, baby," I say softly.

"Oh." A blush burns over her cheeks. "Yeah, I definitely want you to do that."

"I'm going to need a lot more convincing on that."

A wicked gleam flashes in her eyes, lips tipping up. "I think I can work on that."

And while she doesn't convince me to make it so you can see my house from space, we have a fuck of a good time trying.

NINETEEN

Wren

"What are you doing tonight?" Adam calls across our lawns on Friday morning. The snow has been plowed and the walkways shoveled, although a significant bit of it has already melted away. Adam shoveled mine, the gentleman. I tried to help, of course, but he threatened to tie me to his bed if I didn't let him. I think I may have revealed a bit too much when I smiled at his threat instead of backing down easily, but that's neither here nor there. Last night, I slept in my own bed by myself, and I was thrown back a bit when I realized just how empty it felt.

"What?" I ask, smiling and grateful I'm catching him before leaving for work. He takes a step off his porch, and I note with appreciation that he's in his running gear—a black, thick hooded sweatshirt and sweatpants. It shouldn't be hot, but it is, nonetheless.

"What are you doing tonight after work? Want to come over for dinner?"

I purse my lips as I heft my oversized bag higher up my shoulder, then take a few steps of my own down the steps of my porch. I ignore his burning gaze, pretending to dig in my bag for keys that are already in my hand as I answer. "I can't, I have things to do."

"Things?" he asks. His arms are crossed on his chest, taking me in with a disapproving look and a raised eyebrow.

"Yes, things."

"What kind of things?"

"I have to make a photobooth backdrop and accessories tonight."

"A photobooth?"

"Yes. It's for the festival, and before you ask, yes, someone else could be doing it, but their kid came down with a nasty cold, so they don't have the time. I offered to help, and I need to spend time tonight getting it done. *Someone* keeps insisting I go to bed before midnight, so I need to work on it right when I get home." I won't tell him that I'm kind of happy to be going to bed at a reasonable hour, since my body feels so much happier with me because of it.

And I *definitely* won't be telling him that sleeping with him the past few nights has been some of the best, most well-rested sleep of my life, or that I didn't wake up feeling as rested this morning. Sleeping with Adam is like sleeping with the most perfect, heated, weighted blanket. The second we settle into bed, he shifts us so his leg is hitched up over me, as if he's afraid I won't stay put without him keeping me there. His chest is pressed against my back, fighting off the winter chill that has hit Holly Ridge, and my mind quiets its constant repetition of my to-do list once I'm bundled into him.

"Wren..." he chides, and I roll my eyes, moving down my walkway and toward the trunk of my car, opening it before tossing my things inside and diligently ignoring him. I don't want to hear his lecture about how I need to be taking on fewer tasks. I spent the last few days doing not much of anything, hanging out with him while the school was closed for two days. While I brought my laptop over to his place to handle some online work, and he came to mine once the power came back on so I could finish up the quilt, I feel the pressure of tasks and responsibilities building up after my time off.

I'm formulating my response to the argument that is probably unavoidable as I reach up to close my trunk. When it's shut, I gasp with surprise as my body is shifted, Adam's hands on my hips, turning me and pinning my back to my car. Even though I should complain about him getting salt on the back of my coat or something, I can't find it in me to do so, not with his body pressed against mine, his warmth seeping through my clothes. I'm convinced the heat of him has magical stress-relieving properties. When he's touching me, it eases.

"I know," I murmur before he can argue further. "And you're right, I need to delegate more. But this isn't me jumping in where someone is being too lazy. Sophia has three kids, all of whom got sick, which I know because one of them is my student and was out a good chunk of last week. She works for herself, so she took time off to help the kids, but now she needs to catch up on work and family stuff. And, let's be honest, there's a good shot she's also going to get it. I offered not just because it would help her, but because it needs to get done. I'd rather take it on now when I have a little bit of extra time than in a week when she tells me she got sick and I have to scramble."

He stares down at me then, his eyes soft and understanding, before he pushes one of my stray hairs back. "Bring it to my place. I'll feed you and help out."

A beat passes as he stares at me, distracting me momentarily when his eyes move from mine to my lips and back again, but I blink to clear my mind and speak.

"You'll help?"

"Yeah. I'm not spending the night away just because you gotta work on some new craft." I blink at him for a long moment. "So bring it to my place, I'll help out as best as I can."

I give him a soft smile but shake my head.

"That's sweet, honey, really." His eyes go soft with the endearment. "But it's boring and tedious. You don't have to do anything. You can just hang out while I—"

He shakes his head. "I don't do what I don't want to do, Wren. That's the difference between you and me."

I roll my eyes, that familiar irritation sparking to life in my chest.

"Yes, yes, I know. You have all the boundaries, and I have none. You're right, I'm working on it, but—"

"No," he starts. I lift an eyebrow, and he smiles. "Well, yes, but that's not what I meant. What I mean is I don't do what I don't want to do. I never have, and I'm telling you right now to prepare because I never will. So if I didn't want to help you out, I just wouldn't."

I get it then, as I take him in. His face is close to mine, and I take in the handsomeness that is Adam—those green eyes, the small lines beside them that I watched get deeper while he was working in his office, concentrating hard. His straight nose, high cheekbones, and tight jaw irritated me, making it hard for me to understand what he's trying to tell me.

To understand that he *wants* to help, not because he feels obligated, but because he genuinely wants to help *me*. Because he wants to take care of me, and he realizes this is how he has to do it.

It's an uncomfortable realization.

I receive offers to help, of course, from friends, family, and coworkers. I always tell them I appreciate the offer, but not to worry about it. That I've got it covered, giving them the social allowance they need to step away from helping me gracefully. And when I do, I always see the flash of relief cross their faces, relief that they don't actually have to see out their offer. It's what has always confirmed my choice to take on more and more, to take those tasks off the people I care for's shoulders.

No one insists after I tell them they don't have to help me, not when I give them the easy out.

Except for Adam, apparently.

"Okay," I say with a small sigh. It's uncomfortable and foreign, but I accept his help either way. When a genuine, relieved smile spreads on his lips, I know it was the right choice.

"Good," he says. "Now, when do you get home?" I hesitate again, biting my lip. "Wren."

"Normally, the bell rings at two fifty-five, I should be home by three fifteen, three thirty." I bite my lip.

"But...?"

I sigh. "*But*, I offered to cover after-school care today."

His head tips up to the sky, and he sighs, sending up some kind of silent prayer for strength before looking at me again.

Guilt and nerves churn in my stomach at the sight. How long until he realizes I don't have time for myself, much less a *man* in my life? Until he realizes I'm a lost cause?

Unless you start to value your own happiness over everyone else's, Wren, a voice that sounds very much like my grandmother's whispers into my mind.

"Okay. Okay. I can work with that," he says after a moment, and my heart skips a beat.

"You can?" He must see the surprise mixed with a dash of hope I can't seem to hide in my eyes, because his face softens.

"If I get you at the end of it, Wren, I can work with anything." His hand moves up, tucking hair that was moved by the gently blowing wind behind my ear. "But we're going to work on this whole offering yourself up to help everyone but yourself."

With his words, I nod. "Yeah. It's gonna slow down."

Now it's his chance to look shocked. "Is it?"

I shrug, playing off this moment that suddenly feels too big for a conversation against my car before work. "I've never had any reason not to, Adam. Never had anyone who wanted some of my time."

He likes my answer; that much is clear from his face. I expect him to try and pull more out of me, to ask me to expand or make some promises right here and now, but he doesn't.

"Okay. I'll get dinner. You bring your shit over here when you get home. Not sure if I'll be great at crafting, but I'll do my best." He lifts his hand, brushing the back of it over my nose. "Now go, get in your car. You're freezing."

"Well, *someone* pinned me against my car and forced me to talk about my feelings."

His smile widens to a grin. "Brat. Get in the car before I have to make you late for work."

I have never been late for work. *Never.*

But god, right now I'm contemplating ruining my perfect attendance record.

Adam sees the hesitation and smiles wide, shaking his head before pressing his lips to mine. "Not this time, Birdie. Go. Then get back to me as quick as you can, and I'll make good on all of those thoughts running through your mind."

I nod, and he grabs my hand before walking me around to the driver's side, opening the door for me. He turns me, then brushes off the salt from my back, paying extra attention to my bottom, which makes me giggle. Finally, he presses a kiss to my lips, watches me sit in the seat, and closes the door for me. He stands in my drive as I back out of it, waving as I drive off before he goes on his run.

And even though I love my job, I've never been so excited for work to be over that day.

TWENTY

Wren

Warmth slides through me as I come, moaning Adam's name, head tipped back, eyes drifting shut. I'm straddling his hips, full of his cock. One of his hands is on my hip, the other rolling my nipple perfectly, pulling a few extra moments of bliss from my body.

After a moment, I come back to myself, my eyes open again, my breathing heavy as my head tips down again, meeting Adam's wide grin, that dazed look I've become accustomed to seeing anytime I finish clear on his face.

"Good?" he asks softly.

I roll my eyes and push on his shoulder because we both know I just came hard. "Uh, yeah," I say through a small, panted laugh and then grin down at him, my hair falling between us.

It was a good freaking night, and it's only getting better. Adam shifts his hips beneath me, pressing himself somehow deeper into me. A deep groan leaves his lips, and that's when I look down at him, gasping in horror.

"Oh my god, Adam. I can't believe...I...and you didn't. I'm so, so —" A blush burns over my cheeks as I realize I just made myself come on him, completely ignoring *his* needs, and then...stopped.

"If you fucking apologize for giving me the fucking show of a lifetime, for taking the pleasure you needed when I ordered you to do just that, I'm going to have to spank you for real."

His threat is nothing of the kind, and instead, I tighten without meaning to around him.

I just came hard, yet suddenly, I'm feeling needy again already.

"Fuck, Wren," he groans through gritted teeth, bucking up again into me. I give him a devilish look before tightening my inner muscles a second time, though this time it's on purpose. "A fucking tease."

I let out a little giggle, my chest feeling light. I didn't know that sex could be like this—intense and ground-shaking and *fun*—but I should have known that's what I'd get with Adam.

"What are you going to do about it?" I ask, trying to make my voice low and seductive. I think I nail it when his eyes flare with heat.

"Can you take another?"

"I...I don't know?" I say with a giggle.

"Well, we can have fun trying," he murmurs, hips lifting, pushing in deeper. I let out an outright moan at that.

"Okay," I whisper when I catch my breath.

"Like this again?"

In the days since the snowstorm, we've had sex a handful of times, mainly with me on top, *taking what I need*, as Adam likes to say, though we've also moved to him finishing on top *after* I come. I know Adam wants me to make all the decisions for now, so I push back my nerves and tell him what I want.

"Can we, um." I bite my lip, looking to the side as a blush burns over my cheeks. "Can we try from behind?"

He lifts a hand, nothing but gentleness on his face as he cups my jaw and turns it back to face him.

"Tell me exactly what you want, Wren, and you'll get it."

A beat passes before I answer. "Hands and knees?"

He groans deep, closing his eyes, and I can't help but feel pride at pushing his buttons and tugging at the strings of his control. It's gone when his hands move to my waist, lifting my body. I mewl at the loss of him, something that pulls a chuckle from him before he tosses me to the bed and moves to his knees. Gently, his hands go to me, shifting and moving me until I'm on my hands and knees, Adam kneeling behind me. My breath hitches in my chest as he notches the head of his cock into me, then slowly, agonizingly slowly, pushes into me. A low groan escapes my chest at the sensation, at the way he slides against swollen tissue and hits me at a new angle. I tip my hips a bit, taking more of him, and he hisses when he finally sinks all the way in.

"Is this what you wanted, sweetness?" he asks, his hands on my hips. I nod quickly and moan as he slides out, then in again. "You wanted to be fucked, didn't you?" I nod again, then groan when he picks up the pace. I start to back into him with each thrust in, my back arching as I do. He takes the hint and starts moving harder and faster.

"Fuck, you should see yourself like this, Wren. Taking my cock like my sweet little good girl, hips bucking back into me, begging for more."

"Yes," I breathe, my pussy tightening around him. It's building again, bigger than before, and I moan. "Fuck, Adam. I'm close."

A growl leaves his lips, and I tighten. "Tell me what you need, Wren."

I moan as the head of his cock hits my front wall, but I don't speak. I don't tell him that I want him to reach around and rub my clit, to make me come a second time while he finds his own release.

"Wren," he grunts. "Tell. Me. What. You. Want."

He says it, thrusting in between each word, and my vision blurs, my pussy tightening with pleasure as I move closer and closer to the edge. I can't speak, hell, I can barely even breathe. I shake my head, hair falling before me as I feel his fingers tighten on my hips. A deep growl leaves his lips, and I moan at the sound, but that turns into a scream when his hand leaves my hip and comes back down, hard and quick, spanking my ass.

I let out a scream of pleasure, and my body shakes, moving close to the edge. I tighten around him, and he bites out a curse.

"Of course, you fucking liked that," he groans, sliding deeper than before as my back arches deeper. "My perfect fucking woman."

My hands lose purchase, my mind no longer able to concentrate on keeping me up, and I lie down, my chest touching the bed. It changes the angle of his thrusts again, and I moan desperately, my hips moving back, needing more.

Adam's hand moves back again and slaps my ass, the other cheek, and I tighten again, a pained, needy sound leaving my lips.

"Tell me what you want, Wren, or we'll be here all fucking night." There's a plea in his voice, and some primal part of me wants nothing more than to please him, to give him what *he* wants.

Then I realize that what he wants is to give me what *I* want. Our needs and wants form a perfect circle. He wants to give me what I need, and I want to do the same. I push back the hint of embarrassment that still lingers and shout out the answer.

"My clit! I need you to rub my clit."

"That's my fucking girl," he grits out, then a hand leaves my hip one last time, sliding forward toward my belly and strumming my clit. It's oversensitized, and I'm already so close to the edge that it just takes a few firm swipes before I'm tumbling, falling hard and fast. Stars shoot behind my eyes as I scream his name, as my body quakes, pleasure shooting through me with such ferocity, I wonder if I black out for a moment. But I force myself to stay on this planet when I feel his fingers tighten on my hip, when I feel him slam deep.

I love nothing more than witnessing and feeling Adam come, and I'm not going to miss that. I glance over my shoulder to see his head tipped back, divine rapture written on his face as he calls out my name like I am the end-all and the be-all of all things good in his life, and he fills me. I continue to watch as his grip loosens, as his shoulder muscles slacken, and as he blinks, and then comes back to this planet.

He looks down at me, the very edges of his lips tipping up as he looks at me with entertained awe, as if I make his world turn.

"Was that so hard?"

Then I burst out laughing.

"I don't know how much longer I can do this, Adam," I say with a groan. His head snaps up to look at me, hunched over some of the sturdy construction paper as he cuts out one of the paper Santa hats that we'll glue to a popsicle stick as a photo prop with snail-like speed.

It was after I came home from work and went to my place to drop off my things and grab the photobooth material. After Adam showed up at my front door and insisted on carrying all of it over himself. When I protested, he gave me a hard kiss and told me to pick out some sleep clothes for the night, and that was all I was allowed to carry. Long after he decided he needed to have me the second I walked into his house, and long after dinner, which consisted of pasta and homemade garlic bread. Now the photo backdrop is finished, and we're working on the final props together.

"We're almost done," he says. "I know I'm slow, but—"

I laugh and shake my head, then brush the lips I'm gluing to a popsicle stick off my lap onto the coffee table.

"No, no. Not that. Honestly, I got more done than I anticipated with your help, so I can wrap it up and finish tomorrow." I'm done working on these tonight. Right now, I just want to spend the night with Adam. I put on my sternest expression before I relay my next demand. "But I can't deal with your place. If you're going to want me to spend nights here, we're going to have to liven this place up."

He lifts an eyebrow at me, then reaches over to where I sit on the couch and tugs me, maneuvering me until I'm straddling his hips.

"Oh?"

There's a hint of a smile on his lips, which makes me feel more at ease with continuing.

"Yes! It's dead in here. I get it, you hate Christmas, blah blah blah...but you don't even have normal decorations. And you don't have a tree! I struggle to spend long periods in December in a house without a tree. I only get so long to enjoy them," I pout, and he laughs, gripping my waist and moving me once more until I'm on my back on his couch with his body hovering over me. He leans down to press a sweet kiss to my lips before pulling back and taking in my face.

"You want me to get a tree, baby?" he asks softly. My eyes go wide, and excitement races through my veins as I nod. "Then let's go get me a tree." I squeal with excitement and clap. He lets out a laugh before he turns both of us so we're lying side by side on the couch. His hand moves up, tucking a strand of hair back, and I plant a hand on his chest. "You seem excited by that."

"You have no idea. Okay, so I prefer real trees, obviously. A fake one is almost sacrilege in my family, but if you don't want to deal with the cleanup, I'll endure a fake one so long as it's pre-lit."

"Wren, if I'm getting a tree to make you happy, we're getting the kind you want." My eyes go wide with disbelief.

"Really?"

'Yeah, baby. Really."

"Can we go now?" I ask, trying to stand up, but his hands tighten their hold on me, and he laughs, shaking his head.

"It's after nine at night, babe. I don't think anywhere is open." I groan, and he laughs at it, but I don't feel any kind of embarrassment, just excitement. "We'll go tomorrow," he says. "Got anything going on?"

Tomorrow is Saturday, and for the first time in a long time, I haven't offered to do anything tomorrow. Not a fundraiser, not something for the school, not a favor to a friend or a friend of a friend.

I got asked, for sure. In fact, as I was headed out the door today, I was asked by Mrs. Crowley if I could babysit tomorrow. I almost said yes, but I remembered Adam's eager look when I told him I'd do better at slowing down, and I recalled that I don't have to do everything for everyone. Instead of accepting, I gave her an apologetic look and told her I couldn't. I felt immense guilt as I turned her down, especially when I technically didn't have anything happening, but that evaporated when she shrugged like it was no big deal.

"No worries," she said. "I'll ask Jennie. Enjoy your weekend, Wren!"

She wasn't mad at me.

She didn't think I was selfish.

The world didn't collapse.

As seems to be happening often lately, my eyes were opened.

"Nope," I say, giddy to give him the news. "Free all day."

He looks at me, impressed, knowing how rare that is for me, before he pulls me in to press a kiss to my lips, almost like he's proud of me.

"Where should we go?"

I bite my lip, looking anywhere but at him.

"Um," I start, my heart pounding. "So, we could go to Meyers Grocery. They have a small selection in their parking lot...or we could go to one of the home improvement stores and scavenge their stock..."

He scans my face, tipping his head and reading between the lines as he always seems to be able to do. "But...?"

"But..." I sigh. "But my parents would probably kill me if they found out. They own a tree farm, and that's where everyone gets their trees. It's a whole thing—chop down the tree, a little spot for cocoa, and it's all crazy-decorated, of course. I promise I'm not trying to push meeting the parents or anything, it's just a small town, as you know. And news travels fast and—" Nerves are eating at me, and I'm rambling now, but my words are stopped with warm hands on my jaw and Adam pulling me in close to press his lips to mine.

It's soft and sweet and quick, silencing me before he rests his forehead to mine.

"We'll go to your family's farm, Wren."

"I don't want to be pushy, I—"

"Are you mine?" he asks for the second time today.

This time, it makes my pulse pound. With the way he's holding me, the way he's looking at me, it feels more intimate, more important —a bigger question than those three words.

"Yes," I whisper.

"Then it's going to happen one way or another. Better to do it now when we have a reason to be there, right?"

I bite my lip, seeing the truth in his words, before nodding. "Yeah, I guess."

"Then we'll go tomorrow. Get me a tree. But you have to help me get the stuff to decorate it and put it up, okay?"

My chest fills with warmth. "That I can do."

TWENTY-ONE

Wren

We're in the car for maybe two minutes as we take the ten-minute drive up the mountain to get to my parents' place before the word vomit begins. For a moment, I considered winging it, but my inner planner and the need to ensure everyone's comfort and happiness prevailed.

"Okay, so I probably should have asked you this before we headed over to my parents' house, but if my mom and dad don't ask, my brothers absolutely will, and I very much do not want to scare you off because my family is pushy." I try to sound casual, but my heart is pounding with nerves. I didn't want to force Adam into this talk just yet, but I don't see any real way around it. I know my family well enough to know going into this blind would be a terrible idea.

"Oh?" Adam asks. His head turns to look at me, smiling, my clear discomfort entertaining him.

"They're going to ask what we are," I blurt out before I lose my confidence to do so. "And I don't want to push, really. We can even turn around and say you're sick, and Madden and Jesse can help me pick out a tree for you and deliver it tomorrow. I won't be offended, I—"

"We're picking out a tree today, Wren," he says, cutting me off.

I take a deep breath and close my eyes, trying to center myself. "I know, I know, but—"

"Together," he continues.

He's still not getting it, I think, so I try to explain. "Yes, but—"

"And I'm going to meet your parents."

"We—" I try once more to interject.

"Because from what I understand, that's what you do when you're seeing a woman and know there's something there."

My words stop, my mind going blank at everything but what he just said.

That's what you do when you're seeing a woman and know there's something there.

"So if your family asks—" he starts, clearly not stuck on his previous statement the way I am.

"When," I correct with a sigh, trying to focus on the topic at hand. "There is no universe where *no one* is going to ask. They might wait to strike when they think I least expect it, but the question is coming. I'm the baby of the family, with two older brothers. It's impossible to get around that."

He chuckles, then corrects himself. "Okay, *when* someone asks, what do you want the answer to be?"

"What?"

"I don't know how this works, Wren, if you haven't figured this out. My dating life hasn't been...typical. I've never been with a woman who lives in a small town with a family that cares about her. I've never had to meet the parents."

My head snaps to him, and my pulse pounds. "You've never met the parents?"

He gives me a sheepish look, a light blush blooming on his cheeks. "Rock star and music mogul lifestyle doesn't really lend itself to that, Birdie."

"Oh," I say low, and bite my lip. After the snowstorm, I searched for Adam Porter using the new parameters and the intel I had and brought up page after page of him in LA at restaurants with big stars, as well as a few rumored dates and girlfriends. Some musicians, some producers, some freaking *models*, but all of them next-level gorgeous and put together. My breathing quickens as my pulse pounds, and I realize just how different we are.

"Erase that look, Wren." He reaches over and grabs my hand, gripping it right. "Right now. I haven't dated anyone in well over a year, and I'm not sure if any of my past relationships could be considered true *relationships*. I promise I am more out of my depth than you ever will be. I'm here with you because I really fucking like you, Wren. I appreciate that you don't view me as a stepping stone, nor do you seem to care about my past or potential future accomplishments or how they might benefit you. I like that you haven't changed at all since you found out who I am. The only thing you seem to be using your wiles for is to see if you can put Christmas lights on my house, and that is refreshing. It's why I'm here with you, on my way to your parents' Christmas tree farm to chop a tree down in the freezing cold."

I glance over at him and smile, though his eyes are on the road.

"Now, tell me, when your parents or your brothers or whoever asks what we are, what do you want me to respond with?"

"I don't..." That panic returns, with a different font but the same pulse-pounding result, as I try to decide what I think he wants to hear. Does he want me to say we're together or not? I don't want to push things past what he's comfortable with, but we really haven't—

Suddenly, the car veers off the road, and Adam brings it to a stop, putting it in park before turning to me fully. He reaches across the console and slides his hands into my hair, pulling me close and pressing his lips to mine.

"Nothing you say will be the wrong answer, Wren. I'm trying to see where your head is at with this, not send you into a spiral. I don't want you trying to weigh your answer against the answer you think I want to hear, okay?"

"I just—" I whisper, but he cuts me off.

"Let me give you my thoughts first, okay?" Some of that nervous panic leaves me. "I want to be with you. I want to be yours. I would be very much okay if we walked into their home hand in hand and told your family that I'm your boyfriend, even if I'm thirty-five and that makes me feel like I'm seventeen."

"What term would you prefer?" I ask without meaning to.

"Yours would suffice. Or your man. But that's not the point right now, Wren. The point is, in my perfect world, you're mine, and we're together, no matter what you title it. But the truth is, I don't think I've ever been a *boyfriend*, so I don't know how to do this properly. If you're not ready for that, then—"

"No, no," I say, shaking my head at him. "No. I um." I bite my lips, nerves fluttering in my belly.

God, why was it easier to ask Tim Higgins to the Sadie Hawkins dance in seventh grade than it is to tell a grown man whose face I have sat on that I want to be his girlfriend?

"You have to use your words, Wren. You've gotta tell me what you actually want."

His words remind me of many other circumstances where he's said that to me, and it sends liquid warmth to pool in my belly. It also gives me the jolt of courage I need. I take in a sharp breath, and satisfaction spreads over his face, like he knows where my mind went. But I'm stubborn, and I don't want him to win this, so I just glare.

"We're not going anywhere until you tell me what's going on in your pretty little head. Tell me what you want, Wren."

"I want you to be mine," I whisper.

He smiles at me, the real one, the one that meets his eyes, the one that he always gives me any time I tell him an honest answer. He leans in, his hand going on my jaw, his forehead resting on mine.

"Then I'm yours."

"Hey, Mom," I say, walking into the kitchen of the house I grew up in. It smells like cinnamon and pine trees and *my childhood,* and when I see her reach into the stove to pull out a giant tray of cinnamon rolls, I fight back an excited squeal, knowing I'll be sent home with some. At the kitchen table are my two brothers, which tells me my niece Emma is probably in the playroom. My dad is nowhere to be seen, which means he's probably out preparing for when the farm opens at two. Madden and Jesse are probably supposed to be out there with him, but they are biding their time for what I know is coming next. "Jesse, Madden." They both give me grins, and I roll my eyes.

"Hey, sweetheart," my mom says, coming over to press a kiss to my temple before turning to Adam. "And you must be Adam."

He puts his hand out for my mom, but she waves it away, wrapping her arms around him and forcing him into a hug. His eyes meet mine and go wide, and I fight back a laugh. I warned him about my family's inevitable question of *What are you two?...* but I also probably should have mentioned that my mom is a hugger.

When she steps back, she looks him over, her hands going to her hips. "My, you're a big guy, aren't you?" As soon as the words leave her lips, a pink flush I've seen in the mirror on my own face a million times blooms on her cheeks, as if she didn't mean to actually say that.

"Jeez, Mom," I grumble, turning to my brothers, wanting to get this over with. "Jesse, Madden, this is Adam. Adam, these are my brothers. Feel free to ignore them."

Madden turns to give Jesse a wicked, mischievous look before turning back to me and putting a hand to his chest, feigning hurt.

"Hey, is that any way to introduce your favorite brother to your..." The words trail off, and he lifts an eyebrow firmly at Adam, and I know a bright red flush burns on my cheeks without even having to touch them to feel the heat.

"Boys," Mom warns in her stern tone, but Adam was prepared for this.

He steps over to my brothers, putting a hand out to them. "Her boyfriend. Nice to meet you; I'm Adam."

My brothers look at one another before Jesse puts a hand out to shake. It's firm, too firm to be casual and kind. I want to cut in, but when I look at Adam, he's smiling, seemingly entertained by the battle of wills. He repeats the process with Madden, and I relax a bit.

Maybe this won't be too bad.

Maybe—

Then Madden opens his stupid fat trap.

"What are your intentions with our baby sister?" he asks, and I try to seem annoyed and not blush, but I know I fail desperately.

"You guys, stop it. You're being weird," I say, my cheeks now feeling like they were recently doused in lava. "It's weird when a brother is that invested in his sister's personal life. This isn't the 1800s."

He looks up at me with the most innocent expression, the one that absolutely used to work on my mom and *absolutely* works on the women in town now.

"What? We're just trying to get to know the mystery man our baby sister brought to the farm. You never bring men here."

"I swear to God, Madden, if you don't stop, I'm going to throw a temper tantrum." He gives me a deadpan look like my threat doesn't faze him, and I stamp my foot in irritation. I don't know what it is about my brothers, but the second I'm around them, I revert from a full-grown adult back into the nine-year-old girl who was easily teased and taunted by her older brothers. It's a phenomenon that someone should study.

"If asking a few simple questions freaks him out enough to scare him off, he's never going to work," Jesse says with a shrug.

"For whom? You or me? I didn't realize you also needed to have a relationship with *my* boyfriend." Even saying the word brings a blush to my cheeks.

Madden opens his mouth to argue, but then Adam's warm hand is on my hip, pulling me back against his chest. Immediately, a wave of calm moves over me, and no one in the room misses the move. Even Mom lets a little squeak out, though an excited grin accompanies hers.

"Ask away, I have nothing to hide. If I had a little sister as gorgeous and kind as Wren, I'd be doing the same thing," Adam says, and when I look over my shoulder, he has a sincere look on his face. That warmth settles in my chest, and I fight back a girly sigh.

A long moment of silence passes, and I hold my breath waiting for Madden and Jesse to jump on his open opportunity, but Jesse looks at Madden and shrugs. That's when I realize we passed the first test, and I can possibly relax a bit.

"All right, you two, give your sister a break. Everyone, sit and eat," my dad says, walking into the kitchen.

"I guess we're having brunch?" I murmur with apology in my voice at him. He shrugs, then puts a hand to my lower back, guiding me toward the set table. I should have known when I texted Mom this morning to tell her we were stopping by before the farm opened to get a tree that she would put something together, but I thought since I hadn't given her much time, I was safe. I should have known better.

I am her daughter, after all.

I can't think about that too long because Jesse's eleven-year-old daughter walks in, giving me a huge hug. I try not to focus on how big she's getting, already up to my chest. She was born when Jesse was barely twenty-one and I was just fifteen.

"Aunt Wren," she says, stepping back with a grin that looks so much like my brother.

"Hey, girl, how's it going?"

"Good. Sixth grade is a piece of cake."

I grin at her, then watch as she moves to the kitchen table with practiced ease. Jesse has a small house on the property where he and Emma live, so she spends a lot of time at my parents' place.

"Well, you gotta pay attention. I've been telling Mrs. Taylor you were a star student when you were in my class, and I don't want her to think I was just playing favorites." She slides into her chair at the table and gives me a look filled with sass and attitude.

"But I *am* your favorite." I sigh in exasperation, then turn to Adam, who is close behind me.

Mom sets platters of bacon and eggs, along with the cinnamon rolls, on the table, then gestures toward the table. "Come on, sit down, you two." Before we can move, though, my dad steps closer and puts out a hand, giving him a surprisingly kind look.

"Adam, I'm Pete, Wren's dad. Good to have you here." Adam takes the offered hand and shakes it, and a mix of confusion and relief floods me when I note it's not aggressive like Madden and Jesse's. Then he moves to sit at the head of the table before pointing at the cinnamon rolls. "Jess, send me over those rolls, will you?"

Madden looks at our dad, aghast, but Jesse grabs a platter and hands it to Dad without hesitation. I catch Mom's eye, and she winks at me, and somehow, someway, I know this conversation is done and we've survived. I give her a grateful smile.

The rest of the unexpected brunch goes well, with Emma chattering along nearly the whole time, asking a million random questions to Adam—"*What do you like better, unicorns or mermaids?*" or "*Do you think cats are better than dogs?*"—and filling me in on all of the sixth-grade drama.

Well, that is, until I feel it happening.

I'm listening to Emma explain to Adam why his answer—that he would rather fly than speak to animals—is absolutely wrong when I hear my dad and brothers talking at the other side of the table.

"The wreaths gotta be brought down to the senior center. I told Maude I'd get them to her on Thursday, but I'm going to have to be here to receive a shipment at that time."

"Can you drop them on Friday instead?" Madden asks, and Dad shakes his head.

"No, the volunteers are only there on Thursday afternoon."

He's right; I know this because I coordinated those volunteers, which was my first attempt to improve at delegating some of the holiday decoration tasks. The senior center is located next to the community center. Since the holiday festival is taking place at the community center, I would like to add extra decorations to the surrounding buildings. The volunteers are supposed to add the wreaths donated by my parents to as many doors as possible on Thursday afternoon.

"Well, Wren can probably do it on a different day, right? Send her home with them, and she can hang them tomorrow or Monday," Madden says. I fight back my urge to glare at him, and my shoulders go tight. They ease a little when Adam reaches over, placing a hand on my knee. Just his touch is enough to calm my racing mind.

All eyes at the table turn to me, and my heart starts to race.

The thing is, I *could* do it. I could go home with them today and try to pencil in some time in the next day or two to head downtown and hang them myself. I won't be able to do it tomorrow since I'm supposed to spend most of the day at school, setting up for the big Polar Express party I volunteered to head. However, maybe Monday morning before school, I could fit it in.

But the gnawing and uncomfortable fact is that I don't *want* to. I don't *want* to rush and try to fit this errand into my already busy week. And I don't like how that's sitting with me, the one who would usually jump at any opportunity to help.

Does that make me a bad person? Am I a bad sister or daughter if I don't want to pitch in?

Relief washes through me when my mom speaks up, though, easing my own concerns.

"I'm sure Wren has enough on her plate right now, with the decorating committee and whatnot. You remember how busy Grandma always was, and she was a lot better at delegating." My mom gives me a stern look I hope Adam misses, but I return her look with gratitude all the same.

"She always has time to help out," Madden says, and my jaw goes tight. "How long could it really take to drop off some wreaths?"

"Or you could do it yourself," Mom starts, giving him what I know from experience to be a cutting glare.

"I'm busy! I'm just saying she's always free to help out."

"Madden King, I—"

"I can just—" I start, wanting to end this before it becomes a real issue. But before I can, a new voice joins the mini argument, silencing everyone.

"Wren's busy; she can't do it. The woman barely goes to sleep each night as it is, trying to do everything herself."

The glare Madden throws toward me and Adam has me opening my mouth, but again, I'm stopped.

"But I can help."

I turn to look at Adam with wide, shocked eyes, but he keeps his gaze locked on my father. His hand does tighten on my leg, though, in what I think is supposed to be reassurance.

"I've got nothing going on next week. I can come here on Thursday, pick up the wreaths, and deliver them. You can give me directions, right?" Finally, he turns to me, and I see a command to *accept this* written across his handsome face. He expects me to argue, to tell him I'll just do it myself, but all I feel is genuine relief and utter gratitude. Not only did he stand up to my brother for me, but he's also creating a solution that lets me feel guilt-free and doesn't require me to do it myself.

He's perfect.

Absolutely perfect for me.

"Uh, yeah," I say, a blush burning on my cheeks with everyone's gaze locked on me. "I can do that."

Silence fills the room before Mom breaks it, leaning in on my other side. "Oh, I like him, Wren. Keep this one around," she says in an ill-disguised stage whisper.

Madden continues to stare at me pensively while Jesse looks on, clearly entertained. Emma takes the opportunity of everyone being distracted to reach for another sugary cinnamon roll, but I don't stop her.

Madden looks at Dad, then Adam, with a tight jaw, clearly annoyed that someone is stepping in and countering him. He opens his mouth, and my stomach turns, knowing my brother, who is barely two years older than me and always the one to clash with me the most, is about to poke a bear. That is, until Dad speaks up.

"Adam, if you ever have some free time, we'd be grateful if you could offer some time," he says in that *my word is final* way, and stares at Madden meaningfully.

"I've got a truck. Would that work? I don't want to take Wren's car because it looks like it's on its last leg as it is."

That's all that is needed to break the discomfort hanging in the air. I turn to Adam, aghast.

"Excuse me, Bessie and I have a long, healthy relationship."

"That you should end," Adam retorts quickly with a slight tilt of his lips.

"Excuse me!" I stare with wide eyes at him, and his smirk turns into a grin.

"That thing is a death trap," he says.

"I've been saying that for years," Madden says begrudgingly. When I look at him, his irritated glare has turned into begrudging approval. "Maybe you can convince her to upgrade."

I see calculation in Adam's eyes, and considering I'm pretty sure he's loaded, I don't think *buying Wren a new car* is entirely out of the question.

We need a distraction.

"Okay, on that note," I say, standing up, eager to get out of here. "Adam and I have a tree to pick out. Thanks for brunch, Mom, it was great, even if it was an ambush."

Mom smiles without a hint of remorse on her face before she looks at Adam, who has also stood and is holding his plate awkwardly, clearly unsure of what to do with it.

"Leave it, honey, the boys will clean up," Mom says with a wave of her hand.

"Mom—" Madden begins to whine.

"You've been nothing but rude to our guest, so it's the least you can do."

Madden glares at Mom, and I'm pretty sure Dad kicks him under the table, giving him the *be good for your mother* look, and despite him being almost thirty, he sighs and shuts his mouth. I give him a faux sweet smirk before sticking my tongue out at him. He scratches the side of his nose with his middle finger before Jesse speaks, probably trying to keep *all* of us out of trouble, as is his way.

"Yeah, don't worry about it, we've got it. Nice meeting you, Adam," Jesse says.

Then, before anyone can say anything else, I grab Adam's hand and drag him out the front door.

TWENTY-TWO

Wren

"Ready to go pick out a tree?" Adam asks, putting a hand to my lower back as we step out into the cold. There's still a layer of snow on the ground, though pathways are shoveled or covered with a thick layer of hay throughout the property, making it easy to navigate. I start to move us away from my parents' house and toward the barn, which is off in the distance.

"Okay, so the truth of the matter is, I already know what tree you're getting," I say, pulling my fluffy hood up. Adam looks at me as he reaches for my hand, sliding his fingers between mine.

"So what are we doing out here then?" he asks, narrowing his eyes.

"Escaping my family. I'm sorry they're so..." He cuts me off with a loud laugh, shaking his head and then turning to pull me into his arms. I melt when I wrap mine around his neck, the remaining nerves fading away.

"No need, Wren. I've been dealing with you for weeks now, and I figured that stubbornness was a family trait. That meeting with the family was not nearly as much of an interrogation as you led me to believe it would be."

I stare at him, brows furrowed. "My brothers *literally* asked you what your intentions were."

He shrugs. "That doesn't matter, and it's nothing I wasn't prepared for. Your brothers are protective because they're your older brothers. They're going to keep being protective, especially if I'm encouraging you to set boundaries and say 'no' more, something that might not benefit them as much as before. But eventually, they'll get over it and accept me when they realize I'm here for the long run." My heart starts pounding with his words. "Your mom likes me, I think, and your dad seemed to be...fine with me. Other than Hallie and Nat, I assume, those are the people whose opinion you'll really care about most of all, so that's all I'll care about."

I stare at him, warmth moving through me with ease as I realize for the millionth time that Adam notices and catalogs everything. I knew this, of course, from the way he can always tell if I'm tired or if I'm uncomfortable or if there's something I secretly want but don't want to burden others with, but this is more. This involves understanding who I am as a person and what matters to me, and making decisions with that in mind.

"You're perfect," I whisper in awe, unable to stop the words from tumbling free. He holds my gaze, then lifts a hand to cup my cheek before brushing a thumb over the skin there.

"For you, I hope," he says in the same quiet tone.

"I feel like I owe you the biggest thank you known to man. You endured my family, *and* you took on one of their tasks so I wouldn't have to. The amount of brownie points you just earned is astronomical."

"Mmm, I think you can find some ways to express your gratitude later."

A flicker of heat moves through me at his words, and an idea sparks in my mind. A wild one, but one I like a heck of a lot.

"Yeah, definitely. Do you want to see my favorite place ever?"

He lifts an eyebrow, then nods, and I step back, grabbing his hand and moving toward the giant, well-kept red barn off in the distance.

When we get there, the padlock is already off, so I open the doors and step in, reaching to flick the lights on. It's not *warm* in here, but it's much warmer than it is outside. Locking the door behind us, I pull Adam through the spare decoration and sleigh barn.

Every corner of this place is filled with unused decorations that have adorned the farm in years past, either because they need to be fixed or cleaned up over the upcoming summer, or because they don't fit Mom's vision for this year. Some will get pulled out on the last weekend before Christmas when extra decorations go up for "Santa's arrival." That weekend, the sleigh comes out for photos with Santa, and someone dresses up as the big jolly man to take last-minute holiday wishes.

Adam looks around in awe, eyes stopping on different corners that house decor for other holidays as well, such as big eggs for the yearly egg hunt and Halloween decorations for the pumpkin patch that Madden convinced our parents to add two years ago.

I tip my chin toward the red sleigh in the middle. "When I was a kid, I thought my dad was a sleigh mechanic, that his job was to fix up Santa's sleigh. I still don't know how my parents did it, balancing everything so my brothers and I still believed while running all of this."

Sometimes I think it's a miracle that they managed not to spill the beans about Santa and his elves while pulling off all of this behind the scenes. I'm sure they were run ragged running this place and trying to make all of the memories for three kids, but they made it all look so seamless and effortless.

"I can see where you get it," Adam says, looking around in awe before his eyes land on me. "What's the sleigh doing in here? Shouldn't it be out for the decorations?" I had told him earlier about the small "North Pole Village" that my parents set up, where customers pay for their trees. It features a shop with a wide selection of decorations, a hot cocoa shack, and food available on weekends, as well as crafts and activities for kids.

I shake my head. "Santa comes to the farm twice: once the

Sunday after Thanksgiving and a second time on the Sunday before Christmas to get last-minute wishes. If it were there all the time, it wouldn't be as magical, you know?"

He takes me in, and it's as if he's seeing a part of me that I don't think he could have understood without my taking him here. But I still have my idea brewing in my mind, so I tip my head toward the sleigh.

"Come on," I say, moving toward the bright red sleigh. My pulse is beating at the wicked idea that came into my mind. I'm not sure Adam will go for it, but I figure it can't hurt. Adam climbs into the sleigh and then offers me a hand to pull me up to sit next to each other. I lay my head on his shoulder, and he slides his arm behind me, pulling me into his side.

"Thank you for today," I murmur. "I know this isn't your thing. I hope it's not...hard for you." I bite my lip as a bolt of guilt rolls through me, but for not the first time since we've gotten together, I push that aside and allow myself to be selfish. If Adam wants to be with me for any length of time, this—the holidays, Christmas cheer, the family farm—is a big part of me; we won't be able to tiptoe around it.

I'm a bit shocked at how easy it's getting to be selfish, to put my own wants and needs, if not first, then at least not at the very bottom of my priority list.

He shakes his head. "No. It's not. It's...it's getting easier with you. It's not as consuming. I'm trying not to see it as a reminder of what I haven't accomplished anymore." He gives me a small, shy smile, and it sends butterflies swarming in my chest. "I'm trying to see those awards the way you did." I push on his shoulder gently.

"As you should! You should be screaming from the rooftops about what an amazing songwriter you are, Adam."

He stares at me for a long moment before he speaks again, lower and quieter than before.

"I actually think I had a breakthrough. I've been working more on that song, and I think it's actually...something."

I give him an excited smile. "I'd love to hear it."

A blush burns on his cheeks, and it's so damn sweet, yet so out of character for him. But I'm starting to wonder if it really is, or if beneath his gruff exterior lies a boy who wants to feel appreciated and celebrated for his accomplishments. He's spent so much time in a world where his talent was just one of hundreds that he might not see it for what it really is: phenomenal.

"When you're ready, of course."

"Maybe when it's done. I don't want to get too excited. I might still get stuck."

I reach out and grab his hand, twining his fingers with my own, and shrug. "Then we'll just have to get stuck in a snowstorm and have sex until you're inspired again."

A deep laugh fills the barn, and he bends, reaching with his free hand to grab my chin to tip it up before pressing his lips to mine. He probably intends for it to be a soft kiss to my lips, but I reach for his neck, bringing his head to mine and holding it there. I pour everything into him with it—my gratitude, the softness in my chest that I won't name just yet, the need that's slowly brewing in my belly. He instantly catches on, smiling into the kiss and taking over. He puts a hand to my hip and nips at my lower lip before sliding his tongue between them to taste me, and I mewl into it when I taste him, all cinnamon and coffee and everything right in my life right now.

Slowly, with a hint of nervousness, my hand moves between us, cupping his cock through his thick jeans. His hips move up on instinct, and I grin.

"Wren," he says in warning.

I bite my lip, then do my best to stroke him over his pants.

"Come on. I want to show you how appreciative I am," I whisper. Then I'm moving to my knees, kneeling between him as he sits before me on the sleigh. My pulse is pounding, and though some of it is because I'm nervous taking the reins like this, the rest is because I am suddenly so turned on, I can't handle it.

"Wren," Adam says, but the argument isn't even really there. His hips move up into my hand, and I hum to myself. I put my hand over his growing bulge, and a whisper of a groan leaves his lips.

"I've always wanted to do this," I confess, a blush burning on my cheeks.

"Give someone a hand job in Santa's sleigh?"

"Okay, don't make it sound so crude!" I laugh.

"I don't think there's any other way to say it, baby. You're on your knees in this sleigh."

"I just mean...hook up in here." My voice goes low, trying to be sexy even though I feel like I'm totally failing at that. My hand moves to the zipper of his jeans, and I slowly tug it down. He doesn't stop me, which feels like a good sign. Maybe I'm not totally fucking this up. "You know, you always hear about a roll in the hay or teenagers hooking up in the hayloft. I was far too much of a goody two-shoes to do anything like that, but I could daydream."

I slide my hands into his jeans, cupping him over his boxer briefs. He's already hard, and I grin.

"And this is what I always thought about.

"Wren," he says in warning.

"Please," I whisper.

"What if someone—"

"I locked the door and put on the deadbolt that locks it from the inside." It's a feature I later found out was intended to allow my mom to come in here and wrap presents without anyone sneaking in. Right now, I'm grateful for it. "And everyone is busy up at the main house." My hand squeezes him a bit, and he groans, eyes fluttering shut with pleasure. "Please. It's what I really want," I add with wide eyes, biting my lips.

It's manipulative, I know. It's using his own words against him, but if he's going to challenge me and push me into the uncomfortable territory of putting myself first, getting what I want, and asking for what I want, then I'm going to get what I want.

And right now, I *really* want to suck Adam off.

Thankfully, I don't have to ask again—it works like I thought it would. His hand moves to my chin, tipping my face up to look at him better, his thumb brushing along my cheekbone as he stares down at me.

"How on earth am I ever supposed to say no to you?" he asks in a whisper, and it feels almost like a genuine question, one that settles in my stomach sweet and warm before I smile at him.

"You're the one who told me I need to ask for what I want and not worry about what everyone else thinks."

"I did, didn't I? Can't say I thought making you a little more selfish would benefit me so well." That thumb moves along my cheek once more, then slides down to tug at my bottom lip before he speaks again, this time the words low and rumbling.

"What do you want, Birdie?"

There's no hesitation with my answer.

"I want to suck your cock, Adam."

"Fuck," he groans, but he doesn't argue. Instead, his hand shifts his pants aside, reaching in and pulling out his thick, hard cock. I sit back on my heels, watching the show before me.

"Stroke it for me," I whisper, my eyes locked. He lets out an unsteady breath that shoots right to my clit, but does what I ask, his hand wrapping his thick cock and tugging from base to tip.

"Nothing is hotter than you telling me what you want."

I sit back on my heels and watch him fuck his hand. A small whimper leaves my lips as I watch his hand tighten toward the top, a drop of precum beading at the head. My breathing goes ragged, and I lick my lips.

"My turn. Let me suck you."

"Whatever you want, sweetness," he says, voice strained, before I replace my hands with his, using both to pump him. He groans loudly, and it gives me a surge of confidence, making me feel sexy and powerful as I dip my head and run the flat of my tongue over the head of his cock, lapping up the salty liquid there. His breath hitches as I wrap my lips around the head and suck, and a moan falls from his lips as I slide down and then back.

"What a pretty little thing, my Wren. On her knees for me, sucking my cock so good," he murmurs, almost to himself. His hands move, brushing and gathering my hair into one hand, getting it out of my face. "So fucking good, baby."

I thrive at these words, at the confirmation that I'm pleasing him, and I move faster, taking him deeper. My hand wraps around the base to jack the bit I can't fit into my mouth, and my head bobs over him, feeling him lengthen and throb in my mouth.

I begin to squirm, wildly turned on by the noises he's making, by what I'm doing, by the mere fact I'm bringing him so much pleasure. I shift, trying to press my thighs together, to find some angle where I can get the proper pressure on my clit to alleviate the ache between my legs.

With the next stroke, I take him deeper than ever, and his cock slides deep into my throat, and I moan around him as his hand tightens in my hair, the sound garbled. It seems to be a tipping point for him.

"Fuck it," he says, and he's shifting, popping my mouth off his cock and bending to put his hands beneath my arms. Then I'm moving as he lifts me, situating me until I'm straddling his legs, my dress pooling around us, his stiff cock between us. His hand moves, his thumb pressing right where my clit is beneath my panties and tights. "Is this pussy wet for me?" I pant as his lips press to my jaw, and he peppers kisses along my neck. "Wren." It's a command to answer that I hear through a thick haze of lust.

"Yes." The word comes out in a long breath as his hand moves to my hip, pulling me to grind against him.

"From sucking me off?"

"Yes," I groan, tilting my hips, desperate to find some kind of friction for my clit.

"Let me check," he says. I expect him to slide a hand down my belly, beneath my tights, and into my underwear, but that isn't what happens.

Instead, both of his strong hands move to the crotch of my tights, and he grips them on either side of my center. I let out a shocked gasp as the admittedly thin fabric tears, giving him the perfect access to my panties.

"Adam!" I gasp in admonishment, but there's no time for any other argument, not when he's sliding my underwear to the side, not when he's dipping one thick finger into me. He groans at the feel, and I echo it, my hips moving.

"Fuck, you're soaked." His finger moves out, then slides back in, slowly fucking before sliding in a second.

"Adam," I whisper. It's building faster than ever before, the pleasure swirling in my belly, but I still need more. I need his finger on my clit or I need him to fill me more...something. *Anything.*

He knows that, and as seems to be his way, Adam has a plan.

"I gotta get you close, because I am not going to last long. Not with the visual of you kneeling before me, sucking my cock fresh in my mind, not with those little, needy sounds you've been making, and sure as fuck not with the way you're squeezing my fingers." His words are a low growl, vibrating through me and sending me higher.

"Adam," I breathe.

"That's it, baby. Ride my fingers. Fuck, you're beautiful like this. Taking what you want, what you need, asking me for what you want. Being selfish. Nothing turns me on more."

I nod, barely able to push the following words out without moaning to do just that.

"Fuck me, Adam," I groan. He said he wants me to ask for what I want. That's what I want.

He smiles then, wide and proud.

"There she is," he murmurs, then slides his fingers out, pinching my clit and pulling a mewl from my lips as he does.

I open my mouth to argue about his teasing, but then he's lifting me with one hand and using the other to guide his cock between us. Once the head is positioned, I fight the urge to slam down on him, to give myself the exquisite fullness I've come to expect with him.

Instead, I let him take the lead, his hands going to my hips beneath my dress, slowing my descent.

It's torture.

The most beautiful, magical, breathtaking torture as I feel every inch of him filling me, as our labored breaths mingle, as he presses soft kisses to my lips and my cheeks and my jaw and my neck as if he can't stand not touching me incessantly.

When my hips settle on his lap, we both let out a deep groan. I lift my hips once, then drop again, sighing with pleasure, but when I try to do it again, he stops me.

"No, no. Grind on me, baby. Take what you need."

I drop my head forward into his neck, breathing heavily, trying not to scream from the pleasure flooding my body. His hands grip my hips under the floaty skirt of my dress, grinding my hips along him in a way so reminiscent of our first time, encouraging me to take what I need. With each movement, my clit grinds against him, and his cock fills me a bit deeper. The angle is perfect, the way we're both sitting up, meaning I have the most direct pressure on my clit with each movement. I experiment with lifting my hips just a bit, then shifting to grind as I fill myself with him and bite back a shout at the way it makes that tension in my belly tighten faster.

"Fuck yeah," he groans, clearly liking that as much as I did. I do it again and again, and soon I'm teetering on the edge.

"Oh god, oh god, oh god," I murmur. My underwear is cutting into my hip, but it doesn't distract me or take away from anything—instead, it's the opposite, adding to the layers of pleasure I'm feeling.

"Come on, baby. Come on. Fuck, that's what I want. I want to feel you come around me."

That does it.

The people pleaser, who has been pushed back as of late, comes out and gives Adam what he needs—what *we* need—and I come around him, biting into his shoulder as stars burst behind my eyelids, and my body rocks against his. Tremors rack through my body as I come and come, and somewhere through it, I feel his hands go to my hips, lift and drop me a few times, fucking me hard and deep to get himself where he ends up. Finally, a deep groan leaves his chest, and he fills me, triggering a second, smaller, though no less blissful, orgasm from me as he finishes coming inside.

"You know, I really think I'm starting to see the allure of the holiday spirit," he murmurs as we both come down from our high.

I laugh the entire time we clean up.

TWENTY-THREE

ADAM

"Thank you."

The words are a whisper from the woman on my chest. It's long after we left her family's tree farm, after we lugged the tree into my house, and after we brought a box of extra ornaments and decorations over from her place.

After putting the tree in the stand, we hung all the round ornament balls and lights on it. We didn't have a star for the top, but Wren told me she'd look for one that was *just right*, insisting that tree toppers had to *speak* to you before you just threw one on top. We ordered in Chinese and then ate it in front of the glowing tree before she curled up into my chest.

"For the tree? It looks good, Birdie. I'm happy it's here." And despite my general dislike for the holidays and decorations, I realize then that I actually mean it. I like having them here —the calming, soft glow of the lights and the way they fill up the empty space. It's a real tree, obviously, something my neat-freak parents never would have allowed, and I now realize what people mean when they say that they prefer real trees for the smell alone: my entire house now smells like pine.

But it's not just the decorations. It's the little nutcracker decoration she put in my living room, half her size, but something she said I *had to have* when she saw it in her family's gift shop. It's the homemade sugar cookies she grabbed from her freezer and baked after dinner with red and green sprinkles and the mulled cider candle that's sitting on my coffee table.

It's cozy and special, and after today, I further realize that despite her love for decorations and spreading joy, Christmas isn't about commercialism for her. It's about tiny moments like these with the people she cares about, making memories that will linger for years to come.

And I'm finding more and more; it's growing on me.

Wren's version of Christmas is growing on me.

With the dread of the season melting away, I'm starting to remember that I did, at some point, used to love the holidays, before they became a time for responsibilities and missed expectations, before they became a job and a burden.

"Really?" she asks, lifting her head, eyes wide and hopeful. I nod, and she smiles.

"I like the smell."

That smile spreads into a pleased grin. "It smells like home to me. My parents' place."

"We didn't do much for the holidays, but we had a tree. Nothing chaotic and surely not one covered in ornaments made by kids. They had a decorator come in and make one that was aesthetically pleasing, one that wouldn't interrupt my mother's decor. My parents were crazy neat freaks, so we had a fake tree to avoid needles dropping. I never really got the whole smell thing until now."

There's a beat of silence before Wren speaks.

"You don't talk about them often," she murmurs.

I shrug, trying to play it off. "We don't talk much. There isn't much to talk about."

"What are they like?" she asks, shifting to put her hands on my chest, then propping her chin there and staring down my chest at me. "What's your family like?"

"My family is nothing like yours," I say with an embarrassed laugh. I remember having friends with close families growing up, ones who didn't care about prestige or awards or clout, and always feeling embarrassed that my family was the way they were—are, really.

"I didn't ask about my family, Adam. I asked about yours." I stare at her, at her sweet, gentle eyes and the small tip of her lips. "I just want to know you more, Adam. You're very mysterious."

"Have you Googled me now that you know where to look?"

A blush blooms, and I know my answer.

"I promise I didn't look at any tabloid articles, just Wikipedia—"

"Read all you want, Wren. I have nothing to hide." She gives me a look, silently reminding me that I am, in fact, hiding out in Holly Ridge. "Not from you, anyway." Joy lights up her face, and I like seeing it there, so I begin telling her what she wants to hear. "My parents are well-known surgeons, very renowned in their respective fields. They wanted me to do the same. They got me into piano at a young age to improve my hand-eye coordination or some shit like that. Apparently, studies have linked piano playing with surgical skill."

'That's interesting," Wren says, her fingers tracing along mine with a reverence I've never felt before.

"Yeah, well, it backfired. I fell in love with it, with music. It turns out that where they had hoped I would be a great doctor, I was just really good at music. A prodigy of sorts. I picked up instruments fast, often mastering them within a few months."

Her eyes go wide. "Instruments? Plural?"

"I can play a lot of instruments, but I like the piano best."

"But in the band..."

"I was bass. I never wanted to be at the forefront, and drums and bass are typically the most in the background. I wanted to live a normal life. Trent didn't; he loved the limelight, which is why he ended up going solo."

She lets out an interesting noise but is clearly biting back her commentary, hoping I'll keep speaking.

"My parents didn't like the band. They felt it was a waste of all the time and energy they had invested in me. They realized pretty early on that I wouldn't be putting my energy into the medical field, so they shifted their focus. They wanted me to move into classical music, get them the honors they thought they were due that way."

"You didn't want to?"

"Do I look like a tux-and-tails kind of guy, Birdie?" She scrunches up her nose and lets out a little giggle. I feel that urge to kiss her, and I realize I don't have to fight it, not anymore, so I lean down, pressing my lips to hers. Her body relaxes beneath my touch, and I smile into the kiss.

"No, you don't," she responds, a bit dazed when it breaks.

"Exactly. So they were pushing for it, but I was secretly in a band, and we were doing pretty well. I'd say I was at a sleepover or a practice for a sport that was preapproved—couldn't risk my hands, after all." Her jaw goes tight, and I chuckle at her protectiveness. "And we got picked up."

"I imagine they didn't like that."

I shake my head and let out a humorless laugh. "No, no, they didn't. They were pissed, threatened to cut me off and kick me out if I *made a fool of them in that way.*" I shrug, then finish. "But I knew what I wanted, so I left. I didn't talk to them for five years."

"God, that's crazy," she whispers with wide eyes. "So you just... did what you wanted?" She sounds so shocked by that, but I suppose that would be a foreign concept for my Wren.

"Yeah. I knew what I wanted to do with my life, and that it would never line up with what they wanted from me. I wasn't going to live my one life for someone else." Her face goes contemplative with understanding. "I didn't talk to them for five years, until we won Band of the Year. Dad texted me then and congratulated me. Now we occasionally speak a couple of times a year, but they're so different from me, and they don't get it." I shrug, playing it off as I brush her hair back gently. "Your turn."

"What?" she asks.

"I told you something about me, now it's your turn. Tell me something no one knows. Something that's just yours," I say.

She lifts an eyebrow. "I'm an open book, Adam."

"The fuck you are," I scoff out, and she laughs. "Come on. Tell me something no one else knows. Some secret dream you've been too selfless to admit out loud."

Silence hangs between us, and I think for a moment she won't say anything. I won't push it, of course, but I stay quiet in case she finds something, gently brushing my fingers through her hair.

"I wish I could travel more," she says after a while, voice low. "My parents never left because of the farm, though they don't mind. They love it here. But it meant we never went anywhere fun for vacation. I thought when I left for college, I'd go somewhere fun and exciting, but I stayed in-state to save money and then went right into working at the school." She smiles genuinely, and I can see that there are no regrets on her face about that being her path; instead, she's simply fondly thinking of what could have been.

"Where have you been?"

She lets out a small, self-deprecatory laugh. "I've never left Holly Ridge."

"Never?"

She shakes her head. "I was supposed to go to Seaside Point last summer, but that got...postponed." I'm sure there's a story there of some favor she granted, but when she lets out an almost bitter laugh, I focus on her following words. "Well, I was *really* supposed to go to Paris. I impulsively bought tickets last year. I was going to go over summer break, but then my grandmother passed away, and everything got so chaotic...I couldn't do it."

Grief lingers in the words, and I'm so unused to dealing with other people's emotions that I'm not sure what to do. Despite getting her love of the holidays from her grandmother and bending over backward all season to follow in her footsteps, she really doesn't talk about her much. I'm unsure of the right thing to do, to ask, but I go with my gut, which, for the most part, has not steered me wrong with Wren.

"Why Paris?" It's a simple question, an easy one to brush off if she wants, so I'm surprised when she gives me the answer immediately.

"When I was little, my grandmother got me the book *Madeline* when I got my appendix out. It's actually a pretty sad book about a group of little girls living in a boarding school run by nuns, and one of them has her appendix removed, but I found it really entertaining. It's set in Paris. Then she got me *Madeline at Christmas* that same year, and that kind of cemented it." She shrugs then, trying to brush it off and make light of her words. "It's silly, I know, the only reason I want to go somewhere is a book I read when I was probably six. But I must have read it at an influential time because it always stuck."

I shake my head. "It's not silly. Not at all." I often think about how I chose Holly Ridge just because of a woman I met in an airport bar, and that's far more unhinged than picking your ideal vacation destination based on a book you read as a kid, but she speaks before I can tell her.

"Have you been?" Her eyes are wide and excited, and I can't help but smile in return.

Reaching up, I brush one of those loose strands of hair behind her ear. "Why do you think I've been there?"

"You were in a rock band, Adam. You've probably been all over the world. I want to know about everywhere. Where was your favorite? Where did it suck the most? Where was the best food?"

She is the cutest thing on this planet.

"No," I say with a shake of my head. "I've never been to Paris. Maybe one day we'll go together. Use that passport of yours. I'll whisk you away to all of the places you've always wanted to go."

She shakes her head and lets out a small smile, a blush creeping over her cheeks. "You don't have to impress me with lavish trips, Adam. I'm already yours."

Clearly, she doesn't get it.

She doesn't get that I will never take *having* her for granted. All I want to do is spoil her and give her anything and everything. She doesn't get that when I say I want to give her everything she asks for, I mean it.

That's fine.

I'm starting to realize that I'll be content to spend the rest of our lives proving it.

TWENTY-FOUR

Wren

I don't see Adam much on Sunday, leaving bright and early to set up the classroom for Monday's half-day Polar Express party. I came home late, spending the night with Hallie and Nat, having a mini girls' night, gabbing and filling them in on everything new in my life.

We texted a few times throughout the day, but I was crazy busy, and he seemed to be the same. On Monday morning, I feel a dash of disappointment when Adam doesn't step out for his run when I leave, and when I get home just after one (thank you, half day!), I note that Adam's lights are off, including the tree visible from the front window and the twinkling fairy lights I convinced him to wrap around the wreath on his front door.

I roll my eyes and snap a picture before sending it to him.

> I leave you alone for one day, and you turn off your Christmas tree?

I wait for a few moments as I bring my bag into my house and unpack it. It remains silent as I gather my dirty clothes and carry the hamper down to the laundry room, attending to my usual weekend chores that were pushed off. When I throw everything in and start the load, I check my phone and notice that the text is marked as read but unanswered.

Of course, Adam would have his *read* receipts on—he wouldn't care at all if someone knew he read a text and didn't respond. But I *am* surprised he didn't reply. I let it be for another five minutes or so while I carry the clean clothes from my dryer back up to my room. Then, I take a deep breath and decide to send another text, guilt and nerves eating at me.

I know that a big part of our story began when I started bugging him about decorations, but I don't want him to think I actually care that much about it all. I now understand why he doesn't really like Christmas decorations, and even though I'm making it my mission to assign new memories to the holidays, that won't change overnight.

> I'm joking, by the way.

I hit send, then stare at it nervously before deciding to send another clarifying message.

> I really don't care about the tree, promise!

I add an exclamation point because everyone knows that an exclamation point means friendly excitement, and a period means *I'm so mad at you, I might never talk to you again,* before I set my phone down and try to distract myself by emptying the dishwasher. But when I check my phone again in five minutes and see that the text is marked as read but unreplied to, my gut churns. I pace, trying to think of a response that doesn't come across as too clingy, while also wanting to check if everything is okay.

> Are you leaving me on read because of Christmas lights? Be careful, I might think you're flirting with me.

Yet again, he leaves me on read.

If it were any other man, I might think he was ignoring me, that he was over whatever glimmer of a relationship we had, and was trying to end it without actually doing so.

But I'm pretty sure Adam is the type who always tells it like it is and does it straight to your face if he were ending things.

Maybe this is his way of telling me, "Game on?" I had started to miss this aspect of our relationship.

As I glance over at my bin of decorations, I try to decide which to tackle first. I'd planned to go easy on him after our talk, but maybe that was the wrong move. Making a decision, I grab my options and then walk out my door toward his place.

I knock on his door, holding up two different blow-mold decorations in my hands and smiling wide. After a moment, the doorknob turns, and I start my spiel.

"Which do you think would look better for your front porch, angel or snowman? Personally, I think both, but—" My words trail off when I get a good look at Adam, whose face is pale with dark bags under them. He's in a sweatshirt and sweats, along with a pair of socks, but for once, it doesn't look too hot.

He looks *miserable*.

"Tomorrow I'll be ready to battle with you about lights, Wren, promise," he murmurs, and even that sounds like it takes the small amount of energy he has out of him.

"Oh my god, you look terrible. Are you okay?" I set the decorations down and reach for the screen door, but Adam shakes his head.

"No, stay there. You don't want what I have." He holds onto the screen door handle when I try to open it, and I glare at him.

"Adam, you look like death warmed over. Let me in." I tug at the handle, and there's a bit of resistance from where he's holding it, but he's so sick, he can't fight me. When I open the door, he groans and then steps back in resignation. I enter and look around his empty house. Even just from this small glance, I can still tell he's feeling like crap and has been for a bit. There is a stack of essentials he must have had delivered still in bags on the floor and an empty box of tissues on the kitchen table, like he couldn't find it in him to bring it to the actual trash. Empty bottles of sports drink and water are tossed in the sink, and a few of the cabinet doors are open.

"What do you have?" I ask, turning back to him, though I can make my own assumptions, considering it looks like the crud that's been going around. He shrugs.

"Some kind of bug. Killer headache, snot, sore throat, but I think that's just from the cough."

I stare at him, then nod before moving to the bags and taking in the items there. None of them is going to help with what's ailing him, but he's a boy, so I can't expect him to know that kind of thing.

He's so lucky he has me.

I stand and turn to him with a stern look on my face. "Okay. Can you make it upstairs?"

"What?"

I turn to him, stopping to look at my phone, where I'm about to text my mom, and his face is one of pure and utter confusion.

"Can you make it up the stairs to your bed? Or should I set you up on the couch?" He pauses, and I realize that maybe he also has a fever that's clouding his mind, so I explain further. "Wherever you'll be most comfortable is probably best. I'm a sleep-it-off kind of girl, but maybe you're a watch-TV kind of guy? Wherever you set up, I'll bring you meds and some food. Are you hungry at all? Is your stomach bothering you?"

A beat passes before he shakes his head and sighs. "I'll be fine. You really should go, Wren. You don't want to be sick before the holidays."

I shake my head, ignoring him as I bend and start gathering up the things in his entryway to put them away. "That's the least of our worries right now."

"You're not worried because you never worry about yourself, so I'm the only one who *does* worry about you. I can't be the reason you're sick on Christmas."

I stop at the frustration in his words and turn to him, giving him a soft smile, understanding his hesitance.

"I'll be fine, I promise." He opens his mouth to argue further, but I shake my head and continue. "I'm a second-grade teacher, Adam. I'm basically a petri dish, and I'm forced to have the most intense immune system. I promise, this has gone through my classroom four times already. I had it once at the beginning of the year, and I'll be solid for the rest of the season. You should see my immune-boosting supplement regimen." I look him over and cringe. "Maybe we should get you on something similar. But that's tomorrow's worry. Right now, you need rest. So, bed or couch?"

"Wren..."

I step closer, then put my hand on his head. It's warm, and he leans into my chilled hand, his eyes closing like it's a comfort to him. Something in my chest melts, and the urge to take care of him ratchets up. It's not the same need I always feel to help people out. This one is more personal, more intimate.

"Go to bed, Adam. I'm going to clean up a bit and get you settled. I might have to run out, but I'll be back soon." He stares at me, so I add, "I'm not going anywhere, but you look as if you don't sit down, you'll collapse on the floor right here. Chances are, I'll end up hurting myself if I have to drag your big body to the couch from here, but if that's a risk you're willing to take—"

He groans in irritation, but my threat works. He turns around, and as I watch him lumber up the stairs, grumbling to himself, I can't help but let out a silent laugh.

Then I text my mom.

⁂

Over the next hour or so, I send a handful of texts, check Adam's cabinets, and tidy up while I await reinforcements. Thankfully, my mom is free today and able to run to the drugstore and then the grocery store for me, which means she's at the door barely forty minutes after my call. She sends me a text to let me know she's outside so she doesn't wake Sleeping Beauty, who is out cold. I tiptoe to the door, open it, and she hands me a bag with three more sitting at her feet.

"Hey, come in," I say, reaching to take the first from her, then a second. She follows me inside, carrying the other two bags to the kitchen table as well.

"I threw everything in a pot before I ran out, so I'll be back over in..." She turns her wrist toward her to check the time on her watch. "Four hours? Will that work?"

"Yeah, Mom, thanks. I appreciate it."

Quiet fills the kitchen, but it's the kind that sets me on guard, knowing my mom. If she had no other motive, she would have dumped the groceries and run. When she pulls out a chair at his breakfast bar, I know she's settling in for a gab.

"Is the front yard your doing? It's...cute," she says, always diplomatic and kind in her choice of words. I scoff out a laugh.

"It's an ugly hodgepodge, but I'm working on it. He doesn't like Christmas or decorations, but you know me."

"Stubborn in your need to spread joy, just like your grandmother," she says. I preen at what I deem to be a compliment, the warmth of it spreading through my veins. I'm lost in that and unpacking, so I don't see her new angle coming.

"You know, when Hallie told me you were in some feud with a hot neighbor—her words, not mine—I was a little worried. You need another person to take care of, like your father needs more power tools."

I somehow managed to avoid the interrogation at brunch, mainly because there were people around, but I should have known it was coming. Calling her and asking her to bring groceries to my neighbor's house definitely sped up that process.

"Mom—" I start, but she ignores my protests and continues.

"But she said she liked him, that he was good for you."

I groan, sifting through the bags as I silently curse my best friend. Hallie is more like a sister to me, as evidenced by Mom pseudo-adopting her after her mom left their family when we were in middle school. But it also means every little thing makes it to my mom, since both Hallie and my mom love gossiping. Hallie works for my brother, Madden, who manages the wholesale side of the family business, so she's often at the farm.

"She thought he was a serial killer a few weeks ago," I say dead-pan, and my mom lets out a laugh.

"She told me that, too. But she said he's convincing you to put yourself first more, which we all know you need."

I ignore the quiet poke and the discomfort it brings me.

"If you mean breaking into my house and throwing me over his shoulder so I go to bed early or dragging me away from The Mill before I offer to help out with the kittens Stephanie found, then sure." When her eyes don't even change or register shock at my words, I realize she and Hallie have been talking *a lot* about me.

"Whatever unconventional method he's using, it's working. You look tired, but not in the way you did before." I don't speak, busying myself with putting things away. Perhaps if I ignore it, this conversation will come to an end. It doesn't work, obviously. "Your dad likes him."

My heart stutters, and I can't help it. I turn my head to her, confirming she's been watching me closely.

"Really?" I ask, both hopeful and a bit disbelieving. Outside of our family, my dad doesn't like many people.

"Oh yeah. Liked how he stood up for you with your brothers, how he did it firmly but respectfully and took the task on himself." My heart flutters a bit with her words but then dips with the next ones. "You know, we've been worried about you, your dad, and me."

"Mom—" I start, guilt churning in my stomach. The last thing I want is to add *more* stress to the people I love most.

"You say yes to everything and everyone at the expense of your-self." I open my mouth to argue, but she keeps speaking. "And that's a great trait to have, don't get me wrong. It's how we raised you kids, though you took it to heart most of all. And I know I add to it, asking you for favors without asking what else is on your plate, but in my defense, I don't think I really realized how bad it had gotten." She looks at me with that assessing mom look she has long perfected. "You hung up Jed Campbell's lights?" I roll my eyes, exasperated. I bet Hallie told her that, too. "Everyone knows he's just lazy. Hell, you heard your grandmother complaining about him over and over."

I take the opportunity to change the subject quickly.

"Yeah, yeah, I know. I went over there to check in on his timeline, and he mentioned he was busy with work, so he hadn't gotten around to it. I fell for it hook, line, and sinker. But I only did one side. Adam ended up hanging the rest for me." I don't tell her that it was after I fell off the ladder.

"Interesting move for a man who apparently hates Christmas."

I shrug, not wanting to expand. She gives me another look that sears through me, looking past my indifferent mask in a way only a mother can, but her phone beeps with an incoming text, distracting her. Relief floods my veins, and for the first time in my life, I silently hope my mom has to leave.

She looks at her phone, then shakes her head, tutting a bit before sighing. "That's your dad, asking if I'm making *him* soup. I gotta get home before he starts messing around and eats it all before it's even done." She stands, then pulls me into her. "Good thing I made double, knowing this could happen."

I let out a little laugh, then she puts her hands on my shoulders and leans back to look at me. "I'm so proud of you, Wren, and I know she is, too. But promise me you'll take care of yourself, too."

A lump forms in my throat, one I can't speak around.

I've kept myself incredibly busy since school started, feeling as if the holidays are creeping up on me. I knew that with them, grief for my grandmother would come. It was her favorite time of year, and it's mine because of her. When I took on the position of head of the decorating committee, I knew it would be a lot of work. Yet, part of me was grateful for it—grateful not to have any extra time in December to think, much less miss her too much.

Of course, I've been doing everything I can to make her proud and protect her legacy, but the selfish part of it was that I knew if I slowed down, I might have to face those feelings head-on, feelings I don't think I'm ready to face yet. Instead, I've bottled them up and hidden them away. I thought I had been doing a pretty good job hiding it from everyone, but now that my mom is looking at me like that, I'm wondering if I might not be as good an actor as I thought.

I open my mouth, unsure of what to say. Thankfully, I don't have to say anything. Instead, she gives me another soft smile and presses a kiss to my cheek before heading toward the door. We say our good-byes, and I watch her walk off before I finish going through the bags. Then, I bring a drink and some medicine up to Adam, who quickly takes it before falling right back to sleep.

TWENTY-FIVE

ADAM

I spend the day in a sleepy haze, but by six p.m., I'm feeling slightly more human. I don't feel great, but I no longer feel like utter death like I did yesterday or when I woke up this morning. Deep down, I know it's because of Wren. She came up a few times, making sure I chugged an electrolyte drink and took some medicine before I fell back asleep. Although my nose is still running and my throat is still scratchy, the headache that wouldn't end is gone, and I feel like I have control of my limbs again.

I hear a noise downstairs as I lie in bed, assessing my body. When I realize I'm not falling back to sleep, I decide to head downstairs. As I make my way down, I'm hit with the most delicious smell, and despite not having an appetite all day, my stomach growls.

"Oh, you're alive!" Wren says as I shuffle into the living room. She sets her laptop aside and stands from the couch, moving my way. I furrow my brow at her, confused as to why she's still here, but I don't have time for that when she lifts a small hand, resting the back of it against my forehead. "Oh, you feel so much better, thank God."

She steps back, taking me in. I'm sure I look absolutely disgusting, but she smiles at me and nods. "You look better, too. Are you hungry?" I don't answer, but my stomach does, growling loudly. She lets out a small laugh before tipping her head toward the dining room. "Come on, sit at the table, and I'll get you something."

I don't say anything, still confused and a bit sleepy, but I do as I'm told, sitting at the kitchen table. In a minute, a bowl is in front of me alongside a spoon and a big glass of water. She sets a couple of pills on the table as well before sitting in the chair across from me.

"Take those, too. You look better, but let's get it moving faster."

"What are they?" I ask as I lift them, placing them all in my mouth and downing them with a gulp of water in one swallow.

"The same cold pills I've been giving you all day."

"And this?" I ask, tipping my chin toward the bowl of yellow broth.

"Chicken and vegetable soup. My mom made it. It's a miracle cure, I swear. I have no idea how, but it genuinely fixes every ailment."

"Your mom?" She nods, watching me stir the soup to cool it down. I didn't notice before, but there's also a pile of saltines to the side of the bowl.

"Yeah. I'm good with cookies, but I'm shit with soup. She makes the best soup ever. Go, try it."

I stare at her for long moments, but her eager look has me pushing down any more questions and taking a spoonful of the soup. It's amazing—light, warm, yet super flavorful, even for my dulled taste buds. I take a few more bites before Wren nods at me, as if she's satisfied that I'm taking in nourishment, before she disappears. Eventually, she comes back with a bowl of her own in one hand and a can of soda in the other, sitting across from me as I continue to eat slowly.

"Why would your mom bring me soup?"

She looks as confused as I feel by the question, tipping her head to the side a bit before answering.

"Because I told her you were sick." She takes a big spoonful, an egg noodle hanging precariously over the side of the spoon, before she brings it to her lips and blows on it.

"Okay...?" I ask, furrowing my brows.

She returns the look, then shrugs. "It's what we do, Adam. We take care of each other here."

She takes her bite.

"But I barely even know your mom."

"But she knows you're important to me." She says it like it's as simple as that, and I'm confused for a moment before it clears with some understanding. Wren's generosity isn't some personality trait that came from nowhere. It's something her family created, curated, and nurtured. Wren just took it to the next level.

"Does she make soup for everyone who is sick in town?" I ask with a teasing smile, lifting an eyebrow as I scoop up another spoonful of the soup. It's probably in my head or a combination of the hot broth and my body's desperate need for sustenance, but I think I am starting to feel better from the soup.

Wren blushes, then shakes her head. "No, she doesn't," she answers simply.

"But she made soup for me."

"Yeah. She came by earlier, said she hopes you feel better."

We fall into a comfortable silence as we eat, and I finish my bowl, setting the spoon down and taking a bite out of the saltine. I'm much hungrier than I anticipated, and without me saying anything, Wren gets up, grabs my bowl, and returns with a refill.

"You know, I don't think I've ever had soup when I'm sick," I say, feeling stupid saying it out loud. Maybe it's the cold medicine Wren gave me, or perhaps it's the lingering fever weighing my body down, but I don't have my normal filter tightly in place. "I always kind of thought it was something from books and movies, not some actual cure-all."

"Really?"

I shake my head, and I'm surprised when it doesn't throb. This morning, I could barely keep my eyes open with the sinus headache that was plaguing me, but now, with food in my belly and a full day of sleep behind me, I feel almost human.

I get sick like this once, maybe twice a winter, and it usually lasts a few days at minimum, sometimes dragging on for a whole week.

I could tell myself it must be some new strain that has me bouncing back quicker, but I know somewhere deep down that it's not. It's being cared for, getting what my body needed, and not having to do it myself that has me feeling almost normal so soon.

"What did you have as a kid? My mom always made us soup. Sometimes, we'd have pumpkin muffins because they were Madden's favorite, and we didn't realize they had vegetables in them."

I smile when she does, then shrug, embarrassed, and look away when I realize I'm supposed to give her my own anecdotes.

"I don't..." My voice trails off. "I don't think I've ever had real sick food before."

"Your parents didn't make you sick food?" she asks, brows furrowing.

I let out a little laugh and shake my head. "My parents are surgeons, remember? They couldn't get sick, or they'd miss out on a surgery, so if I caught something at school, I was kind of quarantined. When I was really little, I'd have a nanny or a sitter take care of me." Wren's eyes go wide, and I know she doesn't mean to give me a look of pity, but she does all the same. "It wasn't as bad as it sounds, I swear. And when I was old enough to fend for myself, I did. I always thought it was kind of cool—unlimited TV, whatever food I wanted. Then I'd just...ride out my sickness. I've been that way ever since. I'll just hunker down until I feel normal again, then I'll go on with my life." When I look up at her, there's a bit of sadness on her face, but she covers it quickly with a snarky grin.

"That seemed to be going well for you," she says. "I thought you were a zombie."

I laugh, relieved that we're moving off the topic. "I felt like a zombie," I say.

"And now?"

"I feel human. Thanks to you." I reach across the table and grab her hand, brushing my thumb over her fingers. "No one has ever done something like this for me."

She shrugs. "It's what I do, Adam."

I sit up then, remembering. "Didn't you have to go to the community center this afternoon to organize the gifts?" I stare at her, watching her body still, then relax so quickly that I would almost think it didn't happen if I weren't watching so closely.

"Yeah, I got it covered."

"You got it covered?"

She looks up, turns to me, and I see her biting her lip.

"Okay, don't get too excited, I have to go there after work tomorrow to get it done, but I pushed it off." I stare at her, and even though I don't like that she is going to be working late tomorrow because she helped me, I know it's a big moment, even more so when she continues. "I called Sue, whom I was meeting there, to tell her I needed to reschedule, and I was worried that she would be mad, but she didn't mind at all." She sounds surprised by that fact, which is so very Wren.

"You didn't have to change your plans for me."

She shrugs. "You were sick."

"I would have survived. You didn't have to do all of this just for me."

She bites her lip, then reaches over and runs a hand through my hair. I'm sure it's tangled and probably sweaty from my fever, but she doesn't seem to care. Instead, she looks nervous.

I get why when she speaks her following words aloud.

"Are you mine?"

They're exactly like the words I spoke to her a few days ago in the driveway, and I remember them seeming to take her breath away.

I get why now.

They hit me square in the chest, reaching somewhere deep in my soul as she stares at me, nervous and expectant.

It doesn't make sense, especially considering how short an

amount of time it's been that we've been together, but I feel like we were meant to be here, to be next to one another and find each other.

I answer honestly. "Yeah, Wren. I'm yours."

"I take care of what's mine, Adam."

The words are a whisper, but for a man who is becoming more and more aware of the fact that no one has ever taken care of him, it means everything.

TWENTY-SIX

ADAM

"Hey, Will, how's it going?" I ask when Willa Stone picks up on the second ring. Nerves rack through me, and for a split second, I can't remember why I called at all. But then I look down and see the scribbled lines of the song before me. Typically, Greg handles this by calling the artists or their labels with a new song, but I'm hoping that by sharing my vision for the song I've written with the pop star myself, I might get better results.

"Adam Porter, as I live and breathe. How are you? I haven't heard from you in forever," Willa says, a small tinkling laugh in the words.

Again, I wonder if this was a bad idea. This morning, I realized the song I'd been tinkering with wasn't just decent. It had real potential in a way a song hasn't in a while, and I instantly knew who I would want on it.

Still, I don't know exactly what has me picking up the phone and calling Willa *first* instead of Greg. It's probably because the last time Greg called, I snapped at him and haven't heard from him since. Either way, some ghost took hold of me this afternoon, and before I knew it, I was calling Willa to tell her about the new song instead of my agent. He'll probably have a fuck ton of things to say about that, but he'll get over it when I land this and get him a nice little check for it.

"Yeah, it's been a while. I'm calling because, uh...I think I have something for you."

"Oh yeah?" she asks, and even though she sounds intrigued rather than irritated or bored, my pulse still pounds with nerves.

"Yeah. It's, uh." I bite my lip, looking at the song before me, lyrics and notes all over the pages. "It's not totally done, but I think it would be great for you." I take in a deep breath, steeling myself. I've gone over this a dozen times in my head as I struck up the nerve to place the call. If she turns it down, it's no big deal. There are a million other artists who could do something great with his song, which tells me it has single potential.

But Willa would be my first choice.

"I know you've turned down a bunch from me recently, and there's no hard feelings with that, really, there's not. But I think this could be big. It feels...it feels good." There's a pause on the other end as I finish my mini-pitch, and dread fills me as I wait for her response.

"Turned you down?" she asks.

"Well, yeah. I mean, technically, it was Greg you turned down, but—"

"Adam," she says, hesitantly cutting me off. "I haven't seen a song of yours in at least a year, probably more."

My pulse pounds, but my mind is trying to piece things together. "What?"

"Well, yeah. Greg told me you weren't writing, that you had writer's block or something."

I blink, brow furrowing with confusion. "I mean, I did. For the last six months or so. But early this year I sent over..." I try to think of how many songs I've finished and which ones I thought had real potential to perform well with Willa's audience. "Four? Five? And you and the label turned them all down."

Silence hangs heavy, and a pit swirls in my stomach before Willa speaks. And when she does, it's with caution and gentleness.

"Adam, the only things I've gotten from you since 'All Lit Up' were three Christmas songs." The air catches in my chest. "I thought that's all you were working on. I even called Greg to see if I could convince you to write for me, but he told me you were moving to Christmas exclusively after the success of 'All Lit Up' and giving everything else to Trent."

The world stops.

Moving to Christmas exclusively.

Giving everything else to Trent.

"You have got to be fucking kidding me," I murmur. Suddenly, things make sense.

Trent has been the *only* artist to ask me about new songs.

I thought I was because all of the shit I'd sent to the artists I'd worked with previously sucked, so they'd written me off. However, it seems that my agent has been playing games.

"I take that to mean that wasn't the case," Willa says low, interrupting my thoughts.

"I've been trying to get *away* from fucking Christmas music. 'All Lit Up' was the best thing I ever did, but I don't want that to be my legacy. I told Greg that, and he wasn't happy about it, but I think he realized he couldn't argue with me over it. What was he gonna do, force me to write?" I run a hand over my face, seeing the last year for what it really was: sabotage. "Willa, I've been trying to sell songs for a *year* since I told him I was done with Christmas, and nothing has sold except a few songs to Trent that I basically gave him so I'd have *something* coming in." I don't tell her that I took ghostwriting credits on those, something Greg talked me into after nearly six months of no interest from anyone else.

It wasn't about the money. I've always been smart with my investments and never leaned into the extravagant rock star lifestyle, so I technically never had to work another day in my life. It was about the ego of not selling anything. An ego hit that Greg curated.

"Adam, fuck, I'm so sorry. I had no idea."

I shake my head, trying to make sense of it all. And the more pieces I put into place, the more I understand what happened. Greg made a lot of money from "All Lit Up" and wanted to do it again. Why wouldn't he? Bonus points if I basically gave away my songs to Trent, which would benefit Greg just as much.

"Send me the song," Willa says, cutting through my mental sifting of the past year—or longer. "And whatever you were trying to send to me before. Send it directly to me, not through anyone else." I nod, then agree verbally because she can't see a nod, obviously. "Then email Leo. He's taking on new clients to build his agent portfolio; he says he wants to slow down with the PR, and you know how much he hates Greg. He can probably find a lawyer to comb through Greg's contract with you, though I'm sure he's breached it if he's been fucking you over like this."

I nod, already drafting an email, and then type in her address as she rattles it off to me.

"I'm not gonna lie, Adam, I'm relieved. With Stella pregnant and Riggs slowing down to build their family, I thought I was going to have to do this next album all on my own." She laughs as if she isn't fully capable of doing just that before she adds, "I'm also looking for a producer." My chest fills with light as I realize what she's saying: she wants me to be a leading contributor on this next album. "Of course, I'm not sure if you have the time, but—"

"Willa, I just found out my agent has been fucking me over and not getting me any work for a year. I have all the time in the world."

She lets out a laugh before she speaks again, a broad smile in her words.

"Okay, okay. I hear you. We can talk about it after the new year, okay? I just got your email, and I'll look them over in the next few days." She pauses, then lets out an awed breath. "Oh, I *love* the title of this one!" I smile, knowing instinctively which song she's talking about. "That's a hit, Adam." I grin now and nod, knowing somewhere in my gut that she's right. My recent breakthrough is something special, and she's the only person I want to take it on. There's a noise on her end, and she curses. "Okay, I gotta go, I have a video interview in, like, three minutes. But email Leo, okay? We'll fix this."

"Yeah. Thanks, Willa," I say, genuine appreciation in the words.

"Anytime. This industry is full of assholes, so the good ones have to stick together."

And then she's gone. As I sit there, mind reeling, I'm reminded for the millionth time that Willa Stone is absolutely one of the good ones.

I waste no time, deciding to put off a hasty firing of Greg until I get a second opinion on the contract I signed years ago. Instead, I type up a lengthy email, providing Leo with all my information and the story I've begun to understand after my conversation with his client, and I attach the songs I sent over to Willa. I hit send, then sit back and take in a deep breath, assessing myself now that my tasks are finished.

I should feel angry, which I do.

I should feel disappointed, which, I suppose, I do.

But I also feel a deep sense of relief I can't ignore.

My biggest fear was that I was a one-hit wonder for a holiday song. That after that one did well, that's all anyone would want from me, but it seems that isn't the case. Not in the least.

Instead, it's more about trusting the wrong people, getting taken advantage of by those I thought cared for me, and letting that bring me down.

And fuck, is that comeback going to feel fucking *good*.

In just three minutes, I've already received a response from Leo in my inbox.

Fuck Greg; I've been dying to take him down for years. Don't call him until we have a plan, though. Love the songs; they're perfect for Will. I smell a hit, Porter. I'll send this to my lawyer and see what we can do. Talk soon.

I smile to myself, hope blooming in my chest in a way it hasn't in a while. I feel inspired and motivated, and I know, in some small way, that the only thing I have to thank is that song, the catalyst for this entire conversation.

And the woman who inspired it.

As if summoned by my thoughts, I watch as Wren pulls into her drive and steps out of her car, carrying a million bags and boxes as usual, and I can't help but smile.

I should be furious that my career was at a standstill because of a conniving asshole and a talentless fucker, but I can't find it in me to. Not when I know that when I leave this house, I'm going to spend the night with Wren, the kindest, sweetest soul who I know fell into my life to show me what I was missing. Not when I have a future laid out that is looking brighter by the moment, and it's all because of the pretty brunette across the street.

TWENTY-SEVEN

ADAM

"Right there," she says, and I groan as I shift.

"Here?" I'm out of breath, trying to hold it in place.

"Yeah, yeah. Just like that."

"This sounds absolutely pornographic," a now familiar voice calls. I peer around the giant Christmas tree I'm trying to ensure is straight and see Hallie standing beside Wren, her lips tipped in a cocky smile. Wren turns to her, confusion clear on her face, arms crossed on her chest. "Oh, yeah, just like that, a little more, Adam. It's almost there," Hallie says in a breathy voice.

I shake my head, but when a blush burns on Wren's lips, I can't help but smile.

This morning, I woke up in Wren's bed to find her getting ready far too early. When I glared at her, she reminded me that she needed to head to the community center bright and early to help set up, something she had been planning for weeks and had mentioned to me the night before. I wasn't going to argue, not with the festival happening in just a few days and her nerves already on red alert. So, I nodded and then stood, starting to get ready as well.

"What are you doing?" she had asked.

"I'm coming with you."

"Really?"

"I have nothing else going on today, and if I go with you, there's more of a chance you'll get home quicker, right?"

She shrugged, though we both knew it was true. I didn't mention that I also wanted to ensure she wouldn't volunteer for more tasks, but she probably knew that as well.

"Then I'm coming with."

"You don't have to—"

I stopped her before she finished her sentence, pulling her into me before putting a hand to her chin and staring into her eyes.

"This is a fully selfish move, Wren." I hoped that the truth of that was written on my face.

"You're being selfish, huh?" she asked, quoting me.

I smiled and nodded.

"After school tomorrow, I want you all to myself." She lifted an eyebrow, and I smiled wide. "I know on the twenty-third you'll be spending the entire day downtown, probably getting there at five a.m. and not coming home until ridiculously late. I want one low-key evening so you can relax before the chaos starts." I pressed my lips to her neck, and her breathing hitched. I found myself contemplating whether I could also talk her into a quickie.

"The whole day?"

I pulled back, catching the contemplation on her face and knowing I had her.

"After school. You don't have aftercare tomorrow, right?" She nodded, and then I saw her appreciation of my knowing her schedule. "Tomorrow night is mine. I'm going to make sure you relax and take care of yourself before the chaos ensues. I'll go with you, be some muscle you boss around, and help move things along so it gets done on time, but I want you to promise that tomorrow night is mine."

She paused, seeming to think for a long time, and I thought I might be out of luck before she smiled softly and nodded.

"Deal."

Then she dragged me into the shower, and I did, in fact, get my quickie.

Now I'm standing in a gymnasium in the recreation center downtown that Wren tells me is used for the recreation basketball teams in the winter and camps in the summer, moving a Christmas tree for the third time because it just wasn't *right*, and being accused of making *porn*ographic noises in a public place.

I fucking wish.

"Hallie, stop it," Wren says, pushing her shoulder.

I've learned this is their way: Hallie being crude and outlandish, and Wren blushing over it. I twist the pins in the tree base until it's stable on its own before stepping away. I look at Wren, who bites her lip.

"I don't know—"

"It's perfect, and you know it," Hallie says with an eye roll before directing her look to me. "She always gets like this. The perfectionism kicks in, and she starts overthinking everything. Sometimes you just gotta tell her to stop and move on." Hallie spots something over my shoulder and grins deviously.

"Right, Jesse?" she calls out.

I turn to find Wren's brothers behind me and move toward Wren as they approach. Before anyone can hear me, I whisper to Wren, "Once they're gone, I'll move it another dozen times until you're happy, okay?" Wren gives me an appreciative look.

"What are you wrangling us into?" Madden asks, throwing his arm around Hallie. She pushes at his chest, and he stumbles back, laughing.

"Gross, get your stink off me," Hallie says with a grimace. From what Wren told me, Hallie was drawn into the King family fold as a kid and is a second sister to the King brothers. But the way the oldest King scowls at his younger brother tells me there might be something more there.

"Hey, man," Jesse says, reaching over to me and pulling me into a handshake and hug I don't expect, but I play along. Once I'm released from that, I'm pulled into a second one by Madden, and Wren makes wide eyes at me over his shoulder before giving me an excited thumbs up.

"Thanks for helping with the wreaths. Dad said you also stayed on the farm and helped him haul the leftovers into his truck to donate. Saved me from having to do it," Madden says when he steps back.

"And me," Jesse says with a laugh. "Madd and I were ready to flip a coin to see who would get the job, then we found out you already did it."

I shrug and try to ignore the way Wren's eyes burn into me. She knows I picked up and dropped off the wreaths, mostly because she tried to argue that I was still *recovering* and unable to do it, and that she should just do it herself. That night, I fulfilled my threat of turning her over my knee while also proving I was more than okay to lug around some wreaths. I'm happy to report that, as expected, she more than enjoyed it.

But I didn't tell her about helping her dad with the trees.

"Poor Adam had no idea what he got himself into, tying himself with the Kings. He's going to be dragged into every kind of favor known to man," Hallie says to Wren, who just smiles.

"Do you snowboard?" Madden asks.

"Me?" I point to my chest, confused.

Jesse looks around the small group with exaggeration. "There's no one else here whose entire life story we don't know." I blink at him. "Yeah, he meant you, Adam."

Wren lets out a little huff. "Jesse, be nice."

"I am! We're trying to invite him snowboarding!"

Wren glares at her brother, clearly not buying his line, but I shrug, trying to avoid another sibling argument.

"Yeah, I snowboard. Have since I was a kid." Another disappointment, since snowboarding was far more lowbrow than skiing in my parents' eyes, but that's neither here nor there.

"Great. We're going next month. You'll come. Not sure of the date yet, but I'll get your number from Wren," Jesse says.

I blink, confused.

"You could *ask* him," Hallie says. "Like civilized people."

Madden rolls his eyes but asks.

"Would you like to come snowboarding at Bear Mountain some-time next month, Adam? It would be our greatest pleasure to have your attendance," Madden says in a haughty tone before looking at Hallie. "Was that good enough?"

"Next time, add a bow," she says deadpan, and I snort out a laugh. Madden's jaw drops, and I see him rearing up to respond, but I jump in before the two of them go at it.

"Yeah, I'd love to. I haven't been boarding in a while," I say.

"Perfect. It'll be a great time," Jesse says, seeming relieved that I stopped Madden and Hallie from arguing.

"Yeah, and it'll be the perfect opportunity to feed you to a bear if you treat Wren poorly."

Madden and Jesse laugh, and Wren opens her mouth, but Hallie must see some kind of feud brewing and steps in. I wonder for a moment if this is how it always goes with this crew: two fighting and someone else stepping in before it escalates.

"Okay, you two, follow me. I need your help hanging garland, and I've been instructed that Wren is no longer allowed on ladders."

I let out a small laugh, then watch as the force of nature that is Wren's best friend leads the two men off without a second glance.

"They like you," Wren says after they're out of earshot, and I let out a loud laugh.

"I think you're delusional, sweetness."

"I'm telling you, they do," she says. "They like that you stood up for me at the farm."

I pull her into me with a laugh. "Madden threatened to feed me to a bear if I broke your heart."

"That's just what brothers do," she says with a shrug as if threatening murder isn't strange at all. "And he just wants to seem tough. Trust me, if they didn't like you, you'd know." I'm not sure if I would, considering that I'm ninety-nine percent sure that their inviting me to go snowboarding with them next month was so that if I went missing on a mountain, no one would suspect a thing, but I don't get the chance to tell her that.

One of her many alarms goes off on her phone, and Wren glances down to check the time. "It's twelve fifty. I should head outside to wait for the volunteers' lunch. It's supposed to get here at 1," she says. "Wanna come help me bring it in?"

I pull her into my side. "Lead the way, Birdie."

A minute later, Wren glances outside and shakes her head before stepping back into the community center. "Not here yet. We'll hang in here to avoid the cold, though."

I nod, then glance down the hall that is lined with photos.

"Ahh, the Hall of Fame," she says with a nostalgic sigh. "My grandma started it, said we needed to commemorate every event that occurs in this building." She turns to me and explains further. "It was supposed to be torn down in the seventies. It was the old pre-k to second-grade building before they built the bigger one for all of elementary, but she championed for it to be turned into a community hub."

I smile, fully able to see Wren doing something similar.

"This was this year's Halloween haunted house," she says, pointing to a photo of two dozen people all dressed in costumes. I scan the image to find Wren in a Little Red Riding Hood costume.

She looks hot, but I won't tell her that.

"And Saint Patrick's Day."

There's another with a group in green, but Wren isn't there.

"Where were you?"

"Taking the picture," she explains simply—typical Wren.

I move down the hall, my focus on finding Wren amongst the people in the photos, and I smile each time I do, until my heart stops when I see a familiar face. I move in front of it, taking her in. She's a bit younger in this photo than I remember, though not by much, and standing in front of the town hall, all lit up. I supposed I always knew that at some point I'd see the reason I settled on this town, but after not bumping into her, I figured there was a chance she was a part of some lucid dream that had instead led me to Wren.

"Who's that?" I ask, pointing at the woman.

"Who's who?" Wren asks, moving closer to me. A small breath leaves her lips, and when she turns her face to me, there's a melancholy look there, a look that is just as much joy as it is pain before she speaks. "That was my grandmother."

TWENTY-EIGHT

ADAM

The January before last, I had a layover in the Denver airport on my way to New York, but a storm had all planes grounded for the foreseeable future. I was sitting at a bar nursing the dregs of a drink when an older woman sat next to me.

"A glass of white, whatever you recommend," she said, smiling up at the bartender who came over. "And whatever else he wants."

I turned to her and couldn't help it—I smiled. Even though I wanted nothing to do with anyone, being that not only was I stuck in an airport when I should be in the sky, but also because I'd just gotten word that Blacknote Records had rejected all four of the songs I was trying to sell them, I smiled at this woman.

She was in her late seventies to early eighties, by my best guess, with short, gray hair curled on her head and big, wire-rimmed glasses attached to a pink stone chain. She was wearing a light pink cardigan set and had a matching rolling suitcase, which made me wonder if she had chosen that outfit intentionally. The stool was high, and she was short, so she had to give a little hop, grabbing the bar top to help boost herself as she got onto the stool. But once she settled, she let out a deep sigh and turned to me, putting a hand out.

"Dottie," she said.

I stared for a moment, and even though I always made every effort to avoid talking to strangers because there were few things on this earth I hate more than small talk, I shook it. She didn't seem the type that you simply ignored.

"Adam."

"How long have you been stuck here?" she asked.

"Three hours with endless more in sight."

She nodded and smiled. "You looked like you could use some company."

I wanted to argue, to tell her I didn't. To say I didn't need nor want company. But before she had come over to me, I was scribbling out ideas onto a cocktail napkin, trying my best to think of something new to offer the label, and coming up with nothing. Having her here gave me a good excuse not to continue down that depressing path.

"You're right," I said, and when her smile widened and the wrinkles around her mouth deepened, showing me clearly that she did it often, I knew I had made the right choice.

Over the next two hours, she told me everything there was to know about her. She was from a small town and was on a trip because she had gotten a nasty diagnosis recently and wanted an adventure before she was too sick to travel. She was on her way back from an Alaskan cruise when she got stuck in the airport. She had two children, five grandkids, and a great-granddaughter.

In exchange, I confessed my own stories to her, ones I usually kept close to my chest. I was in a band, and I now write music for a living.

I was stuck.

"I'm coming back from a stay in a cabin in Montana. I was hoping it would help with my writer's block," I said as I swirled the dregs of my second drink, casting my eyes down.

"Did it work?" The question wasn't asked the way Greg asked, laced with annoyance or pity. It was a genuine question, like she genuinely wanted the answer.

Still, I gave her a safe one.

"Travel is always worth the adventure," I said, even though I didn't know if I really believed that anymore. She looked me over, clearly reading that it wasn't an answer at all, but appearing to go with it all the same.

"I wish my grandkids were adventurous. They've never left our little town."

I nodded, relieved to be off the topic of my writing. "Oh yeah? And where's that?" I crossed my arms on my chest and leaned back, looking her way.

She smiled widely, as if even the memory of her home brought her joy and peace. "Holly Ridge, New Jersey. The best little town in the whole world."

"Maybe they love it so much they don't want to leave?" I asked, and she shrugged.

"My grandsons, maybe. My granddaughter...she has the bug. She wants to see the world, to travel about."

"But?" I asked. There's always a but.

"But she's so stuck on putting everyone else first. I'm hoping she grows out of that, but who knows." She shrugged, then looked me over. "Maybe she just needs to meet the right person to help her figure out her priorities."

I opened my mouth to tell her that I'm sure her granddaughter would figure it out on her own in due time, especially if she has as close a family as she implied, but a voice came over the loudspeaker, declaring that the storm had eased and my flight would be boarding soon.

"That's me. I gotta go," I said, reaching into my pocket to pull out my card to pay for both of our drinks, but she shook her head.

"No, no, let me."

"Now, Dottie—" I said, ready to argue. If nothing else, my parents taught me manners.

"I've never gotten to buy a famous songwriter a drink. Let me have my moment. You've already paid your dues by spending two hours with me at this bar, listening to me ramble on. I'm sure you had much better things to do."

I stare at her, then shake my head.

"Not much I'd rather have done than hang out here with you."

She gave me that wide smile again.

"I hope you find your muse again, Adam. Good luck."

"I knew her," I whisper, grazing a finger over the glass of the photo and looking more closely. Wren is next to her, and now that I see them both, I see the familiarities. The eyes are nearly the same, and she has her grandmother's smile.

How did I not see it before?

"What?" Wren asks, rightfully confused.

"I met her. Last January. She was stuck at the airport in Denver due to a layover. I was supposed to go home to New York, but the flights were grounded due to a storm. We sat at a bar together. Talked." I shake my head, confused and bewildered by this news, before I turn to her and give her my biggest confession.

"Your grandmother is the reason I'm in Holly Ridge," I say, the words feeling strained as they leave my lips. My pulse is pounding, and adrenaline is making all outside noise dull; my focus is solely on the frame and Wren.

"What?" she asks again, and I shake my head, trying to organize my thoughts and explain to her.

"When I met her at the airport, she told me Holly Ridge was the best little town in the whole world. In October, when I was looking for somewhere to disappear to, I remembered her mentioning it. I found it on a map, found a house, and bought the first one I found." I stare at Wren, stunned silence hanging between us as what I just confessed sinks in.

For a split second, panic fills me, unsure of how she'll respond.

What if it makes her unhappy or sad? What if the grief she's been struggling to contain all month suddenly chooses to surface now? I'll hold her through it, of course, but she wouldn't want to have that moment here, with everyone around.

"Oh my god," she whispers, eyes going wide, mouth spreading in a delighted smile that has my shoulders easing. "She came home and told us she met a celebrity. Showed us a scribbled signature on a cocktail napkin, but she couldn't remember your name, and it was so messy, we couldn't discern it." She lets out a loud laugh. "We thought someone had lied to her to get her to buy him drinks!"

I lift my hands, eager to set the record straight. "In my defense, I wanted to pay for the drinks, really. She insisted."

"Oh, trust me, I know. She was very stubborn." She stares at me, then at the photo, her face etched with awe, though I'm sure it's a different kind than mine.

I move my gaze back to the wall of photos and scan it again, now looking for Dottie King. I see her in almost all of them, many with Wren of various ages at her side, and smile at the way the world works.

I can't believe that the woman I met at the airport, who told me to go to Holly Ridge, is the grandmother of the woman I am quickly realizing I am head over heels in love with.

"I can't believe you met her," she whispers, and when I look back at her, there are tears in her eyes.

"Birdie," I whisper, reaching out to her and pulling her into me, my hand holding her head to my chest as she takes a few deep breaths to calm herself. Then her head tips back to look up at me, her eyes shining but tears not falling.

"I kept thinking she would have liked you, you know? She would have really liked you and been so happy to have someone encouraging me to put myself first, take care of me, and help me set boundaries. She always wanted that for me. But it turns out she already liked you."

"I liked her," I whisper.

She nods. "I'm so glad you met her," she whispers.

I squeeze her a bit tighter. "Me too, Birdie."

She tips her head back once more and stares up at me, and I lift a hand, cupping her cheek and grazing over a single tear that has fallen. I can't help but lean down and press my lips softly to hers. When I pull back, her eyes are dazed, but the grief is gone once more, with adoration and relief and gratitude on her face now.

I've never been in love before, but I know this is the moment. This is when I tell her those three little words.

"Wren, I—"

Then her phone rings, and we both startle. She steps back and lets out a little laugh.

"That's lunch," she says, wiping at her cheeks and shaking her head. "Can you go out and get it for me and bring it into the main room for everyone? I think I need a moment to collect myself."

"Of course," I say, then press my lips to her forehead before she turns and moves toward the bathroom.

As I'm walking toward the door, I realize that's the first time she's ever asked me to do a favor for her without apologizing or feeling guilty. And while it's not those three little words, it almost feels better.

TWENTY-NINE

ADAM

If it wasn't obvious before, I think I've cemented that I will do absolutely anything for Wren. It's why I spent the entire day with her, prepping for tomorrow's holiday festival outside in the freezing cold with her brothers, making the best Christmas gift I could think of.

It's my small way to prove my commitment to the town in a way Wren would understand. Well, maybe the second-best gift, but the second one is going under the tree.

Turns out, she and Hallie were right: her brothers don't actually hate me. After watching them interact for six hours today, I realized that constant poking and prodding is simply how they treat each other. I just couldn't understand it because I don't have experience with brothers, which is what I think they now, in some twisted way, consider me to be.

I think the whole King-brothers-hating-their-little-sister's-new-boyfriend-on-principle thing was also appeased when I got Jesse's number from Hallie and told him my master plan before asking for his and Madden's help. It was a big task to do in one day, so I needed all the help I could get.

An hour passes after her brothers help me clean up and head out so as not to ruin the surprise, and I spend it pacing, both indoors and out, keeping an eye out for her arrival home. I do this both to catch her when she gets home and to check how obvious my surprise was if you weren't looking for it. I'm inside when her car pulls into her drive almost an hour later than anticipated, and I feel like a kid excited for Christmas.

I can't help but smile, wondering if this is how Wren feels every day.

I send her a text telling her to come over when she's finished putting away her stuff, but she doesn't respond right away. After a few minutes, I send her another, and when that one goes seemingly unopened, I decide just to go over and drag her ass over here for our date night. I don't feel the kind of embarrassment I usually feel when showing someone I'm excited about something because I'm headed to arguably the most excited person in the world.

Plus, she is going to love this.

But when I knock at the door, she doesn't greet me with a smile and a kiss in casual clothes like I expect for our night in. Instead, she flings the door open quickly, then moves back to the kitchen, the tails of her hair bow floating behind her as she does.

"Hey, babe, come in, come in!" she says, sliding long tubes into a giant trash bag. There's a massive pile of wrapping paper on the table, along with ribbon and bows, and a dozen reels of tape.

I stare at the mess, confused.

"Uh, what's going on?" I ask, staring at that giant pile of things. All of them are red, green, and holiday patterns. "Everything okay? I texted you."

She turns and grimaces at me before continuing her task. "Shoot, sorry, I haven't checked my phone. I'm just trying to get some things together before I head back to the community center."

I halt and blink at her.

"Back to the community center?"

"Yeah, I have to help wrap the gifts for Santa."

I stare at her and feel my chest sink to the ground. "I thought you had the night off." An unfamiliar dread is curling in my gut, disappointment mixed with frustration.

"I did, but Stevie needed to head out early to help with her kids, so I offered to take over it for her."

I blink at her and try to bite back the flash of anger that moves through me, swift and unexpected. "You offered?"

She pauses what she's doing, clearly hearing my tone, and stares at me with a furrowed brow.

"Well, yeah. If I hadn't, it wouldn't have gotten done, and there's enough to do tomorrow morning that adding that would be cutting it too close. Santa's coming tomorrow, and the gifts have to be wrapped and assigned."

"You offered," I repeat, and this time, it's not a question but a statement. Now the words are low and pointed, and I can't seem to keep the frustration out of them. But I'm finding I also don't want to. That's how I feel, after all, and a part of me wants Wren to know that.

"I didn't really have a choice, Adam. If I didn't, it wouldn't get done. That's how it always goes."

I shake my head and let out a disbelieving laugh.

"Or it would have when they realized you weren't going to swoop in and save the day." Venom is in the words, and she must notice it finally. She drops the ribbons in her hands and turns to me fully now, confusion and a hint of irritation marring her pretty face.

"Why are you making such a big deal out of this? I know I promised to stop offering to help, but we're in a bind, and this has to get done for tomorrow. It's going to be so busy, I won't be able to find the time in the morning."

I stare at her, remembering all the times in my life when I was never put first. Every time, I was made to feel like a nuisance as a child or like I didn't matter as an adult.

The only person who has never made me feel that way was Wren. The first person in town who made an effort to try to get to know me. The one who persistently poked at my shell until it fell apart. The first person to ever take care of me when I was sick.

I try to remind myself of those things as I say my following words with as much neutrality as I can muster.

"We had plans," I say, feeling stupid and childish when I say it aloud. She stares at me, blinking twice, then her face becomes a mask of apology.

She forgot.

"Oh, shoot, Adam, I'm sorry! I should have called and told you. We can do it tomorrow!" She hesitates, then gives me a slight grimace, as if she knows that won't work, not with the festival being tomorrow. "Or the next day?" Another grimace. "Crud, that's Christmas Eve." She hesitates, then takes in a deep breath before giving me a big smile that seems forced. "I'll make it up to you, I promise." She turns back to the table and starts packing, her mind moving a mile a minute. It's obvious she has her long to-do list in her mind, the burden of it weighing on her.

It's precisely why I planned tonight, not just for my surprise, but because I wanted her to have one night of relaxation, a night to get a good night's sleep before the chaos of the holiday truly hit.

"Sure, you will. Unless there's some other crisis that you need to step in for," I say under my breath without even thinking.

She stops what she's doing, noticing something on my face, and then throws up her hands.

"What's wrong, Adam? I'm sorry, really I am, but I have to help. It's what I do, who I am." She takes in a deep breath, and an apology crosses her face. "I am the one people can count on to pick up the slack. I'm the one who says yes. You knew that when you got into this with me." She waves her hands between us, indicating our relationship, I suppose. "I'm working on it, really, I am, but right now, these things need to get done."

I run a hand through my hair and shake my head. "I just don't get why it has to be you. You've been there since six a.m. You've done everything for this. There are a dozen people who could step in; you just have to ask them."

She shakes her head, as if I just don't get it, but I'm beginning to realize it's Wren who doesn't get it.

"Everyone else has things to do. They have families and people waiting for them."

I stare at her, waiting for her words to sink in, and a small, bitter smile spreads on my lips. "I guess that's the problem, isn't it? You drop everything for everyone but won't do it for a date with me."

She looks at me a bit closely, then her face shifts like she's realizing something, like she is surprised by something she sees written on my face. "Are you mad at me?"

I sigh, running a hand through my hair. "I...I don't know. I don't want to be," I tell her truthfully.

She hesitates, and her eyes go pained when they meet mine. "But you are? Mad at me?"

I take in a deep breath, trying to center myself and organize my thoughts, separating them from the hurt feelings and disappointment. "I'm frustrated. I'm disappointed. I'm not convinced you can put yourself first, which makes me worried about what a future between us would look like. I'm frustrated because it feels like the only people who care about you are me and Hallie. I'm aggravated that you think you have to do everything for everyone. I'm annoyed that I asked you to give me tonight, and as soon as someone else needed something, you forgot about it. It makes me feel like I come in last in your world, when I'm starting to realize you come first in mine."

Pain moves over her face, and she steps closer, putting a hand to my chest. "You don't come last, Adam. I'm sorry I forgot, really. It's just such a crazy time, but it's just because it's Christmas. Of course, I would rather spend the night in with you than go back downtown. Of course, I'd rather eat junk and watch movies and cuddle instead of taking on another task that someone else was supposed to do." Her voice wavers, and she takes in a deep, shaky breath. "I'm exhausted, and I want to go to bed, and I want you to hold me, but you're angry at me now. And I get it, I do, I'm the worst, but I don't know—"

Tears well in her eyes, and I sigh, wrapping an arm around her waist and pulling her into my chest. Tears begin to soak my shirt, and I rub her back.

"Wren, baby, it's fine. It's fine. I'll..." I sigh, pushing back at the disappointment. "I just worry about you. I want you to do things for yourself, not for everyone else. I just don't understand why you can't do something for yourself. I don't get why you have to work yourself to the bone, why you always have to be the one to step in and save the day."

"I have to, Adam," she says into my shirt.

I move back, hands cupping her cheek to force her eyes to meet mine before I ask my next question.

"Why?"

"Because...I have to. Because it's who I am." Her eyes go a bit frantic, and panic and uncertainty are written on her face before they spill from her lips. "I have to help. I have to because if this festival isn't amazing, what kind of legacy am I holding for her? The holidays and helping out were her thing, and it's my job to take over it now."

And there it is.

As a tear rolls down her cheek, I get the whole picture.

It's not about upholding some long-standing tradition, not about making the entire town happy.

It's about making her grandmother proud. My sweet girl is still grieving and has channeled all of that into this festival, into the holidays, into filling shoes that she's afraid to walk in. I swipe the tear away with my thumb and shake my head.

"She wouldn't have wanted you to run yourself ragged, Wren. She loved you, and anyone who loves you doesn't want this for you," I say. Her body goes still with my words, and if I were in a different frame of mind, I'd probably realize I should step back now and give her some space. But I'm not, so I don't.

"That's not fair," she says.

"Isn't it? This isn't your job. It's a volunteer position, and it's surely not life or death. No one will get hurt if it's not totally perfect. You don't have to work yourself to the ground just to make everyone else happy." She shakes her head and tries to back away, but I hold her tight.

"It's what my grandmother would have done."

"No, it's not," I say confidently, and she stops everything to look at me, blinking. "And it's definitely not what she would have wanted."

"You don't—"

"I met her, Wren. She talked about you, and I'm telling you, she wouldn't want you doing this to yourself, taking on everything and then some, just to uphold some town's stupid tradition. And she surely wouldn't want you doing it in her name."

She steps away from me then, and I let her as hurt flares in her eyes, though it's quickly smothered by anger. It's foreign to her, but I get that it's easier to be mad than it is to be hurt.

"Oh, fuck off, Adam. You had a drink with her in an airport bar while she was on vacation. I grew up with her. I am who I am because of her."

I shake my head and step closer, reaching for her hand and twining my fingers with hers. "No, you're not. You're you because you're Wren. My sweet Wren, who worries that people won't like her if she doesn't do everything for them. Wren, who believes that with a little more effort, she can tackle anything. If she gives a bit more of herself, everyone will be perfectly happy, even if it leaves nothing left for her. Wren, who is grieving the loss of someone important to her, keeps herself busy to avoid dealing with her emotions. I may not have known her for years and years, but I do know this isn't what she would have wanted for you."

I dip my head a bit, leaning back to look into her eyes better, spotting the hurt and betrayal on her face, but sometimes, you have to go with your gut. And I think it's time for Wren to hear these truths finally. "This isn't the way you should be honoring her, Wren."

It's too far, I think, because she steps further, wiping beneath her eyes, which now have a shield pulled up.

"I have to go," she says low, turning away and moving toward the bags, lifting one over her shoulder.

"What?"

"I said, I have to go. I have things to do."

I shake my head at her in disbelief. "We're in the middle of a conversation."

"No, we're in the middle of you telling me who I should be and what I should do and how things are. I'm sorry that you're unreachable and you only care about yourself, but that will never be me. If you don't like how I have to help the people I love, help my community, then maybe we should end things now."

"That's not fair, and you know it," I say, taking a step closer to her.

She throws her hands in the air like she's done with all of it. "Fine, you care about yourself and me, for some unknown reason."

My own anger sparks. "Don't play that game. We both know the reason, we just haven't had a fucking chance to talk about it because you're too busy wearing yourself to the bone day in and day out! I care because I'm falling for you, Wren! I'm so sorry if my feelings are inconvenient for you, if they get in the way of your working yourself into the ground for people who won't even remember to throw a thank you your way."

Silence fills the room, and my words hang like an anchor between us.

"You're falling for me?" she whispers.

"I've been falling for you since you duct-taped a wreath to my door, but you've been so busy jumping in to help everyone, you haven't been able to notice." She looks at me with hesitation and a touch of uncertainty in her eyes. I sigh and reach out for her hand, and relief washes through me when she lets me hold it. "Please. Stay. Talk to me. This all can wait, Wren. The world won't stop turning if you don't get there right away."

A beat passes, and I think she's going to stop, to stay and talk to me, but then her phone beeps with a new message, and it's like some kind of bat signal, reminding her she's needed elsewhere.

She shakes her head, and I'm relieved to see a bit of apology there.

"They're waiting on me. I can't keep them waiting."

I don't tell her that I was waiting for her. I don't tell her. It won't be productive, because it really won't matter. I've already said too much, pushed her too far. I don't want to push her away for good.

So I nod.

"Okay. Then come to my place tonight," I ask in a whispered plea. She looks at me, a mix of frustration and hurt on her face, the same look I know is mirrored on mine. "I don't care how late it is. Just come over. We'll talk things out, figure it out."

"I don't know, Adam," she sighs, exhaustion in the words, and my stomach drops to my feet.

"Come on. Just come over. We don't even have to talk about things. Let me feed you, get you to bed, hold you. I have something to show you." I don't tell her that a part of me desperately wants to show her my surprise, to just make one shining moment in this terrible mess.

This afternoon, I was so high on excitement and joy, and love. How did it spiral this badly?

"It's going to be extra late," she says.

"I don't care how late it is, Wren. Please."

She bites her lip and opens her mouth to speak, but then her phone rings. She reaches over and checks the screen, then sighs. "That's Nat. I gotta go."

She steps away, slinging the large bag over her shoulder, and then moves to the door, looking at me. I follow slowly, feeling dread in every step, knowing this is going to hang between us until it's fixed, and not entirely knowing if she'll want to fix it if she gets the opportunity to distance herself from it. From me.

Wren doesn't like messy emotions, and she might realize she can avoid them altogether if she avoids me.

I walk her to her car and open the door, watching her slip in. "See you tonight?"

A single strand of hope sparkles between us, and a moment passes, feeling like an eternity.

"We'll see." I know she sees my face dropping, because the smallest sad noise comes from her. I try to mask myself, not wanting to add even more to her full plate.

"Okay," I say with a reluctant nod. "Keep me posted."

She nods, then silence fills the space.

"Later, Birdie."

"Bye, Adam," she says, and I don't miss that she says *bye* instead of *see you later*, and it pierces my chest. She pulls her door shut and starts the car before giving me a small, sad wave.

Then she drives off, taking every ounce of holiday spirit with her.

THIRTY

ADAM

She doesn't come to my house that night, and in my mind, that's her answer. Her car was still missing by the time I begrudgingly went to bed, not that I slept much, keeping an ear out for the sound of tires on her drive. When I woke up to find her car already out of the drive-way, I wondered if she had even come home the night before.

Even though I'm pretty sure she won't be coming home later in the morning since she's planning to do setup and finishing touches at the community center, and the doors open at four, I spend the whole day with an eye on her house, ready to head over there and try to iron this out the second I see her.

I don't, though.

By four, I'm pacing my house and know that the very early part of the celebration has begun, and I can't keep pacing my place indefi-nitely. Without any real plan, I get in my car and start to drive. I drive past the community center, noticing the lot is full and the entire place decked out in Christmas lights, before continuing down the road. In contrast, the lot for The Mill is nearly empty when I pull in, and if I didn't see the neon *open* sign lit up, I'd think it was closed.

The inside looks downright depressing when I walk in, just four customers scattered through the usually busy bar.

When I sidle up to the bar, leaving my phone face up just in case someone reaches out to me—in case *she* reaches out to me—Colton comes up in front of me, an eyebrow raised high.

"Surprised to see you here."

I shrug in indifference. "Surprised you're even open."

"In a small town like this, after the festival starts to wind down, people without families to get home to will need somewhere to go. By nine, this place will be packed."

I nod but don't say anything more. I don't even order a drink; I'm not in the mood at all. In fact, I'm not really sure why I came here, other than that Colt is the only other person I really know in town, and I couldn't stay in my house a minute longer.

"You're not going to the Christmas festival?"

I let out a humorless laugh, thinking about Wren and her family and the whole damn town enjoying a festive time together. "I don't think I'd be very welcome."

Colton's laugh actually contains humor. "Why, because you're the least cheery fuck around?"

"No," I say with a sigh, and then, because I think I crossed the town limits and every aspect of my personality changed, I share. "Wren and I got into a fight."

"Mmm," he says, then pours a beer and slides it over to me. I cup my hands around it, though I don't drink it. "I'm assuming that's why she slept at Hallie's last night?"

"She did?"

He shrugs. "We live in a split house; she's right next to me. Heard them stumble in late last night, and they were chatting a bit early this morning."

Well, at least that explains where she was last night. I'm a bit relieved that she stayed with Hallie, since driving home late and exhausted would have been dangerous.

"What was the fight about?" he asks.

I am not a sharer.

I am not the kind of man who spills personal details with friends or asks for relationship advice. Part of that is because I haven't had a proper relationship to speak of, but also because I value my privacy and prefer to keep things to myself.

So it's a surprise when I find myself spilling it all to Colt.

"We were supposed to spend the night together last night. I had a big surprise for her, and I wanted her to have a relaxing night before her big day. But she forgot that we had made plans and took on another task, which someone else had fallen short on. I was mad, and then she got mad. Then she never came home so we could talk it out, so I kind of figured that was her answer." That all-too-familiar pain lances through me, the same one I felt every time I glanced over at her empty drive.

On the drive here, everything reminded me of her. Every light, every bow, every decoration made that vice on my heart tighten. I didn't miss the irony of coming to Holly Ridge to avoid the holidays and the dread and failure that accompanied them, only to fall in love with Christmas spirit personified. If things between Wren and me are unfixable, I know that the pain I used to feel around the holidays will be a pleasant contrast.

Colton nods as if his argument makes sense to him. "Sounds about right. She and Hallie have had that fight a dozen times over. You should know, if you stay with her, that's a fight you'll probably be fighting for the rest of your life."

I nod, knowing that to be the truth.

But something about the way he says it makes me realize something new: I'm okay with it.

I'm okay with having this argument, standing firm when I know she needs me to, and being flexible when I must. Part of what makes Wren *Wren* is the way she gives so freely. I realize now that I don't want to change that, as I think she fears. I simply want to protect her so she always has the energy to help where it will be most effective, while also prioritizing her own needs.

Even more, I know I let my emotions and disappointment cloud the big picture yesterday. It wasn't the right time to push her, and it surely wasn't the right way. I can't help but wonder how things would have played out if I hadn't. I should have offered to come to the community center and help, even though I can't wrap a gift to save my life. I'm sure she could have found a job for me, something small to get off her plate.

Regret is flooding my veins and my mind, and I almost don't hear Colt when he speaks next.

"You know, the pianist is sick."

My head raises, and my brows furrow in confusion. "What?"

"Yeah, the pianist for the festival. Mr. Mooney. He's been playing there for as long as I can remember, and he provides the only music at the festival, aside from the performances. Something about live piano makes it more festive than a recording or some shit." He shrugs, as if it makes no sense to him, before continuing. "Anyway, he got that nasty cold that's been going around, along with the chorus teacher. I think Wren's going to try and scrounge someone up, but it's also the last minute and the day before Christmas Eve."

My mind is reeling on so many fronts that I don't know where to start.

But mostly, it settles on how stressed Wren must be. If it's a big part of the vibe and experience of the festival, and there is no piano on the first one she's been in charge of, she's going to be a mess. Did she find a replacement? And if she didn't, what would she do? Is she okay?

For a split second, an idea rolls into my mind, but panic surges with it.

I could go.

I could easily play the piano for the festival.

But it would be one step closer to losing the anonymity that I've learned to cherish here. I always told myself it wouldn't be that great.

While it might be nice to grocery shop without being stopped or to meet someone and know there were no other motives to their kindness, that didn't make it *worth it* for me.

But I was so wrong.

It's fucking amazing, and with that burden lifted, I've even gone and made friends with people who I know for a fact like me because I'm Adam Porter, a regular resident of Holly Ridge, not Adam Porter, songwriter or bassist or connection to big names in flashy magazines, for the first time I can remember.

But I only feel that way, feel so settled and accepted here, because of Wren, who, when I told everything to her, didn't even bat an eye. She didn't treat me any differently, didn't stop arguing with me all the time, and didn't start cozying up to me to get something.

Would anything really change if everyone found out who I really was?

I shake my head, trying to knock the thought from my mind. It doesn't matter. If she wanted me to be there, she would have called and asked for my help.

Would she have? The annoying conscience in my head that's starting to sound way too much like Colt's says. *The one time she even joked about it, you freaked out.*

I'm lost in my thoughts, but Colton's following words knock me out of it.

"It would be a great time for some wunderkind musician to come in."

My heart skips a beat, but when I look up at Colt, he's wiping down the bar. I almost think I imagined his words, but a slight smirk plays at his lips. I continue to stare at him until finally, he puts down the rag and leans into his hands on the bar top, looking at me.

That's when I see the truth there: he knows.

"You know?"

"Yeah. I was a huge fan of Midnight Ash. First day you came in, I knew who you were."

"You didn't say anything?"

He shrugs before explaining. "Didn't seem like you wanted anyone else to know, so I kept it to myself."

For the first time in a while, I find myself completely and utterly speechless. This whole time, I thought I was hiding from who I was, that I was experiencing being treated normally for the first time in forever. But maybe that isn't the case at all. Perhaps I just found a place where no one genuinely cares.

"Does anyone else know?"

He shrugs again, which seems to be his primary method of communicating. "I think a couple of people around town have put it together."

I shake my head in disbelief. "No one's ever mentioned it to me."

"Why would they? It's a small town, but we respect boundaries here." I give him a raised eyebrow, and he lets out a laugh. "For the most part. They're a bit nosy, but they mean well."

For a moment, I want to say that no one respects Wren's boundaries, but that's not fair either. Wren hasn't set boundaries for herself, so there aren't really any to respect.

It's something I'm determined to continue to work on.

For as long as she'll have me.

I shouldn't have given Wren so much shit about wanting to help. It's who she is. Sure, she could prioritize herself a bit more, but that's not something that's going to change overnight, much less just because a new man came into her life.

Yesterday, it felt big, the disappointment of it, but the reality is, it's something that, if I want to be with her, I'm going to have to accept, and we're going to have to work on it together. Probably for the rest of our lives, something I'm realizing more and more is what I want with Wren.

But first, I have a festival to get to.

"I gotta go," I say out loud, standing and moving for my wallet, fumbling and dropping it as I do. I grab it and then try to get some cash out, dropping the whole thing once more.

Colt lets out a laugh and shakes his head, waving a hand at me. "It's all good. This one's on me, man. Merry Christmas."

I hesitate for a moment, wondering how the fuck this man turns a profit before realizing I have a mission to get on with. I give him a broad smile and a nod, then head for the door.

"Merry Christmas, Colt," I call over my shoulder, pulling my phone app up to make a call.

THIRTY-ONE

Wren

If I never see another roll of wrapping paper, it might be too soon.

It's all I can think about as I smooth out another red and green striped swath of paper and place a toy on it before slicing the paper to size.

This should have been finished yesterday, but last night we got about halfway through the wrapping before a terrible crash came from the other side of the room, and I looked up to find the stage we had set up the night before had collapsed. It seems the volunteers missed a few nuts and bolts in the assembly. Thankfully, no one was hurt, and even more thankfully, it happened yesterday instead of today with people on it. I called my dad sobbing, and as is his way, he came downtown immediately with my mom and stayed until almost two a.m., fixing and redecorating the stage.

Since it was so late when I finally packed it in, Hallie insisted I stay at her place, not wanting me to drive while so exhausted. I woke up bright and early with a pit in my stomach, and I've been anxiously checking my phone and email for a last-minute piano player, but to no avail. Because apparently, *nothing* can go right, I received a call last night that Mr. Mooney, the pianist, was down with a cold and unable to play. Just my luck, my backup, the choir teacher, is also down with the same thing.

We've *always* had live music for the festival, with my grandmother insisting it made everything more cheerful and intimate in a way that prerecorded tracks never could. However, this year it seems that's one thing that isn't going to happen.

I tell myself that it will be fine, that the festival will still be amazing, and I'm just getting the hiccups out of the way early as I smooth the paper over the side of a box holding a doll.

The decorations are up, and they are more spectacular than ever. The stage is perfectly decorated and even more secure than before. On one wall are more baked treats than I think have ever been at this event, and despite myself, I know it's because I insisted I couldn't be the one to take it all on. Instead, I called my mom and told her we needed baked good donations, and she called up her friends, all of whom eagerly pitched in.

People will help; they just need to know you need it. I can almost hear Adam saying that in my head, but I brush it away quickly. Guilt over forgetting our date remains intertwined with the hurt and anger from our conversation. Still, I don't have time for anything other than productivity and holiday cheer, so I've forced myself to put it off and deal with all of that later.

For now, I'm finishing up wrapping the gifts for Santa to give out to all the kids tonight, and even though my brothers are supposed to be helping me, it's just me on my knees getting papercut after papercut while they pretend to do their own but haven't wrapped more than a gift each. Mom is making sure the treat table is all set up with boxes for people to take extras home and plenty of tongs to keep germs away while Dad lugs in the drinks.

When I look around, I know I've done a great job with the decorations, craft tables, activities, and more. It's the best holiday festival to date and one people will be talking about all year long.

And I've never felt less festive in my life.

"Dude, you need to get out," Madden says, leaning back against a wall, a roll of wrapping paper spread out in front of him, though there isn't even a gift on it. He's not even bothering to pretend. Though I try to ignore the irritation their blatant lack of help brings me, it bubbles beneath my skin.

"Yeah, I'll be sure to fit that in between work at the farm, keeping my house clean, and making sure my daughter doesn't grow up with daddy issues," Jesse says under his breath.

"When was the last time you went on a date?" There's a beat of silence, and Madden groans. "Dude." Jesse, to his credit, is pretending to wrap a gift, though he's doing it painfully slowly. In the time I've wrapped five gifts, he's still on one. "That's it. We're going to the city the Friday after Emma goes back to school. You're getting laid."

"And this is when I remind you that I have a kid and can't just fuck off wherever I want. You know that Mom and Dad go on their trip the first week of January."

They've done that since we were kids: prioritizing their relationship after the chaos of the holidays and spending a week somewhere tropical to decompress. Every year, when my dad gifts my mom the trip, she acts shocked and confused, but by now, everyone knows they'll be gone and plans for it a month in advance.

"Oh, well, Wren can watch her," Madden says with a shrug. "What about Friday? We can go to the city and hit a couple of bars. I'll pick you up at six; you just gotta drop Emma at Wren's for a sleepover at five. That way, you don't even have to worry about feeding her."

This isn't happening.

This can't be happening.

There is no way they are making plans about me without *consulting* me, right? Surely, Jesse, my older, wiser brother, will mention how crazy that is. Surely—

"I mean, I guess that could work. I'd have to be back the next day by three to receive a delivery at the farm, though." Jesse turns to me, finally, and I wait for him to ask if it would work for me.

That doesn't happen.

"She has ballet in the morning at nine, you could take her to that, right?" Jesse asks.

My hands shake a bit as I sit back, staring at my brother with wide eyes.

Something in me snaps.

Something that no amount of Christmas spirit, a fake smile, or putting on blinders can mend.

The fact that no one *bothered* to ask if I had anything going on, and that my brothers are making plans involving me without even *consulting* me, reminds me of everything Adam has said in the past month or so.

I need to put myself first more. I need boundaries. I need to be comfortable saying *no*.

It's not about being selfish, though. That's where he got it wrong, I think. The word *selfish* makes it sound bad, like I'm screwing everyone over despite something stupid and silly for *myself*.

The fury rushing through my veins is not about being selfish. It's about demanding the respect I deserve.

I'd be happy to give up every Friday for the foreseeable future to help my family, support Jesse, and spend more time with Emma.

But I *deserve* the basic decency of being *asked* if I am willing to make that change in my schedule.

I toss the scissors down and turn to my brothers, rage in my veins. "Are you fucking kidding me?" I ask, loudly. Both of my brother's eyes go wide, though I don't know if it's because I just threw a pair of scissors or cursed. Both, probably.

"Wren Taylor King!" my mother says, aghast, head snapping my way despite her being across the room. "Be careful with that!"

I have no patience or mind for my mother, though. My ire is directed wholly at my brothers, even though it's something that's been welling and not just from them.

"Why is it always assumed I can just drop everything and help?" I snap.

"What?" Jesse asks.

"Everyone assumes I'll just *drop everything* and fix every single problem. That I'll cancel whatever I may have had going on to help out. You don't even bother to *ask* anymore! It's like I'm just someone you all go to when you *need* something, but no one ever thinks about what *I* need. Or what I can handle, or what I *want* to do!"

"Wow, Wren, calm down," Madden says, eyes wide and tinged with humor, which makes my anger bubble over even more. I stand then, take a step toward him, and push him on his chest. He's sitting and topples a bit, catching himself on his hands.

"No! I won't calm down. I'm tired! I'm *exhausted*! I haven't had a full night's sleep that wasn't plagued by my to-do list scrolling through my head in a long time. God, I don't even know how long it's been. The summer? Because I'm always doing things for everybody else! Everyone just assumes I'll do it. Popcorn garland? Oh, Wren can stay up late three nights in a row and string popcorn until her fingers bleed. After-school care? Wren loves those kids! Of course, she'll take on *everyone's* duty for it! Bottle-feeding fucking *kittens*? Let's ask Wren, even though she doesn't even know anything about fucking kittens!"

My brothers are both staring at me now with wide, shocked gazes, and my eyes are starting to water, my throat beginning to burn as months' worth of frustration, disappointment, and exhaustion explode from me.

"I am so fucking *tired*. No one ever asks *me* if I need anything!"

"Wren, honey," my mom says softly, and somewhere, I register that she and Dad are nearing me with that look you have when you step toward an injured, wild dog, but I don't stop.

I *can't* stop. It all spills out.

"The only person who ever cared was Grandma; she was the only one who cared if this festival was good, if the school was decorated, and if every kid on the gift tree got something, and if the fucking streets were all decorated, and she did it for *years flawlessly*. Now I'm stuck doing it, and everybody assumes I'm just going to *do* it and do it just as well as her for my first time and not need anyone to help me at all, while also continuing to do *everything* for *everyone*." I take in a jagged breath that hurts as it enters my lungs, as I fight back the tears that have wanted to spill over all day.

"And even though I'm terrified of disappointing everyone, I'm doing it. I'm doing it the way she would have wanted, to make her proud, but she had *me* to help her, and I have *no one to help me now*. And I scared off the one person who tried to convince me to put myself first! Not even all the time! He just wanted me to set boundaries once in a while so I wouldn't burn out like I am *right freaking now!* And now I'm probably going to die alone, and this is the first time in twenty-seven years that the festival won't have music, as someone so kindly reminded me, and the first time in sixty that Blue Bird Lane won't be totally lit up, and I'm *failing!*"

A tear falls, and a part of my mind is together enough to note with relief that the only people in the room right now are my family. I'm not sure if Mom and Dad ushered them out when they noticed I was breaking or if it's been just us for a bit, but I'm relieved all the same. My shoulders drop with exhaustion, like that outburst took the very last drop of my strength from me. "But sure, I'll watch Emma while Jesse goes and gets his dick wet."

"Wren, I—" Jesse starts, eyes filled with remorse.

"Stop. It's fine. It doesn't..." My voice trails off as I put my head in my hands, a million thoughts and feelings flashing through my mind. Grief and disappointment and heartbreak and fear all course through me on loop, and my breathing comes in shorter and shorter gasps as I try to keep it together. I know my brothers are staring at me, shocked and bewildered and unsure of what to do, and that's not fair to them. I shouldn't be doing this right here, right now. It's not fair that I'm directing this outburst at them.

I need to get it together. I need to take a few deep breaths in and—

"Wren, honey, come here," a familiar voice says, and when I lift my head, I see him.

My dad.

The quiet, easygoing man who does what my mother asks without question, who shakes jingle bells outside every kid's house on Christmas Eve to make them think that Santa is here just to keep the magic alive. The one who quietly delivers trees and lights to houses that remain unlit, the one who grew up with my grandmother telling him nothing is more special than Christmas spirit and community.

The one who lost his mom nine months ago.

His eyes are warm and knowing, and he opens his arms for me. Like I've done a million times in my lifetime, I run into my dad's arms.

"Dad, I messed up," I say, sniffling and biting back tears. That single statement encapsulates so, so many things, but I don't have to expand: it's my dad. He knows.

"No, you didn't, sweetie. You were doing what you thought was right, trying to make everyone happy. But you need to learn to say no every once in a while. That would solve a lot of these problems," he says, rocking me back and forth and rubbing a hand on my back.

"I know," I whisper.

"And you need to share your problems."

"I know," I repeat. A long beat passes, and I think he's just letting me collect myself before he speaks again, and I realize he was actually weighing his words.

"This isn't what she would have wanted for you."

My body goes still at the familiar words, but in my dad's arms, I don't feel the same uncalled-for anger I did in my living room when Adam said it. Instead, I feel a terrible mix of guilt and grief washing over me.

I pull back to stare at him. "That's not fair—" I start anyway, he shakes his head, pulling me in tighter, his voice going lower.

"I miss her, too, honey. So much. And I know this is your way of keeping her alive. And I'm sure she's up there watching and in awe of all you've accomplished by yourself. But she's also frustrated that you haven't asked for the help you need, that you look like you could fall asleep standing. She was always busy this time of year, but what you don't realize is that all the years you saw her running this thing, she was retired. Sure, she was taking on a lot, but she didn't have a classroom of kids to manage every day." I scrunch my nose. "She also said no and delegated more. If she saw how thin you were, wearing yourself down, she'd be worried, Wren. This isn't what she would have wanted."

I let a lot of time pass as his words sink in, creating and discarding a million different responses before one slips through the cracks.

"Adam said the same thing," I whisper around the lump in my throat.

"He's a smart man," my dad says simply. "I like him for you."

"I yelled at him when he said it."

My dad pulls back to look at me and raises an eyebrow before he laughs, shaking his head.

"Now that? That's your grandmother through and through. Acting on impulse and then coming down from it and having to put the pieces back together."

Despite it all, I give him a small, sad smile. With his words, memories of my grandmother's temper return, the way it would flare hot and she'd snap, but then how she'd come back and talk it out after.

You always have to talk it out, Wren. Life is too short to let a little argument ruin a friendship, she told me once, when I asked why she was being kind to one of her knitting circle friends whom I had watched her fight with the week before.

If it's too short to let bickering ruin a friendship, it's undoubtedly too short to ruin what Adam and I have.

I nod then, stepping back and out of my dad's arms. When I turn, Mom, Madden, and Jesse are all watching me, Mom, wiping a tear from her eyes.

You always have to talk it out.

"Sorry, I snapped at you. I was generally frustrated by people asking favors of me and assuming I'd step in, and you were an easy target. I'm still annoyed that you didn't ask, but I get that we're family, and I have made it clear that I'm always available to watch Emma," I say to Jesse, then turn to Madden. "I love you, but you take my kindness for granted, and it's unfair."

"I know, Wren. I'm sorry. I'm a dick," he says, a genuine apology written on his face.

I nod, then give him a small smile. "You are, but I forgive you."

He lets out a laugh, then reaches over and pulls me in for a hug. After Madden, Jesse tugs me over to him, and he gives me one as well.

One more person to talk to, but he's going to have to wait.

But not for that long. I turn to my dad.

"Can you and Mom handle cleanup at the end?" I ask. "Just the basics. I'll do the big cleanup and breakdown after the holidays, since it can wait. Just any food and trash cans, and whatnot. I know you have so much—"

"I have been waiting for you to ask for my help, Wren, sweetie. My god, you're stubborn," my mom says, coming over and brushing a tear from my cheek. "Are you going to talk to him after?"

I nod. "He won't come today, not after the way I left and then ignored him last night." My mom raises an eyebrow, but I shake my head, not wanting to get into it. "I can't fix things right now, but I want to get over there as soon as everything is over."

Mom nods. "That's a good plan."

Before I can say anything, Hallie enters with Emma, and everyone uses it as an opportunity to change the subject, which I am grateful for. Madden and Jesse return to wrapping and accomplish a surprising amount with the patient guidance of Mom, while I put out fires and complete the finishing touches. However, the whole time, I repeat my new plan for the night in my head.

I'm going to make it through this festival. I'm going to do it with a smile, and everyone is going to enjoy it because it's a fabulous event that I put a ton of work into and because it's just what Holly Ridge does. We come together, and we celebrate the community we've created.

And then when it's over, I'm going to be selfish.

I'm not going to worry about take-down or cleanup. I'm going to trust that it will get handled.

Instead, I'm going to find Adam and tell him I'm head over heels in love with him and hope against all hope he'll forgive me.

"Okay, so it's a bit of a different concert tonight, as Mr. Mooney came down with the flu, and despite my many talents and my mother's disappointment, I've never learned to play more than 'Twinkle Twinkle Little Star' on the piano." The room laughs, and it eases me a bit despite the ache that the night at Adam's piano causes in my chest.

Tonight is not going to be a failure.

And if things go my way, I'll have a lifetime with Adam to teach me how to play the piano, in case this happens again.

THIRTY-TWO

ADAM

"So we won't have any live music to go with the performances. Thankfully, we were able to unearth an old CD player, so we're just going to—" My excuses are interrupted, though, when someone plays a line on the piano, almost like they're testing out the keys, seeing if it's in tune before it moves to a jazzy rendition of "Jingle Bells."

The room breaks into excited whispers before I turn toward the piano to see who is making the noise.

My heart skips a beat when I see familiar hazel-green eyes locked on mine, a familiar crooked smile on full lips, scruff that absolutely needs some trimming, and dark hair that looks like rough fingers have gone through it a dozen times in the last hour.

Adam.

Adam is here, and he's sitting at the piano.

My heart pounds when his face goes soft and a smile tugs at the corners of his mouth.

"Uh, give me a second, will you?" I say into the microphone before sliding it into the stand and scurrying over to the piano. Adam's eyes and then his body follow me, turning on the bench as I round the corner to him before tipping my head for him to follow me.

"What are you doing here?" I ask as soon as we move away from the stage. The high school dance team is doing a last-minute rehearsal in the corner, and the middle school kids are still sorting themselves out onto the risers on the stage, but I can't focus on any of that. All I know is that Adam is here, in front of me, love in his eyes.

"I heard you needed some music," he says when we stop moving. He steps closer to me until we're just a foot apart, and I stand there, awkward and unsure of what I should be doing or saying.

He's here, helping me after I was a total brat to him.

How did he know?

Why is he here?

Is he mad at me?

"You didn't have to come, Adam," I say. I so badly want to reach out, to grab his hand, for him to put a hand on my hip and pull me into his chest, but I don't.

"I know," he starts. The dimple in his cheek deepens, and I desperately want to brush a thumb over it. "I wanted to. As you know, I only do things I want to do." My heart throbs just a bit with his words, and my throat swells. His hand comes up, brushing along my cheek, and I melt a bit into his touch. "And I wanted to be here. For you."

"I thought you were mad at me."

"I was frustrated and disappointed, but I wasn't mad at you. I wanted to talk last night, but—"

I sigh, nodding and cutting in. "It was a long night. The stage collapsed, and it was a scramble to fix it and redo everything. By the time we were done, I was too exhausted to drive home safely, so I crashed at Hallie's."

A beat of relief washes over his face, and I realize then that I should have set my own nerves and embarrassment aside and at least sent him a text. He opens his mouth to say something, but before he can, I interrupt.

"I'm sorry," I say quickly.

"Wren—"

"No, please. I need to say this."

He shakes his head, but he doesn't stop me when I continue.

"I'm sorry I forgot about our plans, and I'm sorry I played it off like it wasn't important. It was, and you are. I'm not used to having someone hold a mirror to my face like that, and I wasn't prepared for the way it made me feel, but that's on me, not you. I was hurt and sad, and I took that out on you. I promise that starting today, I'm working on finding a balance of wanting to help everyone and prioritizing myself and my happiness." I give him a wonky, watery smile, then shrug. "I even asked my parents to head the crew cleaning up after the festival so I can go home quicker. I needed...I needed to talk to you as soon as possible."

"You asked them for help?"

I nod, then bite my lip. "It was after I shouted at my brothers and had a meltdown."

His eyes go wide then, and I can't help but laugh a bit before I shake my head gently. "It's been a very long day. I'm just trying to say that I'm sorry, and I had made plans to come to you as soon as I could to beg you to forgive me. I know I'm a mess, and I promise I'm working on it. You've been so patient. I just—"

I don't get to finish my rambling because he cuts me off by pulling me into him and pressing his lips to mine. Instantly, all the nerves, stress, and overthinking from the last twenty-four hours leave my body. His lips move over mine, soft and sweet, as his hand slides up and under my hair, pulling my face closer to his. In the simple kiss, we share everything: apology, acceptance, joy, love, and maybe even a little bit of Christmas cheer.

It's the best kiss I've ever had.

"Uh, Wren," Nat says in a whisper, breaking our kiss. "Love that you two are making up and all, but the crowd is getting restless, and we've got, like, a minute before the middle schoolers start telling fart jokes on stage."

I let out a laugh and look up to Adam.

"Sorry. I—"

"I know," he says. "Come on. Let's do this thing."

That's when I realize he means together.

And at the end of the day, despite the hiccups, it's the best holiday festival Holly Ridge has ever seen.

THIRTY-THREE

Wren

Hours later, my dad promises to drive my car back later, and Adam drives me home, his fingers entwined with mine the whole drive.

We move down Blue Bird Lane, and despite it all, when I see the one house nearly perfectly dark, disappointment fills me.

It's the only house not lit.

It's fine, I tell myself. *It doesn't matter.* My dad is right. Grandma wouldn't care. In fact, she would absolutely get a kick out of the man I fell for, not being a fan of Christmas and decorations, though she would encourage me to continue bugging him about it, if only because she loved drama.

When we park in his drive, he turns to me, leaning forward and pressing a hard kiss to my lips before beaming at me, seemingly giddy.

"What?" I ask with a grin of my own, a bit confused, but the look on his face is absolutely contagious.

He shakes his head, not answering before he tips his head to the side. "Come on."

Then he steps out of his truck, the door slamming shut. I watch as he jogs around the front, comes to the passenger side, opens it, and pulls me out.

"*Come on,*" he repeats, then takes my hand and tugs me to the sidewalk outside his house. He stands behind me, hands going to my shoulders before turning me to face his house. Looking over my shoulder at him, I raise a confused eyebrow.

"Stay here," he whispers before stepping away.

"What?" He's getting more and more confusing, and I can't help but wonder if maybe he got as little sleep last night as I did.

"Stay here. I have to show you something."

"Adam, it's freezing," I say with a laugh.

"I know, I know. But just stay here. It'll be worth it."

I roll my eyes, then watch as he jogs into his house. I stay where he left me, watching him unlock the door and then enter, leaving it open. Then he pokes his head out, the widest smile on his lips. He looks like an excited little boy, and my intrigue goes even higher. What is he doing?

"Oh, I can't wait to see this," a voice says, and when I turn, the Caufields and their two girls are staring up at Adam's house.

"See what?"

"He was working on this all day yesterday with your brothers."

I turn fully to her, confused. "*My* brothers?" They didn't mention Adam at all today.

"It didn't light up yesterday, so I figured there was a problem," Mr. Caufield muses.

Light up?

"Ready, Birdie?" Adam calls, and when I look at him, I notice something I didn't before.

A cloud must move, revealing moonlight that shifts, glows, and gleams, reflecting on tiny dots all over his house.

My heart skips a beat.

Is that....

Then it happens.

Adam hits a switch or plugs something in—I can't tell because I'm lost in the shock of the moment—but the next thing I know, *I'm blinded*. Thousands and thousands of tiny lights glow from his home, illuminating every corner of his house. It's so bright I have to squint a bit, and clapping erupts from behind me, accompanied by cheers from what I now realize is a good chunk of the neighborhood.

There aren't any crazy decorations on the lawn other than the ones I've been sneaking on, and it's just a fuck ton of white lights except for a few strands of green garland that I know to be new, but the house is all decked in lights, perfectly decorated. My eyes start to water as I look up at him on the steps, his grin illuminated by the lights.

He did this for me.

"Ready?" he calls out down the walkway.

"There's more?"

Somehow, his grin gets wider before he looks down at his phone and hits something there.

That's when the music starts.

My heart beats rapidly as I watch it happen, as the lights start to blink in time with an all too familiar holiday song: my favorite holiday song.

One the man in front of me wrote.

"All Lit Up."

I shift my gaze back to the steps, looking for Adam, but he's already moving toward me, then stepping behind me, forcing my back to his front and putting his hands on my hips. He ducks down, his chin resting on my shoulder.

"What do you think?" His voice is low in my ear, words only for me.

"Adam... this is..."

The house starts twinkling along, and tears fill my eyes, especially as I look down the street both ways and realize it's completely lit up. Every home is glowing, the magic of the season fully activated. The music plays, the lights blinking on and off in time with the song, and I have to swallow a lump in my throat before I turn in Adam's arms. "You didn't have to do this for me," I say low.

"Are you mine?" he asks, and there's a twinkle in his eyes as he says the words we've exchanged a handful of times now.

"Yeah, Adam. I'm yours."

"There is nothing I wouldn't do to show you how I feel about you."

"All Lit Up"—his song, the song he told me he hates, the one that sits as a reminder of things he hasn't accomplished yet—rings out loud as the lights adorning every inch of his home blink on and off.

But all I can do is stare at him.

"You hate this song. And you hate Christmas."

He shakes his head. "I might not love the holidays the way you do, and I'm warning you now, I probably never will."

I look at him through watery eyes. "I don't think anyone loves Christmas the way I do, Adam."

A soft expression takes over his face as a hand on my waist lifts to brush away the tear I didn't realize had fallen. "But I came to Holly Ridge, and I found that there's a bright side to Christmas. It's not the lights, and it's not the tree, and it's not the songs or the presents."

My lower lip wobbles, and even though I tell myself it's because it's been a long, emotional day and I'm running on little sleep, I know that's not why.

He pulls me in closer and whispers, "It's that right there." My brow furrows, but he doesn't make me wait for the explanation. "It's the way your face lit up when the lights went on, when you saw the way it was bright and shining. That? That's the brightest part of my year, Wren. I can't be mad at Christmas or Christmas lights, not when they brought me you."

"Adam, I—" I start but stop when his hand moves, tucking a few loose strands behind my ear, and he gives me the softest, sweetest smile.

It's one I've seen before when my dad looks at my mom, and my heart begins to race.

"I love you, Wren," he says simply. He's a man who has written some of the most heartfelt lyrics I've ever heard, someone who is a master of words and making them count, and somehow, I can't imagine more beautiful words coming from his lips.

"I love you, too," I whisper. The song continues to play behind me, the lights flickering on and off, my neighbors becoming carolers as they sing along, as Adam dips his head down.

And then he's kissing me, and the world feels magical and perfect and bright.

And it has nothing to do with the lights.

EPILOGUE

ADAM

"So, here's the thing," Leo says into my ear as Wren brushes something over her eyelids in the bathroom, a room over. She turns to me as if she knows I'm watching, her eyes lighting up when they meet mine before she blows me a kiss before returning to her makeup. "I can't guarantee anything. Despite what anyone tells you, I'm human. However, I do have a large network of contacts. If you want to disappear into bumfuck nowhere and never have the press bother you, I can work some magic. But that's also assuming no one in the town wants to out you, et cetera."

I nod with understanding, even though he can't see it, then turn my back to Wren so I can focus on the conversation at hand.

Leo and I are in the final conversation about him taking me on as a client after his lawyer reviewed my contract with Greg and determined that nothing legally tied me to my former agent. While Greg would continue to receive royalties for previous projects I did with him as my agent, he has no legal tie to anything moving forward if I so choose.

When Greg caved and confessed that he had wanted me to do more Christmas songs, as they *were an easy sell and less work for him*, I fired him on the spot, which means I'm in the market for a new agent.

I just finished telling Leo I would like to write and produce, but would be doing so primarily from Holly Ridge, and I would like to do so without attracting too much public attention. I want to live a simple life now that I've gotten a taste of it, and it seems Leo is on board with that.

"That's fine. I don't mind doing press junkets when needed, but I want the focus to be on the music, not me. I want to be as uninteresting as possible, so no one even cares about me."

"Got it, we can make that happen," Leo says. Another weight leaves my chest, though I wasn't actually worried about his accepting that demand. It's more about having confirmation that I can actually balance both aspects of my life, which eases the small bit of nerves lingering in my chest.

I turn to the balcony of the room Wren and I are staying in, the Eiffel Tower beyond lit up as Leo continues to rattle off terms for the contract he's sending over for me.

I took Wren to Paris.

It was her Christmas present, something I had coordinated and planned in under a week with the help of Hallie. She contacted everyone whom Wren had promised favors to on my behalf and quietly asked them to find someone else, knowing that would be Wren's first reason to turn down my gift. School would be the second reason, but since New Year's landed in a weird spot this year, it meant winter break was a bit longer than usual.

I jumped on the opportunity to take her away as soon as possible, before she could overthink anything. I gifted her the tickets, along with some luggage and a few odds and ends, on Christmas Eve when we exchanged gifts (a necessity since she didn't want to gift me risqué lingerie in front of her parents, whose house we went to bright and early on Christmas morning), and we left on the twenty-sixth. We're only here for a week, heading home on the third so Wren can get back to work on Monday, but I'm already dreaming up plans for spring break and a longer trip over her summer vacation.

Wren wants to travel, and I'm going to give everything to the woman who gives everything to everyone else. That unused passport is about to become mighty full if I have my way.

Our first day here, we attended the last day of the Christmas market in Strasbourg, knowing from my research that Wren would find it absolutely magical. We then explored the city of Paris, finding every other Christmas market that was still open for the season. Yesterday, I took her on a self-guided *Madeline* tour I found on the internet, and she had a blast pointing out all of the different locations with awe and excitement.

Now she's getting ready for dinner at the Eiffel Tower while I wrap up my call with Leo, who, as soon as I sign the contract, will be my new agent.

"It all sounds great," I say, even though I'm barely listening. My new lawyer has already reviewed the contract, one not recommended to me by Greg, to confirm it looks good, and I've received the go-ahead. "You're hired, Leo."

"Perfect. I'll send the contract to you now. In about an hour, some onboarding documents will be sent to your inbox. Take your time filling them out; there's no rush. Our first project together is already a sure thing. Willa's been sending me concept ideas for a music video for 'Are You Mine'? Already."

My heart pounds with his words.

I finished the song on Christmas Eve while Wren baked more cookies than anyone could eat to take to her mom's house the next day, and she cried when I played it for her.

It's the song I started the first night I had Wren.

"I don't want to be pushy, I—"

"Are you mine?"

The title I found the first night she let me help her out.

"Are you mine?"

"Yeah, Wren. I'm yours."

"I take care of what's mine, Adam."

The bridge I wrote as soon as the headache wore off after she took care of me.

"Are you mine?"

"Yeah, Adam. I'm yours."

I finished the song the day after I told her I loved her.

And now Willa Stone is telling me it's going to be the lead single for her next album.

"It's going to be a hit," Leo says. "I have a solid eye for this kind of thing, and I'm telling you, it's going to be Song of the Year, if I have my way."

My breathing hitches in my chest at the thought. "The contract should be in your inbox," he says, as if he didn't just promise me my biggest dream. I shake my head to clear it so I can focus.

"I'm on vacation now, but I should be around to sign the contract tomorrow morning."

"Great, I'll keep an eye out for it." There's typing in the background, and even though it's New Year's Eve, I know Leo takes breaks for nothing. "I think this is going to be a great relationship, Adam. Enjoy your vacation, and we'll start the new year off with a bang."

"All right, sounds good. Talk to you later," I say, then hang up.

Endorphins rush through me as I toss my phone to the bed, and I let out a deep breath, hoping to release them a bit. When I spot Wren leaning over the vanity in the sweet little silk robe I bought her in one of the gift shops we visited the other day (she told me she couldn't accept it and had no use for a silk robe, to which I told her it would really be a gift for myself, something I'm realizing was absolutely the truth), I get a better idea and move across the luxury hotel we're in.

When I make it to where she is, I reach for her, pulling her up and into my arms and giving her a hard, deep kiss. Her body melts into mine, her hand moving up to cup my chin and moving to her tiptoes to better reach me. My hand slides down to her ass, and I cup a cheek, squeezing it as I break the kiss.

"What was that for?" she asks with a giggle as I rest my forehead against hers.

"I need you," I say, pushing her hips into mine so she can feel *exactly* what I mean by that.

"Adam, we can't, we don't have time—" she starts, but I cut her off, bending down to press a kiss to her neck.

"Are you mine?" I ask, low and gruff.

She hesitates, and her breathing hitches, the pulse in her throat speeding up beneath my lips.

"To do with what you please," she whispers, and I groan into her neck, then put my hands to her waist, lifting her and placing her on the edge of the vanity. Makeup tubes scatter, but they're the least of my worries.

I press kisses to her lips, chin, and neck as my hands move to her shoulders, sliding the robe off. It slowly slides down, revealing her full breasts, and her arms shrug out of it completely before she lifts her hands to pull my face down to hers. The kiss is hot and messy and filled with a need I know only she can ease.

I slide my hands down her sides and realize she's not wearing a bra, something I take full advantage of when I cup her full breasts, tweaking the nipples between thumb and forefinger. She arches into my touch, a soft moan falling from her lips. One hand travels down further, and as I graze over her soft belly and hip, I realize she's not wearing *any* undergarments. I groan when my fingers touch her hot pussy, already wet for me. She moans as I ghost my fingertips over her clit before going lower. She leans back a bit, tipping her hips so I can have better access.

I slide a finger into her, and a breathy sound falls from her lips as her pussy tightens around me. I groan at the feel, then slide out and add another finger, slowly fucking her. I don't have time to drag this out, to give her orgasm after orgasm as I enjoy doing, but I always have time to play with this pretty cunt.

"Adam," she moans. "Please. More."

"You'll get what I give you right now," I say, my gaze shifting from her center to her eyes. "And right now, I'm giving you two fingers." She pouts, and I laugh despite my hard cock. "I give you everything you want, but we're on a time limit, Wren. So I'm taking the lead. But I always make you feel good, don't I?"

She licks her lips before nodding.

Then, as if to tell me she trusts me completely and to do whatever I want, she leans back slightly onto her hands and spreads her legs wider before looking down her body at me. Her lips part, and her breathing becomes heavier as she watches me finger her. When my fingers pull out, glistening with her wetness, she moans.

"My Birdie likes to watch, doesn't she?" I ask, thinking of all the ways I could make that happen in the future, wanting to give my girl anything she wants. She nods, eyes not leaving where my fingers continue to thrust into her. I add a third finger, stretching her to take me in a few moments, and her pussy tightens around me. Her breath hitches as I bend them a bit, grazing against the spot that makes her body quake.

"Yes, yes," she whimpers, hips moving.

I can tell she's close, but this is not how she's going to finish.

Not today, at least.

My hand slides free of her, and she mewls out a protest, but I silence it by sliding my wet fingers into her mouth. The mewl turns into a groan as she sucks, and my free hand moves to the fly of my pants, undoing the button deftly before pulling my cock out and sliding my fingers out of her mouth.

"Please," she whispers, reaching for my cock and widening her legs, but I shake my head in a taunt.

"Not like this."

Her brows furrow in confusion, face tinged with irritation. "
Adam—" she starts, but then I'm grabbing her by her hips, lifting and
turning her before using my foot to turn the chair so the back is to the
mirror, and setting her on her knees into the chair.

The angle is fucking perfection, just like I thought it would be.

"You want to watch, sweetness?" I murmur, gripping my cock
and stroking it as my other hand moves to the small of her back,
pushing and sliding up as she bends at her hips over the back of the
chair. She looks fucking gorgeous like this, bending over, hands on
the vanity, back arched to show off her pretty, dripping cunt. I can't
help but trail a knuckle through her.

"Yes. Fuck, yeah."

I smile at her in the reflection, eyes wild with need and lust, hips
moving and shifting, trying to find some kind of relief. "You want to
watch me fuck you?" I step closer to her, a hand resting on her ass.

"Please, Adam," she moans as I notch the head of my cock into
her, then hold her eyes in the mirror. "I want to watch you fuck me. I
want to watch you make me come, and then I want to watch you fill
me up."

I groan at the determination in her words, the iron will that is so
new and so fucking sexy, the one she really only pulls out when we're
like this, when she knows I won't do a thing until she asks for what
she wants.

And so I give it to her, slamming in deep and without warning.
She drops forward, hair grazing the counter as a deep, guttural moan
leaves her lips. I hiss at the pleasure of it, then move a hand, gripping
her hair and lifting her head back until she's facing the mirror again.

"Fucking watch, Wren," I say, holding her hair tight in my hand
as I slide in and out of her with ease, making her tighten around me
again. She likes it when we get like this, when I tell her what to do,
when I give her my *own* demands. She's never tighter around me
than when I start bossing her around like this.

My perfect little people pleaser.

"It's so hot," she murmurs, panting.

"Fuck," I groan, loving that I get to watch both angles like this, my hands framing the vision of her pussy taking my cock, her ass bounding with each thrust, as well as being able to watch every single change across her expressive face.

I'm shocked we've never done it before.

I sure as fuck will be doing it more, now that I know it's an option.

We continue like this, my hands on her hips, holding her where I want her, fucking her hard, my gaze moving from the mirror to watch her tits bounce and her jaw drop when I go particularly deep, to her cunt that's taking me so fucking perfectly. After a minute or so like that, her hand leaves the counter and moves to shift between her legs, but I grab it, setting it back on the counter before returning to holding her hips. She gives a confused look, then tries again.

This time, I pull back a hand and smack her ass, her own halting on its journey to her clit. Her eyes are wide, both with shock and desire, when they meet mine again.

"Adam—"

"No hands. Only my cock this time." I now know from experience that Wren can, in fact, come from my cock and my cock alone, and that's what I want. "Keep your hands on the vanity."

"Adam," she whines. "I can't—" She tightens around me all the same, liking when I lay down the rules of what she can and can't do. Wren likes to take charge, to demand what she needs when we're together, but she likes it even more when she doesn't have to think and can simply do what I ask and take the pleasure I give her.

"Yes, you can, Wren. I think we've proven that." I think about Christmas Eve, when I fucked her under the tree and refused to touch her clit to make her finish. My cock jumps with the memory.

"Please, please..." she whimpers as if she feels it, her eyes hazy with need in the mirror. I continue to fuck her hard and deep, speeding my thrusts and hearing her moans grow louder and more high-pitched. Her knuckles are white on the edge of the vanity as she fights the urge to finish herself off.

"You look so fucking pretty, taking my cock like this, Wren. God, it's a masterpiece." Her ass moves back with each thrust, cheeks spread with the angle I have her in, and it gives me an idea. My hand shifts, sliding up, my thumb moving to press on her asshole. Her body tightens, but so does her cunt as I press harder, and I groan at the feel.

"One day, my sweet Wren, do you want me to take this?" A deep moan leaves her lips, and she groans, nodding. I stare at her in the mirror, watching every pleasure-filled change on her face. "You want me to fuck your ass, don't you, baby?"

She nods again.

"Yeah, god, fuck." A deep rumble of satisfaction leaves my chest at the mere idea of taking Wren here. "Fuck my ass. Please, Anything." She's desperate to come in any way, and I can't help but grin at that.

"Mmm, not today. But maybe I can..." My words trail off as I apply more pressure, my hips still rocking into her, my balls tightening with the need to release, but I won't let myself come until Wren does. I slide the very tip of my finger into her ass. A shout leaves her lips, and I grin.

Somehow, I knew she would like this.

"How about this? How about my finger?"

She nods frantically. "Fuck, yes. Finger my ass, Adam. Fuck." This is the only time Wren curses, the only time filthy words leave her lips, and they always turn me on like no other. I fuck her with just the very tip of my finger, adding a tiny bit more each time.

I wasn't kidding when I said I wanted to fuck her ass one day, but I can't go too much, too soon, and scare her off from it. After a minute of easing to the first knuckle, of hearing her moan and beg for more, I slide my thumb in completely and begin to fuck her with it, alternating thrusts so it slides in as my cock slides out. I can barely focus on anything but maintaining the rhythm, on making sure she's enjoying herself, for fear that if I don't, the overload of sensation will end this early.

"I'm close, I'm close," she moans.

Thank fuck.

"I know, Wren. Fuck, come for me, sweetness. Fucking *come for me*," I groan, both a plea and a demand as I slam in deep, my thumb filling her at the same time, and she screams, shattering around me as she comes and comes and comes. I make sure I lock my eyes on her in the mirror, desperate to commit this to memory. She tightens around me like a vise, her body quaking as I push in deeper and fill her, coming alongside her in the most intense orgasm I've had yet.

It takes an eternity to catch my breath, and I finally slide my finger out of her, pulling a hiss from her lips. I smirk down at her, a smirk that moves to a grin when her ass tips just a bit as if she's looking for more again.

Oh, hell yeah. I am absolutely going to fuck her ass one of these days.

She's slumped against the vanity as we catch our breath, and I slide out of her gently, reaching for a tissue to clean her up. I press a kiss to her shoulder, then her spine, then her lower back. Her head lifts, a sparkle in her eyes as she meets mine in the reflection of the mirror.

"Go get ready, Wren. We're running late now." I lift my pants that had fallen past my ass and tuck myself away, Wren's watchful eyes following each movement with intrigue as if I didn't just fuck her hoarse.

"And whose fault is that?" she asks, the sass kicking in now that her orgasm has faded. I reach down and pick up the long-forgotten robe, sliding it over her arms and pressing a soft kiss to her lips. She looks up at me with soft eyes, pleased by the tiny gesture.

God, I fucking love this woman.

"I love you, Wren."

"I love you too, honey," she whispers, then puts a hand to my neck to pull me down for another, harder kiss. I groan into it, pulling her into me, her naked front against my clothed body. She mewls as she shifts, trying to get more of something, and I grin to myself.

The woman just came hard from nothing but my cock and finger in her ass, and she still wants more.

My fucking woman.

"You know, maybe we could skip dinner," she muses breathlessly when I break the kiss.

I hesitate for a moment, then catch the lit-up Eiffel Tower from the corner of my eye through the balcony windows before I shake my head.

I want to show Wren the world, to give her every experience she never thought she'd have.

Starting with this trip.

"Not this time. Plenty of time to enjoy you, but you only get so many chances to eat dinner in the Eiffel Tower on New Year's Eve."

She gasps, her eyes going wide. "No way. Really?"

Her voice is giddy, and it makes me laugh before I nod and push a strand of her hair behind her ear.

"Yeah, sweetness. Now let's get going before we miss our reservation."

She moves, quickly tying up her robe, sitting in the chair I just fucked her on, and turning to face the mirror. She picks up one of the fallen makeup items and moves to do something to her eyebrows. But when she leans in, her eyes catch mine in the mirror, shining bright.

"Happy I get to be yours, Adam."

My heart fills with warmth, and I lean down, pressing a soft kiss to the top of her head before I plant a whisper there.

"Mine."

Two years later, I'm on a stage holding an award, and the crowd cheers loudly, deafeningly, as Willa Stone finishes her acceptance speech for Song of the Year. The music video for "Are You Mine?" plays on a large screen behind her.

It's a surreal moment, a life-changing moment, one I dreamed of for as long as I can remember, but when I look out into the huge cheering crowd, the only thing that matters is the pretty brunette with a red bow in her hair, tears in her eyes, and my ring on her finger.

The brightest light in my life.

ACKNOWLEDGMENTS

Writing a Christmas book in the middle of August is always an interesting experience, but I loved this one so much. It made me so eager for cool weather and setting up my Christmas village, and I hope you loved it just as much!

As with all books, this one would not exist if it weren't for the people holding my hand, listening to me crash out, and helping to make this thing the story it is.

First and foremost, forever and always, Alex. Thank you for listening to me when I crash out because something isn't working, and for giving me the easiest fix. I'm sorry, I sometimes tell you it wouldn't work, and then a week later, tell you you were right all along. We both know you're the brains in the relationship, so we really shouldn't be surprised. Thank you for always dropping every thing for me, for being the best husband I could have ever dreamed of, and the best dad. I love you forever. You will always be the best thing that's ever been mine.

To Ryan, Owen, and Ella, thank you for being the best kids on this planet and letting me have the honor of being your mom. We're going to pretend that if any of you are reading this, you just flipped to the back to see the acknowledgments, okay? Either way, you're grounded because you know the rules!! Love you guys the most.

To Rae, the world's best PA, which always feels weird to say because we all know you're not just my PA. Thank you for always being patient with me forgetting things, for reminding me a dozen times and sometimes just doing it on my behalf. Thank you for enduring my random Sunday afternoon texts with ideas (in my defense, I ALWAYS tell you not to even touch it until Monday!) and for always being open to beating a dead horse into dust when needed. I am so grateful I ahve you in my life. I fear you're stuck with me, especially since my kids think we adopted you.

To Ashleigh, my pretty, pretty princess, thank you for being the kindest, most understanding person I know. I finished this book in record time because I knew I needed it done by your bach, so maybe we need more trips to get me productive? By the time this book is in your hands, you might already by married (!!!) and I cannot wait to celebrate you soon!!

To Taj, the best agent I could ask for. I'm so grateful for everything you've helped me accomplish and continue to encourage me to try. Thank you for championing me and for not getting mad when I fall off the face of the earth.

Thank you to Becca for sitting with me on a call and letting me pick your brain, only for you to tell me I was totally overthinking everything. You were right.

Thank you to Lori and Christine for editing and proofreading and helping me refine things.

Thank you to Cat at TRC Designs, who is not just a genius with design, but the kindest person alive! Thank you for dealing with my never remembering to send you things or responding to emails!

Thank you to my alpha and beta teams who helped me make sure things made sense (they didn't) and told me when the spice was spicing (Marlee, Sophie, Malitza, April, Cait, Amanda!!)

To Kayla for being the biggest help with keeping my social media running smoothly and getting the word out, and to Catherine for doing the most phenomenal content pulls always. I'm so grateful to you both!

Thank you to the moon and back to my ARC and content team for being absolutely amazing. I love each and every one of you, and I can never fully tell you what your love and support mean to me. I know that the success of this book is in huge part due to all of you, and I can't possibly thank you enough.

Finally, thank you, dear Reader. I once thought there was no way I could finish writing a book, and this is now the twenty-third one I've finished writing and the twenty-second I've published. Whether you're a long-time resident of the Morganverse or taking your first visit, I'm so grateful that you chose to bump my story up on your TBR and give me a shot. I can never tell you the way you've changed my life.

Love you all to the moon and to Saturn.

ABOUT THE AUTHOR

Morgan is a born and raised Jersey girl, living there with her two sons and daughter, and mechanic husband. She's addicted to iced espresso, barbeque chips, and Starburst jellybeans. She usually has headphones on, listening to some spicy audiobook or Taylor Swift. There is rarely an in between.

Writing has been her calling for as long as she can remember. There's a framed 'page one' of a book she wrote at seven hanging in her childhood home to prove the point. Her entire life she's crafted stories in her mind, begging to be released but it wasn't until recently she finally gave them the reigns.

I'm so grateful you've agreed to take this journey with me.

Stay up to date via TikTok and Instagram

Stay up to date with future stories, get sneak peeks and bonus chapters by joining the Reader Group on Facebook!

f ⓘ

ALSO BY MORGAN ELIZABETH

Enter the Morganverse by catching up on your favorite Morgan Elizabeth books!

All books are interconnected standalones, which means you can jump in wherever you'd like, regardless of series or number in that series!

The Springbrook Hills Series

The Distraction

The Protector

The Substitution

The Connection

The Playlist

Season of Revenge Series:

Tis the Season for Revenge

Cruel Summer

The Fall of Bradley Reed

Ick Factor

Big Nick Energy

The Ocean View Series

The Ex Files

Walking Red Flag

Bittersweet

Evergreen Park Series

Passenger Princess

If This Was a Movie

Never Been Worse

Down the Shore Series

Tourist Trap

Mavens Series

Maneater

The Mastermind Duet

Ivory Tower

Diamond Fortress

All My Love

Printed in Dunstable, United Kingdom